# THE
# GOBLIN
# WAR

# THE
# GOBLIN
# WAR

HILARI BELL

An Imprint of HarperCollinsPublishers

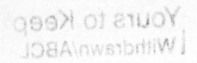

HarperTeen is an imprint of HarperCollins Publishers.

The Goblin War

For information address HarperCollins Children's Books, a division of
HarperCollins Publishers, 10 East 53rd Street, New York, NY 10022.
www.harperteen.com

Library of Congress Cataloging-in-Publication Data
Bell, Hilari.
The goblin war / by Hilari Bell. — 1st ed.
    p. cm.
Sequel to: The goblin gate.
Summary: After crossing over from the Otherworld where they have been
trapped in mortal danger, Tobin and Makenna must figure out how to help
Jeriah stop an army of barbarians from taking over their Realm.
ISBN 978-0-06-165105-2 (trade bdg.)
[1. Goblins—Fiction. 2. Magic—Fiction. 3. War—Fiction. 4. Fantasy.] I. Title.
PZ7.B38894Gnr 2011                                    2010040322
[F]—dc22                                                      CIP
                                                              AC

Typography by Hilary Zarycky
11  12  13  14  15   LP/RRDB    10  9  8  7  6  5  4  3  2  1

First Edition

*For those wonderful readers who've been sending me fan email, posting great online reviews, and talking up my books to others who might like them—you know who you are. But what you may not know is how much I appreciate you!*

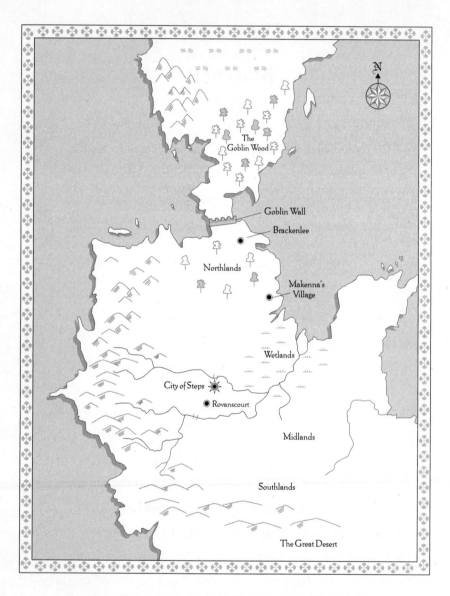

The Goblin Wood

Goblin Wall

Brackenlee

Northlands

Makenna's
Village

Wetlands

City of Steps

Rovanscourt

Midlands

Southlands

The Great Desert

REALM OF THE BRIGHT GODS

# CHAPTER 1

# Makenna

SHE WAS BEATEN. SHE'D NEVER accepted that before; not when the villagers she'd grown up with had drowned her mother. Not even when she'd taken her goblins to war against the whole human race. But now she knew that, sooner or later, the spirits were going to win.

Probably sooner.

Makenna gazed out between the flaps of the big tent. Goblins were only two feet tall, so several dozen goblin families had sacrificed the tents they'd carried through the gate with them to create a shelter for Tobin. And others had donated the thread to sew it together, after the nettle flax that had seemed so sturdy and promising had turned fragile as cobwebs almost as soon as it left the spindle.

There was something wrong with the very fabric of the Otherworld, but it wasn't until Makenna had tried to investigate what was happening to their building materials that she'd realized what it was. She had thought her magic was weaker because she'd drained herself casting the gate, but the goblins' magic had vanished too—because the Otherworld itself was draining all of them.

Makenna scowled at the array of goblin tents scattered along the shore—a shore that had receded almost a hundred yards in the scant week they'd been camped here. At least the spirits hadn't been able to make the whole lake disappear overnight, but the stream that had fed it had dried to a trickle in the first day, and the lake itself was vanishing at an unnatural rate. It would be gone in another week. The nearest lake her scouts had found was smaller than this one, and far enough off that they needed to set out for it now, before food grew scarcer. Before the evaporating water grew more foul.

They had to have water, therefore they had to leave. Makenna had ordered the goblins to take down their tents and prepare to depart . . . but she knew why they hadn't obeyed her.

Tobin's ordinary face was thin now, and flushed with fever, his brown hair wet with sweat. Makenna wasn't a healer—that had been her mother's gift. But even before Charba told her, she'd known that Tobin was too weak to survive another move. The last one had been hard enough, even though the goblins had carried him on the stretcher they'd rigged, using new-cut pines for the poles. When those poles had rotted and broken within a day, they'd simply cut more. Tobin had been conscious then, some of the time, and he'd hated being a burden. But he could no more stop the drain of strength from his body than the rest of them could halt the slow seeping away of their magic. And none of the goblins was willing to leave their soldier behind.

"He saved us all from that priest's army," Miggy had told her. "So we're indebted. Even if this place isn't exactly working out."

*Isn't working out.* What a kind way to avoid saying that Makenna had led them to their deaths.

Tobin would only be the first. The Greeners already had to go too far afield to find enough edible wild plants to feed them, and they couldn't simply move from lake to lake forever. And even if they managed to adapt to that roving life, scavenging enough to survive, the spirits would find some other way to destroy them.

It was Regg's little brother, Root, who'd told Makenna that the strange inhabitants of this place called themselves spirits. They'd let no one but the youngest of the goblin children close enough to learn even that much. But Makenna was enough of a tactician to read their purpose from their actions. They were trying to drive the invaders out of their world, just as she'd driven so many settlers out of the Goblin Wood. And like her, they really didn't care if they killed a few in the doing.

Makenna rubbed her face with her hands, brushing away tears, but the facts didn't change. She should leave Tobin behind. With inadequate food and spoiling water, they'd soon be too weak to pack up and escape themselves. Since

Tobin couldn't survive being moved, they had to leave him . . . and she couldn't, no more than the goblins could.

He'd risked his life for her, and for her people. How could she abandon him to die alone?

As the goblins' commander, could she do anything else?

She was wasting precious water, allowing the tears to roll down her face, when a small hand fell on her shoulder.

"Gen'ral?"

Cogswhallop was the only goblin who called her that, but she'd missed him so much, so often mistaken another's voice for his, that she didn't lift her head.

The hand on her shoulder tightened and shook her. "I thought you'd more iron in you than to sit there spouting like a lass at the first sign of trouble. We're not beat yet."

No other goblin spoke to her with that gruff tenderness. Makenna's eyes snapped open.

"Cogswhallop?"

If this world started throwing hallucinations at them, they were done for—but the familiar long-nosed face didn't vanish.

Cogswhallop snorted. "You didn't think you could leave me behind for long, did you? A good thing too, from what I'm seeing here. Bend down."

Still half disbelieving his presence, Makenna bent her head.

Cogswhallop slipped a chain over it, the green and brown of unpolished copper, and a crude medallion thumped against her chest. It was round, with runes inscribed around a hole in the middle—though they were nothing like the runes in her mother's books.

"What's . . . ?"

The moment her fingers closed around the medallion, the aching drain on Makenna's magic stopped, as abruptly as turning off a tap. Makenna stared at her small lieutenant for a moment—then she pulled off the chain and spun to slap the charm against the exposed flesh of Tobin's throat.

If she'd hoped for a miracle, it didn't happen. Perhaps his eyelids fluttered, but they'd done that before in his feverish dreams.

"It should stop the life drain," Cogswhallop told her. "But I don't know much more than that. And we've enough to go round."

Another chain fell over her head, and she slipped a hand under Tobin's sweat-soaked hair and pulled the chain of the first amulet around his neck, settling the medallion against his damp skin.

"Will it save him?" She had a thousand questions, but that was the one that mattered.

"I don't know," Cogswhallop admitted. "But the answer may be here." He pulled out a bundle of notes, in a neat cramped hand that Makenna recognized. Her breath caught.

"Aye," Cogswhallop confirmed. "It's the priest's own spell notes—all that's known about the Otherworld, and casting gates. There's a bit about these amulets as well, including how they're made. Nasty, that."

Makenna didn't care. "Will they get us home?"

"Am I a hedgewitch?" Cogswhallop asked sardonically. "There's a lady priest as thought they might, but she said you'd have to figure out a way to cast the spell, in the midst of a world that sucks up magic like a drunkard sucks up beer. Or a Bookerie sucks up knowledge."

"I heard that." Erebus popped his head through the tent flaps. He'd hardly left his post outside since Tobin had finally collapsed, and Cogswhallop must have passed him on the way in.

Their familiar bickering brought such a painful rush of joy that the tears started down Makenna's cheeks once more. She had to swallow before she could speak.

"I'd appreciate it, Erebus, if you and your folks could go through these notes and organize them for me. If there's anything on healing someone stricken sick by this world, Charba needs to hear it now. Then I need to see everything about the nature of the Otherworld, and any clue about building a gate out of it. I don't care who's looking to kill us back home. It's got to be better than staying."

Erebus cast Tobin a concerned glance and took the notes away at once. Cogswhallop cleared his throat.

"As to folks killing us, there's been some changes since you've been gone, Gen'ral. Turns out the soldier's brother isn't quite the feckless fool we thought him."

It didn't sound like much, but from Cogswhallop that

was high praise. Especially for a human. The same human whose bungled plots had put Tobin in the power of an evil priest and nearly gotten all of them killed. Makenna didn't think much of Tobin's brother Jeriah, no matter what he'd done recently.

Charba slipped into the tent, and Makenna led Cogswhallop out, guiltily glad to be away from the stench of illness and Tobin's rasping breath. She was a terrible nurse. Evaluating a situation and deciding what action to take was something she was better at, but the story Cogswhallop told her strained that capability.

"So Master Lazur, the Dark One seize his bones, was cheating on his own people as well as trying to destroy us," she finally summed it up. "And he got caught, and hanged, and now it's safe for us to go back."

"He didn't so much get caught as young Jeriah exposed him," Cogswhallop said. "He wants his brother back, and I more or less promised to deliver him—though I didn't realize it was so urgent at the time. What's going on here, Gen'ral?"

"It didn't seem so bad when we first arrived," Makenna told him. "The Greeners soon found plants we could eat. And it was beautiful."

She gestured around them, although the lush forest no longer looked beautiful to her, and the drying lakebed stank.

"But then we tried to build. The Stoners were the first to come to me, when they started working on the foundations. They said the stone was funny. I was in the midst of settling some dispute, and . . . I just ignored it. We were beginning to notice the power drain, and there was so much else going on. . . ."

Cogswhallop listened quietly as she told him about stones that looked like granite but cracked like unfired clay. About timber that dried straight but warped a day after you pegged it into a wall.

"And then the stream dried up," said Makenna. "No, that's not right. The stream stopped. We went to bed with it bubbling away, and when we woke in the morning, there were only puddles among the rocks. I went with the scouts who tracked it back to see what had happened. There was a hill right across the streambed. A whole hill, with grass and well-grown trees. The second stream—"

"A whole hill?" Cogswhallop asked incredulously.

"With grown trees," Makenna confirmed. "But it's not such a feat as all that when you know the trick."

"What trick?"

Makenna smiled grimly. "There's a reason I asked the Bookeries to pull out any notes Lazur had on the nature of the Otherworld. Because I've come to think that the spirits themselves created it, shaping it out of magic like a child pinching clay. If that's the case, it's not so surprising that they could move a hill, or change the nature of wood and stone, or even drain a lake at will."

Cogswhallop walked in silence for a several seconds. He must have arrived a little ahead of the rest of his party.

Dozens of goblins ran among the tents, looking for loved ones amid shrieks of welcome. Joy glowed in their small, sharp-featured faces.

"Then it seems to me," said Cogswhallop, "that you'd best be making peace with those spirit folk. If they can command the earth itself to change, there's no way you can beat them."

"We've tried that," said Makenna. "They won't talk to us, won't let anyone but the children come near them. But the Bookeries have managed to piece together a little, from the bits the children have told us. As far as we can tell, they don't want anyone to live in this world except them. They don't like goblins, and they hate all humans with a bitter passion. They want us out, or dead, or both. The Bookeries say which one they want might vary a bit from one spirit to the next. They have no idea why the spirits hate us so much—though they've plenty of theories, which they argue about. . . . Well, you know Bookeries."

"If you can't make peace with them, then you'd best get out as soon as you can," said Cogswhallop. "I shouldn't be keeping you from those notes. I can tell you the rest of it later."

A mob of goblin children darted past like swallows—Onny and Regg, reunited with their friend Daroo. They were heading in the direction of Tobin's tent, where Onny and Regg had kept watch even more faithfully than Erebus.

Cogswhallop had been searching for his son when the gate closed, trapping him and his family in the real world.

Trapping Makenna and her goblins in this one. But now, feeling magic seep back into her bones, Makenna knew she might finally have a chance to free them all.

The first attempt failed. The glowing gate runes still sank into the trees she'd chosen as an anchor, just as the healing runes she'd placed around Tobin's bed had vanished into the ground.

The amulet he now wore—as did every goblin Makenna had dragged into this world with her—prevented more of his life energy from draining away, but he was still terrifyingly weak and had barely surfaced to consciousness a few times. He'd survived being carried to the next lake, and Charba said he'd probably grow stronger on his own, eventually. But Makenna wasn't sure.

Master Lazur's notes had revealed that all the humans who'd gone into this world without the ability to work magic had died within three months. And those who had magic must also have died at some point. At least, Makenna had seen no sign of them.

Ruthless as he'd been about collecting his information, the priest had learned less about the nature of the Otherworld than she had—though that didn't surprise Makenna. She'd been living here for over two months; all Master Lazur had done was thrust a handful of condemned criminals through a gate, then open a few holes to get back reports.

The only part she hadn't known already, aside from a

few refinements on the gate spell, was his speculation that the spirits who controlled this world might be related to the barbarian's "gods," and that was why the barbarian blood amulets worked here.

If Makenna and the goblins couldn't use magic to affect anything in this world, then getting their power back wouldn't do much good.

"We've got to find a way to get the earth, or wood, or whatever, to stop sucking up the magic we're trying to use on it," she told Cogswhallop. "I think, given these notes on power sharing, that I could link together a group of goblins large enough that I *could* cast a gate. At least a small one."

"But all our powers are different," Cogswhallop objected. "The Greeners' power only works on plants, the Stoners' on stone, the Bookeries' on useless scribbling."

"Not so useless," Erebus put in. "Galavan, in *Essential Nature of Things*, speculated that all magic was the same at its source. Maybe we could pass the pure form of it on to the mistress, and she could use it. Or perhaps passing it to her, or through her, might transform—"

"I think it would," said Makenna, absently rubbing her amulet—a nervous habit a lot of them had adopted. "But none of that will do us any good unless we can keep our power from sinking into this world and feeding it. If this world is made of magic, maybe it needs to eat magic to survive? But if that's the case, what does it eat if it doesn't have folk like us?"

"Maybe it eats the spirits' magic," Cogswhallop said. "It may be eating thistledown and moonshine, but I don't see how that helps us! We need a plan, Gen'ral."

Makenna shook off speculation. "As it happens, I've got one. If the spirits control the nature of this world, then maybe one of them could stop it sucking up our magic long enough for us to cast a spell or two. That seem right to you?"

"Aye, could be. But they've shown precious little interest in helping us so far. And since the children started wearing the amulets, the spirits won't even talk to them. Much less a 'filthy human' like you."

"Then maybe it's time to try something stronger than asking them nicely. You're a fair hand at ambushes, Cogswhallop. Could you capture a spirit for me?"

He must have thinking along the same lines, for he answered instantly. "I might. The pen pusher tells me they're avoiding these amulets like plague, so I'm thinking they might make a fair trap. And I've some ideas about where to set the snare as well. Though if I'm wrong about how they react, it might take one or two tries before we succeed."

"Set your trap," Makenna told him—and for once she'd no compunction about using those words. "And if you're looking for a target, I know just the spirit I'd like to have a chat with."

One of the things about the Otherworld Makenna found most disturbing was that it was so similar to the real world but not quite the same. It grew dark at night. The moon—now nearly full—sailed through the sky and changed its phases just like at home. But the stars around it formed different patterns, and they were too large, too bright. The scent of damp earth was familiar from dozens of night raids and watches, but the branches that brushed her face had a subtly alien smell.

"Are you certain the spirit will show up here?" she asked Cogswhallop.

"No," he said promptly. "But digging a trench across that ridge is the simplest way to stop the stream that feeds this lake, the Stoners have their foundations built, and the woodworkers are starting on the frames. According to the others, that's the stage they'd reached when the first stream vanished. It's the closest thing to bait we've got."

But although they watched till nearly sunrise, no spirit appeared, and the stream continued to flow.

Makenna had been a commander too long to let herself become impatient. They waited out the next two nights as well, crouched in the bushes above the small valley. On the fourth night, Makenna was almost asleep when Cogswhallop's elbow dug into her ribs.

A column of water rose out of the stream, spinning, slowly coalescing into a human-shaped form. A woman's form, Makenna saw with astonishment. Surely only creatures who bred required two genders. But she knew nothing about the spirits. Maybe they did breed. Maybe they had hordes of little spirits, and complained about having to cook for such a mob, while their husbands grumbled about how hard they'd worked trying to drive off the goblins all day.

If Erebus was right about these amulets repelling the spirits, she might have a chance to find out.

She leaned forward, heedless of the stones digging into her knees, and watched the water spirit flow up the stream to the place where the spirit would need to shape a trench across the ridge if she wanted to send the stream down a different course.

The spirit bent, laying shimmering hands against the ground, and before Makenna's astonished gaze, the solid earth began to melt like butter on a hot griddle.

She'd guessed that the spirits could do this, but seeing solid rock crumble at the thing's whim sent a chill down Makenna's spine. She shrugged. She'd been frightened before; she never let it interfere with strategy.

Makenna waited till the spirit was fully involved in her earth shaping. Then she stood, silently raising an arm.

Even knowing where they were hiding, Makenna could hardly see the goblins as they crept forward. She gave them a few seconds to get into position; then her arm flashed down, and half a dozen amulets splashed into the stream—both above and below the spirit's position.

They hadn't known what to expect. Erebus could only speculate that the spirits, whom Master Lazur had also reported to be "repulsed" by the barbarians' amulets, might be unable to pass them.

Makenna hadn't expected the blood-curdling shriek the creature emitted. And she certainly hadn't expected the ice that spread over the surface in curling splinters, stretching out from every amulet the goblins had cast into the stream, growing till they touched the spirit woman's feet.

At that point Makenna half expected her to freeze to ice and die—and a lot of good that would do them! But although the ice ran partway up the woman's skirts, the spirit remained flowing and alive, watching Makenna and her allies hurrying down the slope with an expression of hostility that looked downright human.

Makenna slowed her approach, strolling the last few yards.

Human shaped the spirit might be, but she didn't appear to have bones, or blood, or any internal structure Makenna could see—and she was as transparent as the water she was made of. Water bound into that shape with magic, Makenna supposed, just like all else in this accursed place.

The creature hadn't been schooled in the finer points of negotiating—she spoke first.

"Get those disgusting *things* out of my stream, human. Or you'll never see water in this world again."

Something that looked like that should have a crystalline voice, but instead the words bubbled like a boiling pot.

"I'd think the wood and meadow spirits might object to that," Makenna told her. "Let me propose a different bargain. You stabilize this world so it stops sucking down every rune I set, and we'll all leave. And take our amulets with us. How about that?"

The spirit's eyes narrowed. "I refuse to deal with anyone who wears one of *those*." She gestured to the medallion on Makenna's breast. "None of us will. So you might as well give up now."

"But you just offered me a deal," Makenna pointed out. "Water for your freedom."

The spirit blinked. Powerful, but not too bright, Makenna realized. She'd seen that combination in enough priests and village elders to be wary of it. Sometimes a powerful stupid enemy was more dangerous than a smart one.

*So don't antagonize her if you don't have to.*

"Why do you object to these amulets, anyway?" Makenna asked. "I'm told they're made with human sacrifice, but given how you feel about humans, I wouldn't think that would trouble you."

"They're made of death." The spirit shivered, droplets falling from the ends of her hair. They froze when they hit the ice.

Was it the spirit's own horror of those amulets that had frozen the stream? If so, Makenna probably shouldn't point that out.

"It'd take a fair amount of effort to remove them," she said instead. "We'd have to chip through the ice."

She cast a glance at Cogswhallop, who nodded and murmured to another goblin, who hurried off. Hammers and chisels would arrive shortly.

"I'm thinking we should get something in exchange for our effort," Makenna went on. "Water's a start, but you wouldn't have to give us water if you'd make it possible for us to leave."

"We'd rather see you dead." The bubbling voice was full of malice.

Makenna folded her arms. "I'm not feeling all that bad about seeing you freeze there, either. We've no intention of dying anytime soon, but if we did, would one of your fellows be willing to chip those amulets out for you? Or be able to touch them long enough to do it, even if he wanted to?"

The spirit's lips clamped shut.

Makenna waited for the truth to sink in before she continued. "Then maybe you'd best hope we can keep ourselves alive a bit longer."

"What do you want?" the spirit asked sullenly.

"I've told you. We want to get out of this world," said Makenna. "And given how much you'd like to see us gone, that shouldn't be too bitter a dose to swallow."

The spirit shook her head. "I don't have enough power to create a world bubble large enough to release you all. I've already offered you water—"

"Not precisely," said Erebus, who'd been taking notes. "You threatened to withdraw all the water if we didn't free you."

"And you've been doing that since we arrived," Makenna

added, "so it's not much of a threat. Now if you'd offered to leave the stream be, so we could use it . . ."

The spirit looked around, like a child hoping someone would come along and rescue her from having to confess to breaking a dish. It worked no better for her than it did for five-year-olds.

"Very well," she conceded. "I'll leave the stream to flow for you."

"And what about the rest of it?" Makenna asked. "Crumbling stones, rotting flax, plants that shrivel no matter how well the Greeners care for them?"

"I have no power over the others," the spirit told her. "Only this stream is mine."

Makenna shook her head. "Water alone won't do us much good. All your stream can do is make our deaths slower."

In truth, more time to scheme and struggle was always good, but she saw no reason to tell the spirit that.

"I can't control what the others do!" the bubbling voice wailed. "I really can't!"

"Then," said Makenna, "let's talk about my request. You say you don't have the power to let us go—I'll accept that for now. Could you stop this world from draining the magic out of my runes long enough for me to cast a gate?"

The spirit looked around again, but the situation hadn't changed.

Makenna waited.

The translucent shoulders slumped. "Oh, very well. I'll do

what I can. And if I do, you'll get the death touch out of me and never never try that trick again! Agreed?"

Makenna shrugged. "I'll promise not to do it to *you* again. We may need to bargain with others in the future."

Given the spirit's conviction that her own folks wouldn't come to her aid, Makenna wasn't surprised when she nodded. "Agreed. Do you have an empty flask?"

Makenna's waterskin wasn't empty, but she solved that by pouring its contents on the ground. "I do now."

"Bring it here."

Makenna walked over the ice and held it out. The spirit extended a delicate hand, and water flowed from the tip of her finger into the flask. If she was thinner by the time it was full, Makenna couldn't see it.

"There," said the spirit. "Anything saturated with this water will resist the magic thirst. Mind, once the water has dried, it won't work anymore. That's the best I can do for you."

Makenna eyed the plump skin bag. "There's not a lot there."

"Then I suggest you use it wisely," the spirit said. "All in this world are watching to see if you keep your word, human."

Whether the whole world was watching or not, a bargain was a bargain. Besides, if Makenna didn't keep her end of the agreement, it would make any future negotiations much harder. If it took more than one attempt to make a gate large enough to return them all, she and the goblins might be here for some time.

"Send for some hammers and chisels," she told Cogs-whallop. "And when they come, get those amulets back. We're likely going to need them."

Cogswhallop frowned. "I already . . . Aye, I'll get right to it."

The spirit looked suspicious but said nothing, so Makenna walked away and Cogswhallop followed.

"The chisels will be here any moment, Gen'ral. You know that."

"Aye, but I want you to stop them before they get here, and don't bring them till enough time has passed for someone to walk to and from our camp. A slow walk."

"You don't trust her?" Cogswhallop asked.

"Let's just say I'd like to use this water before she has a chance to change her mind. This world is made of magic—I don't think it'd be hard for them to stop us if we give them time to plan."

They passed out of sight of the stream then, and Makenna set off at a run, clutching the precious skin against her ribs so it wouldn't bounce.

She'd already assembled and trained her fellow casters for the failed attempts, so the others knew what to do. Drawing runes in water was something a priest could do, but no mere hedgewitch could manage it. After a bit of thought, Makenna tacked thick cloths to the two trees she'd chosen to anchor the gate and chalked the runes onto the rough surface. She took a moment to make certain her helpers could dampen the cloth without disturbing the marks, praying there would be enough of the precious water to soak them all. Then she sent several dozen of the watching goblins—and the whole village had gathered to watch—to bring Tobin from his tent. While they were waiting for him, she and the goblins who'd agreed to feed her power settled into a circle in front of the two trees.

They were a pair of saplings whose white bark resembled birch, though their leaves were shaped more like a maple's. But they were much the same size, about three feet apart, and their young branches arced together overhead, forming something enough like a gate that Makenna thought she could anchor the spell there. She nodded to the water bearers, who carefully wet their cloths—time to begin. "From this world to ours," she said.

The circle of goblins echoed it back. "From this world to ours."

The priest's books had given her a proper spell chant in the old tongue, but Makenna's mother had said that a chant was simply a way to focus mind and will, and it didn't really matter what you said.

If the chant did matter, then they were doomed from the start—Makenna didn't know how to pronounce half those words.

She reached out and took the small hand of the goblin to her left. She'd lived with them so long, so closely, that the disparity in size felt more normal to her than the clasp of a human hand. The goblin to her right laid a hand on her ankle, leaving her right hand free. And the power that flowed through those small hands felt as strong and real as rain after a long drought.

Makenna traced a finger over the chalk lines of the rune of "here," for the gate began here, and the damp cloth beneath the chalk began to glow.

"This world to ours," the goblins chanted.

Makenna forced down a surge of triumph. They still had a long way to go.

Runes of travel, runes that described the earth, air, and reality of the world from which they'd come.

She had to stand now, and the goblins beside her transferred their grip to her ankles. Makenna was only vaguely aware of other goblins laying Tobin on the grass—still unconscious, even though the fever was gone. Too thin, too pale, he looked terrible. *Concentrate!*

Runes of safety, runes for preserving health, a rune of stability, which she had a hard time forcing to life and whose glow wavered more than she liked even as she moved on. She was sweating now, and the power that flowed from her goblin allies was weaker.

Makenna took a deep breath and turned to the rune of opening, pouring her magic into it with profligate haste. It sprang to life all at once, blinding bright.

The gate opened.

It didn't fill the gap between the trees, as she'd hoped. In fact, it was barely big enough for a goblin to walk through, and the edges blurred and wavered—but through it Makenna could see the edge of a dusty road and a crowberry bush. The real world.

"Do it!" Dozens of goblins carried Tobin forward, stumbling over the spell caster's joined hands, and the rune of stability began to flicker.

Makenna had speculated about what might happen to someone if a gate failed when they were halfway through. She had no desire to learn the truth the hard way. She traced the dimming rune once more, pouring power into it, first from her goblin helpers, and when that ran out, her own. She could feel the drag, the drain of more and more energy as the goblins thrust Tobin's head into the wavering disk of light.

She'd expected him to fly through, like a smith feeding a log into a furnace. It was actually more like someone pushing a pillow into a jar, and Makenna fought back a hysterical giggle as they finally shoved Tobin's feet through the gap.

His eyes opened. She had time to see that much, at least. He looked up at the sky, then turned his head and looked at her, just as the rune under her fingers flickered out.

The gate collapsed, and power lashed back through her on a pulse of pain.

When the stars that clouded her vision faded, Makenna looked around. Most of the casters were sitting there, clutching their heads, but a few were already standing up. No one dead.

She'd cast the most complex spell of her life, under bad conditions—and while it hadn't been perfect, it hadn't killed anyone.

Soon someone would come along that dusty road and pick Tobin up and nurse him back to health. Health he could never have regained here.

She'd gotten it right. He would be safe and well, no matter how much she'd miss him.

So now all she had to do was figure out a way to get the rest of them back to the Realm, and then bargain out a place in it for goblins before the Hierarch stopped feeling properly grateful or some other piece of murderous scum took over the church.

Makenna sighed. If she could pry some escape out of the spirits, the rest of it ought to be easy.

# CHAPTER 2

# Tobin

A HARD KNOB PRODDED TOBIN'S side, waking him. He tried, sleepily, to move away, but it shoved him again, digging into his ribs.

He rolled over and looked up at a circle of white-painted faces. Their hair, also saturated with the clay they coated their bodies with before a battle, stood out around their heads in rough spikes. They wore the leather armor and loincloths of barbarian warriors.

Fear surged through him—if Tobin hadn't known that it had to be a nightmare, he'd have screamed. But he wasn't on the border, fighting the barbarian clans who'd swarmed out of the desert half a dozen years ago. He was . . . Where was he?

The dragging undertow of weariness that had been leaching his strength from the time he first stepped into the Otherworld was gone. But if he wasn't there, then . . .

Tobin tried to sit up, and the spear that had prodded him reversed, the point poking his breastbone, forcing him down.

The hard-baked clay of the road beneath his hands, the sunlight beating on his face, and, above all, the sharp spear point . . . This wasn't a dream!

The burst of terror he felt then was so fierce that his constricted throat emitted only a stifled squawk, like an outraged chicken. And he would soon be doomed to the same fate.

How in the Dark One's name had he gotten here? He'd been in the Other—

"You were right, Machi. He is alive," one of the barbarians said. "I guess your clan gets to keep its storyteller a bit longer."

Tobin blinked. The words in his mind didn't match the harsh syllables of the language the barbarian had spoken. And "storyteller" wasn't quite right, for the barbarians' term also carried a connotation of "keeper of history and tradition," though the storyteller was clearly an entertainer as well.

"It's always worth checking," another of them said. "But he looks pretty sickly. We'd better wait a bit, to make sure his flesh won't poison us."

Tobin's heart sank. Deep down, he'd always believed that the rumors whispered around the army campfires had to be false, that surely no human being could eat another. But it sounded like they were true.

"You say it so casually," he murmured. "Like I wasn't—"

He'd spoken in his own tongue, the only language he knew—but the barbarians jumped and stared down at him.

"Scorch it!" one of them swore. Somehow Tobin knew it was a fairly strong curse. "Get his shirt open."

The spear point pinned Tobin against the ground, holding him helpless as half a dozen hands yanked at the fabric of a shirt he'd have sworn he remembered his goblin nurse helping him into in the Otherworld. How had he gotten from there to . . . the Southlands? The dust-scented air, the fields of grapevines with new leaves sprouting from their gnarled stems looked like the Southlands. But how—

One of the brighter barbarians gave up trying to tear the cloth and pulled out a knife. Tobin yelped as he knelt, and the point of the other man's spear popped painfully through his skin. But the barbarian with the knife only slit open his shirt, and then swore at the sight of an amulet lying against Tobin's chest. The same sort of amulet they all wore, crudely cast copper, with runes inscribed around it.

The same sort of amulet Tobin's troop had been ordered to remove from barbarian bodies, because it was said that if the barbarians captured a spy who was wearing one, they wouldn't kill him.

"That's right," Tobin said. Could they understand him? And how in two worlds was he understanding what they said? "I'm wearing one of your amulets. So you can't kill me."

He prayed to all the Bright Gods he was right.

"Maybe. Maybe not." The barbarian seemed to expect Tobin to understand him, even though he still spoke the

27

rough barbarian tongue Tobin had never heard before, except for a few battlefield shouts. "I think stolen amulets should be different from ones warriors have earned. And you reek of the Spiritworld. If you're their spy—"

"That's not for you to judge," another barbarian said. "It must be decided by the storyteller and the clan chiefs. So we'd better take him with us."

That, at least, they all agreed to. The spear was removed, and Tobin was foolish enough to struggle as they tied his hands behind his back and bound his kicking legs. He was still weak from the illness that had attacked him in the Otherworld . . . so how could he now be in the real one, being captured by barbarians?

His weakness, and the fact that he remembered being in the Otherworld when he was dressed in the clothes he now wore, made nonsense of his tentative theory that he'd been hit on the head and lost days? weeks? months? of memories. Besides, his head felt fine. In fact, he felt better than he had in weeks, until they picked him up and bound him, stomach down, over the back of someone's saddle like a newly shot deer.

The barbarians' coarse-coated horses were smaller than the Realm's chargers, though sturdy and courageous in battle. Some of the taller bushes they passed through brushed Tobin's face or tugged at his feet, and the rapidly growing discomfort of being carried in that position reinforced his conviction that, however he'd gotten here, it wasn't a dream.

The barbarian camp was only a short distance away, but his back muscles were on fire and his stomach was churning by the time they arrived.

His head spun as they pulled him off the horse and thrust him into . . . a cage, Tobin noted grimly. A human-sized cage, mounted on a two-wheeled cart, perfectly designed for carrying your "meat" with you to keep it fresh—just as the worst of the rumors had claimed.

Would they really *eat* him? It seemed more horrible than simply being killed, and so outrageously unlikely that Tobin clung to hope despite the rough wooden bars surrounding him. He struggled to his knees, which was tricky with his hands and feet still bound, and studied the barbarian camp.

Round tents, made of stitched leather spread over arched wooden poles, were scattered through a large field—probably the communal pasture of the burned-out village he could see in the distance. Tobin had heard that they'd conquered a large strip of the Southlands not long after he'd left to try to capture the "sorceress" of the Goblin Wood. But this was the first time he'd realized what that conquest meant in loss of lives and property.

Hopefully the people who'd lived and worked in these charred ruins had been evacuated in time. Tobin didn't see the mounds of any recent graves. Of course—a chill roughened his skin at the thought—the barbarian method for disposing of enemy bodies might not leave graves.

But he didn't understand why they'd burned the village

instead of moving into the houses themselves. A tight wooden cottage had to be drier than those tents, and the late spring could be stormy this far south.

Cooking fires burned in front of many of the tents, and Tobin was relieved to see that the meat on their spits looked like sheep or goat. A herd of goats milled in the small corral the village must have used—which they hadn't burned, for some reason. Why destroy the houses but not that?

Tobin had no time to notice more, for a group of barbarians, clearly a committee, was stalking toward his cage, arguing as they approached.

Some of the men weren't painted with the white clay that had covered all the barbarians Tobin had seen. They had the same brownish skin as Southlanders, though their hair was generally a lighter shade of brown, sometimes with a reddish tint.

They were smaller, by and large, than Tobin's people—but he had fought them, and he knew those lithe, white-painted bodies were unbelievably agile and strong.

He'd been told that their warriors went nearly naked into battle to prove their courage. The men who'd captured him—a scouting party?—had worn only stiffened leather strapped around their limbs and torsos, and loincloths for modesty's sake. The men who now approached wore very loose britches, gathered at the ankles, and embroidered vests over long tunics, whose sleeves were gathered at the wrists.

The women were similarly clad, even wearing britches like their men, and there were others in the camp Tobin took to be servants, wearing rougher, drabber cloth.

". . . high time we began to differentiate between us and our enemies," one of them was saying as they drew near. "Stealing an amulet from one of our dead doesn't make him Duri. In fact, it makes him less than the chanduri, for even they have more honor than that."

The word "Duri" came to Tobin's mind simultaneously as warrior, clansman, and lord, all three meanings clashing and blending into the word itself. A barbarian term for which his language had no matching concept? "Chanduri" came to him as "lesser Duri"—not warriors, less in rank, less worthy than the Duri.

It had to be the amulet that was letting him understand them, but he had no time to contemplate that realization.

The men had gathered around the cage now; several Tobin thought he recognized from the scouting party. Were the rest the clan chiefs they'd spoken of? Though the word also seemed to have some connotation of "law keeper."

They were older than the scouts, but not nearly as old as a group of village headmen would have been. Tobin had no doubt that these men could lead their clans into battle when the time came. Except, perhaps, one of them. He was much older than the rest, his hair threaded with gray, and he wore a patch over one eye. Though his clothing wasn't as drab as the servants', it wasn't as rich as the warriors' either.

"I didn't come here to spy on you." Tobin decided to speak to the oldest man. "I came . . . I think I came here by accident."

Now that he'd had a few minutes to think, he had a vague memory of many hands shoving him, and of looking back at Makenna through a shimmering curtain that had to be a gate. There was only one known method to pass from the Otherworld to this one, so somehow they'd managed to make a gate and shoved him out—right into the hands of the barbarians.

The oldest barbarian looked at him blankly.

"He says he isn't here to spy," one of the other barbarians told the one-eyed man. "As if we care."

One-Eye shook his head. "No, our enemies are enemies, more chan than the chanduri. Our tradition is clear on that."

"Yes, but it's also clear that even a Softer can't be killed if he wears the blood trust," another man said. "If you start making exceptions because the man who wears the blood trust is our enemy, how long will it be before we start thinking of this clan or that one as enemies, and we end up wasting our strength fighting one another once more?"

"But I'm here by accident." Tobin tried again. "I didn't come to fight you or to spy."

The fact that he'd fought them in the past wasn't something he wanted to dwell on now—though for all the attention they paid him, he might as well have shouted it. Only the one-eyed man even glanced at Tobin when he spoke, and he seemed not to understand.

"So if our enemies come against us in the final battle, wearing the blood trusts they stole from our dead, we're supposed to lay down our swords and let them kill us?" one of the scouts demanded.

"Of course not," another replied. "If they come weapon in hand to fight, then clearly we've been challenged."

"Yes, but what about when they've been disarmed?" another asked. "What if they're wearing the blood trust then? By the strict interpretation of tradition/law/right"—another word clearly not in Tobin's language—"we'd have to let them go. I don't know about you, but to me that sounds like a fine formula for losing a war!"

It sounded like that to Tobin too, and he made a mental note to report this whole conversation to his old commander when he got back. Then he realized that the only reason they'd spoken so freely in front of him was because he wasn't going back, and he missed the next few sentences as the blood drained out of his head and the edges of his vision darkened.

"Not only is our tradition clear on this," One-Eye was saying when the ringing cleared from Tobin's ears, "but our history as well. Before we shared in the sacred blood trust, our clans spent all their might fighting one another—and with warriors so proud and fierce, there is little doubt that if the blood trust could be violated, our clan wars would erupt again."

Tobin thought he detected a sardonic note in that last sentence, but none of the others seemed to notice it.

"He's right." The clan chief sounded reluctant but resigned. "If we start saying the blood trust doesn't apply to enemies, soon we'll be calling everyone we take a dislike to 'enemy,' and that will be the end of everything. Besides . . ." He gestured to Tobin. "As you all know, there are ways. We haven't even captured a spirit yet. We can feed him up, make sure he's not so sick he'd infect us, and . . . Well, there are ways."

They moved off, chatting among themselves, and only One-Eye looked back at Tobin as they left.

Tobin tried to fight off terror and depression by considering how much even that short conversation had told him. First, the amulets must be this "blood trust" they kept talking about. It really did keep them from killing—not only an enemy spy but also one another. If it kept them safe from their own gods, too, which was what the priests had claimed, no one seemed to care much about that.

It also had to be the amulet that let Tobin understand them, so the amulets weren't just symbolic but real magic. He lifted the medallion and looked it over, but the simple copper round hadn't changed. A magic that could translate a foreign tongue in his own mind should look more impressive. And was it only one foreign tongue? Did the barbarians have more than one language? If so, it made sense that translation would help keep peace among them, but it sounded like the amulets did more than that.

Well, Tobin knew they did! They were said to be part of the barbarians' battle magic, although Realm knights had been forbidden to wear captured amulets into battle because they were reputed to have been made with human sacrifice—and by now Tobin believed every wild tale he'd ever heard about that.

The wave of terror that washed over him was so intense, his vision blurred again, and he had to put his head between his knees.

But clearly the amulet would protect him for a while.

There were ways. Ways to take the amulet from him? To trick him into taking it off? Ways around their tradition/law that he couldn't begin to guess?

In that case, maybe Tobin could keep it on and survive long enough to escape.

As the day wore on, Tobin's fear slowly turned into something that was closer to boredom than terror.

The changing angle of the sun told him he'd been captured in the morning. Around midday, everyone seemed to return to their tents for a meal, and if there was some rivalry between the different clans that Tobin could exploit, he didn't see any sign of it. They all seemed to be milling around together, not clustering in groups. No one wore different colors or flew banners that might indicate some sort of clan allegiance—at least, none that Tobin could recognize.

Soon after midday a young woman, not much older than he was, carried a bowl and a waterskin up to his cage. Her expression was as calmly indifferent as a woman feeding chickens, so when she drew her dagger and held it through the bars, Tobin extended his feet for her to cut the ropes. His hands were even more painful, but he preferred to test her intent before he turned his back on the knife.

She sliced neatly through the bonds on his ankles. "Turn around. You'll need your hands free to eat."

"Thank you," said Tobin. "I don't suppose you'd throw that knife in, and let me do it myself?"

She gazed at him blankly. "Turn around, so I can cut your hands loose. I know you understand me."

She gestured to his amulet, and Tobin realized she wasn't wearing one.

"So I can understand you, but you can't understand me? Is that how it works?"

She sheathed her knife and folded her arms. The bowl sat on the ground where she'd placed it, and her message was plain with no words at all.

The hair on the back of Tobin's neck prickled as he turned his back and pressed his hands against the bars, but she only cut through the rope around his wrists, handed him the bowl and waterskin, and departed.

The stew was goat, vegetables, and some grain Tobin didn't recognize. Once he got over a vague reluctance to eat with his fingers, the food was good, though the seasoning tasted a bit odd. They wouldn't skimp if they were fattening him for the slaughter. But Tobin's half-formed plan to appear more ill than he was by picking at his food gave way to hunger. Besides, he needed all his strength in order to escape.

Watching the common business of the camp kept Tobin occupied till dark. The scouting parties, easily identified by their white-painted skin, had been coming and going all day, but by evening most of them had returned.

They washed off the white clay in the stream, Tobin saw, yelping at the chill and splashing one another. But even without their paint, he was fairly certain it was a group of the warriors who finally approached his cage after darkness fell. Their faces, alive with mockery, held none of the woman's half-kindly indifference.

They said nothing to him, though one of them murmured something Tobin couldn't hear and several of them laughed.

There was enough firelight for him to see the glint of blood amulets on several chests, but Tobin knew that pleading with bullies only encouraged them, and taunting them would only give them an excuse.

Not that they needed it.

At least it was just the spear's butt that shot through the cage bars, striking his ribs with bruising force but not penetrating for a lethal blow.

Tobin scrambled to the other side of the cage, but they

surrounded it and started poking at him from that side. He crouched in the center and waited for several long minutes, doing his best to dodge their thrusts. Then he made his snatch, closing both hands around a spear butt as it surged toward his shoulder.

The young warrior on the other end of the spear almost lost his grip in sheer surprise, but his hands tightened reflexively when Tobin pulled. Then his face hardened.

Tobin shifted his grip and tried to thrust the sharp point into the warrior's stomach, but the sturdy wooden bars got in the way and the warrior dodged.

Another spear butt slammed down on his wrist, numbing it, and the warrior yanked his spear out of Tobin's hands.

He tried to get hold of another, but now they were watching for it—and if the wariness of the men in front of Tobin hindered their blows, it freed those behind him to strike at will.

A hard rap on his skull set him swaying, dizzy. A thread of hot blood crept down the back of his neck.

The smartest thing Tobin could do now was lie down and fake unconsciousness, but he was too angry, too frightened.

He grabbed for another spear and missed. A shrewd blow struck his elbow, and pain shot down his arm. He was gasping for breath, and the cage seemed to revolve slowly around him. Soon his unconsciousness wouldn't be feigned.

"This is not the conduct of warriors," a man's voice said coldly.

The blows stopped.

The one-eyed man gazed contemptuously at the warriors who surrounded Tobin's cage. They looked down or aside and shuffled their feet, like boys caught in mischief.

"A true warrior doesn't attack those who are crippled or bound," the older man went on. "Like the slaughter of animals, such tasks are the province of women, and no warrior would stoop to them."

A couple of the younger men flushed at this.

"You know why we're—" one of them protested.

"I know exactly what you're supposed to do and say," One-Eye interrupted. "And for this night, that's enough."

"Well, you don't have to insult us," another grumbled.

But they departed, and Tobin dropped gratefully to the cage floor. Now that he had time to feel it, every muscle in his body throbbed and ached.

"Thank . . ."

One-Eye turned and walked away.

Later, when the camp slept, Tobin tested the cage. For people who lived in tents, their carpentry was good. The bars that made up the walls and roof were set into a frame of thick, squared timbers and then, as far as Tobin could tell by touch, nailed into place.

When the goblins had held him prisoner, only a few months ago, Tobin had freed himself by working the metal bolt that secured his chains back and forth till it ground away the wood around it. The sharpest tool he had here was his belt buckle, and filing through one of the hardwood bars with that would take days, at least.

Tobin didn't think he had days. Though hadn't someone said something about having to capture a spirit?

However small the chance, it was the best idea he had. He took off his belt and began scraping at the base of one of the bars, where it shouldn't be too obvious in the daylight.

His eyelids were drooping as the shock of the beating added itself to the residual weariness of his long illness. But sleeping through the day would have the added benefit of making him look sicker than he really was. And if he began tiring, Tobin told himself firmly, all he had to do was think about what the barbarians planned for him, and he'd wake right—

"I see it takes more than a few bruises to stop you. That's good. For my sake as well as yours."

It was the one-eyed man. Tobin's hand closed instinctively over the buckle—though if One-Eye had approached so quietly that Tobin hadn't heard him, he might have been watching for some time.

"Put your belt back on," One-Eye said, confirming his guess. "If you're going to vanish, all your clothing should disappear with you. It's more dramatic that way, and as a storyteller . . . Well, drama can make the difference between success and disbelief."

Tobin's mind spun, but he grasped the important point. "I'm going to vanish?"

"Into the air, like water poured on rocks under the desert sun. Of course, they expect you to escape eventually."

Tobin blinked. Either he'd been hit on the head harder than he thought or this conversation was taking some odd turns. "They do?"

"They do. Like this." One-Eye grabbed one of the cage bars and pulled. It snapped like a rotten twig.

Tobin was so startled he didn't even move. "How did you . . . ? Why . . . ?"

"This bar is always rigged to break. In a few days, one of them, in the process of taunting you, would crack it with his spear. You'd be stiff and weaker by then." The old man worked the bottom of the bar free of the frame. "That night they would watch from the shadows, waiting for the moment you picked up a weapon. Can you get out now, if I give you a hand?"

Tobin hesitated. This whole conversation made no sense—but he couldn't be worse off out of the cage than he was inside it. He thrust his head and shoulders through the bars and squirmed.

"Go back to the part where they *expect* me to escape. Why?"

The old man grabbed his shoulders and pulled, then kept his hold so that when Tobin's feet were free, they swung to the ground, which kept him from falling headfirst.

"That part's a bit complicated," One-Eye said. "Let me take you somewhere we can talk."

If it hadn't been for his throbbing bruises, walking through the center of the sleeping camp would have felt like a dream. The old man stopped beside the glowing embers of a cook fire and lit a candle stub he pulled from his pocket. To Tobin, the light seemed to present more danger than it was worth, but the stranger had kept him safe so far. The surreal feeling increased when One-Eye led Tobin into one of the largest tents and carefully closed the flaps. Tobin stared around him at racks of swords, chests full of spears, and more racks of the short, curved bows that could send an arrow twice as far as the longbows of the Realm's foot soldiers.

"Now I know I'm dreaming," Tobin said. "You're going to give me a weapon?"

"Not at all," said One-Eye. "I'm going to explain why you must never take any of these weapons, or any other, and also what makes this the perfect place for you to hide—at least till the first search is over."

The need to flee into the night pulsed through Tobin's blood. And curiosity was his brother's fatal flaw, not his. Tobin was the practical one. But there was something about the old man's steady gaze . . .

Tobin sat down on one of the spear crates. "I'm listening."

"You heard Rocza this afternoon, saying that there were ways of getting the blood trust away from you?"

"Yes, and I know you can't kill me as long as I wear it. Though I don't understand . . . Wait a minute. How can you understand me now, when you didn't earlier?"

One-Eye opened his shirt, displaying the now-familiar copper round. "They keep these here as well, what few spares we have. Only warriors, the Duri, are entitled to wear them, but I stole this one long ago. I knew that one day I would need it—it took the fools longer than I expected to bring in a Softer knight—but we don't have time for that tale now. The only way to take someone's blood trust from them, without violating sacred law, is to convince them to challenge you. If two people are determined to fight, the blood-trust laws don't strictly forbid it."

Tobin remembered another shred of conversation from the morning. "So if I came at one of your warriors with a weapon in hand, that would be a challenge and they could fight me, even though I'm wearing the amulet?"

"Yes, and if they succeed in disarming you, or kill you, then your amulet is forfeit. Which is why so few warriors are willing to challenge each other—the penalty for losing is too serious to risk lightly."

It made a twisted sort of sense.

"Is that why they set things up so I can escape? They figure I'll find or steal a weapon and fight them. Then, when they win, they can take the amulet and kill me at will?"

"Exactly." One-Eye nodded encouragement. "And I'm glad to see that blow didn't damage your wits. You'll need them in the next few days."

"Then why bring me here," Tobin asked, "if you're not giving me a weapon?"

"Because this is the first place those who escape are expected to go." The gleam in the old man's remaining eye reminded Tobin of Jeriah at his worst, and his misgivings increased. "By the time they're shown the flawed bar, they've watched people going into this tent empty-handed and leaving with weapons often enough to know what's stored here. So this is the first place searchers will look for you, and when they don't find you—"

"Why won't they find me?"

"Because . . . Here, I'll show you."

One-Eye opened a crate of spears and began pulling them out. "They'll expect you to spring out at them with a weapon, especially in here, so they're not likely to look very hard. And even if they did . . ." He lifted up the bottom of the long crate. But it wasn't the bottom, Tobin saw as he peered inside. It was a false bottom that covered a space that might well hold a man—if he hadn't eaten much for the last few months, and maybe held his breath.

"You've been planning this a long time," said Tobin, staring at the well-made secret compartment. "Why?"

For the first time, One-Eye hesitated.

"Our blood trust—you call them amulets, as if that was all they are—do you know how they're made?'

"I've heard it involves human sacrifice," said Tobin. "And I've seen nothing to change my mind."

"Human sacrifice," the storyteller repeated, as though the concept was strange to him. Did that phrase come to his mind with multiple connotations, as so many of his words did to Tobin? "That's part of it, but really the least part. The human death is only a carrier for the magic of the spirit."

"Explain," said Tobin. "Quickly."

"Still not made up your mind? Then listen carefully, for there are things you need to know if you plan to flee. To make these amulets, our shamans must first capture a spirit. Which isn't as easy as it used to be, for they know the fate they'll meet at our hands. At this moment no one has even located a spirit, which gives us a bit of time."

"More quickly," Tobin said. He didn't know how many hours remained till dawn, but if he was going to run—which seemed a lot smarter than hiding in a chest in the middle of the barbarians' camp!—he wanted to do it long before sunrise.

"It takes the time it takes," the storyteller said reprovingly. "All of this is important. And the more you interrupt me, the—"

"All right, go on."

The storyteller seated himself on a chest with unnecessary deliberation. "To sum the matter up, the shamans must capture a spirit, and also a human they're willing to kill. As the molten copper is poured to make the medallion, they open the human's veins. His death—his knowledge of his impending death is part of what makes this possible—opens up a void in his body so the shamans can force the spirit into it."

The hair on the back of Tobin's neck had risen. "They force a spirit to occupy a human body? While the human's still in it?"

"It appears to be painful for both of them," the storyteller confirmed. "But the fact that the human is dying somehow makes it possible. And when a spirit is bound in a body of flesh and blood, it dies too. The blood must quench the medallions while the human-spirit is still alive, for only while it lives will the spirit's magic transform simple copper to a thing of power. So the bleeding out is made to last as long as possible, that more trusts can be awakened."

Tobin's stomach was rolling. This was worse than cannibalism. "Then you don't eat people after all?"

"Oh, yes. As soon as the body dies, our warriors eat the flesh. It's consuming that flesh, which still holds part of the spirit's magic, that awakens/ignites/restores their inborn power."

Tobin rose abruptly to his feet. "Thanks for warning me about the weapons. I'll make sure not to pick one up if I'm captured."

"You will be captured," the storyteller said calmly. "One of the powers that are kindled in our Duri is the ability to sense . . . the shamans call it 'disruptions in the magical field.' They can sense the presence of a blood-trust medallion several hundred yards away. Some can sense them even farther off. So as soon as one of the searchers passes anywhere near you, they'll know you're there, and in approximately which direction. It would be much harder for me to free you a second time."

"So I'll take off the amulet. . . . Oh." If he wore the amulet, they could use it to find him. But if he took it off and they caught him without it, he would die as soon as they captured a spirit. Or maybe before, if another prisoner was taken and they no longer needed him. And Tobin had no way of knowing if anything he'd just been told was true, either.

"But if I hide in the chest, won't they sense my amulet and find me instantly?"

"There are half a dozen amulets stored in this room," the storyteller said. "Hundreds within sensing distance, and thousands in the greater camp, which those with the farthest-reaching senses might detect. I'm told it's like trying to pick the scent of one flower out of a bouquet, or one voice out of the chatter of a crowd. Whereas if you're walking through empty country with just a few companions, and a voice comes to you from another direction, you hear it clearly. Do you see?"

Tobin did. "So if I stay here, my amulet will be one of a crowd and not noticeable. But what about the rest of me?"

"I have a plan for that," the storyteller told him. "We can dye your hair and skin and dress you as chanduri. No one really looks at the chan, anyway. And there's one other thing I can do. As I said, I've been planning this for some time."

"Why?" Tobin asked again. And this time it was the only question that mattered.

"When we have prisoners," said One-Eye slowly, "we keep them for making the trusts. Sometimes they dwell in that cage for months, until a spirit can be found and snared. But have you thought about what we do for the human part of the trust if we don't have a prisoner? We made thousands of trusts before we went to war with you."

The horror of the only possible answer shocked Tobin even more. It was one thing to kill an enemy, no matter how vile the method. To murder your own people . . .

"I was born with only one working eye," the old man went on softly. "So I could never be a warrior, never Duri. I became the tradition/history keeper because that's the most worthy position any chan can achieve. The Duri spoke to me as an equal—superior to the younger warriors when I trained them to honor our laws. And for years, watching those too old to work go under the knife, I thought I'd made myself safe. But I am now over sixty years, and there's a young storyteller in another camp who listens very carefully to my histories. Softer, if I can get you back to your own people, will you take me with you? And keep them from killing me until I can demonstrate how useful my information could be?"

Tobin considered. If the old man was telling the truth, his motives made perfect sense. Sense enough for Tobin to trust him with his life? A barbarian guide and helper would give him a far better chance to escape. One-Eye hadn't had to let him out of that cage. If Tobin had found that cracked bar in a few more nights, stiff and weakened by repeated beat-ings, he'd have grabbed the first weapon he could lay hands on. He sorted carefully through his memories of the barbar-ian camp—he'd watched them for most of the day—and he didn't remember seeing any old people.

"Yes," said Tobin, making up his mind. "If you can get me over the border alive, I'll take you with me. When do I have to get into that box?"

One-Eye told him not to climb in till his escape was dis-covered, since he'd have to stay there till the search had moved out of camp, and maybe for some time afterward.

He showed Tobin the trick he'd worked out, filling the chest's lid with spears and then looping a string through the catch. Tobin could lie down in the box, settle the false bot-tom on top of him, and then pull the lid closed, tipping the spears into the chest.

They practiced it several times before the old man was certain Tobin wouldn't pull the string too fast or too slowly. Then the storyteller departed, saying it would be better if the alarm found him sleeping in his own bed than lurking in a weapons storage tent where he had no business.

He took the candle with him, so Tobin pulled the tent flap a little wider and let his eyes adjust to the darkness.

The temptation to snatch up a weapon and run was strong, but the storyteller had no motive for lying that he could see. What would it be like to spend your whole life knowing that when you grew old, your own people would kill you, in a horribly painful way, just so their warriors could steal some sort of magical power? And what kind of power did the spirits' magic and death give them?

Tobin had spent two winters with the army on the border, and he'd heard plenty of rumors about "invincible" barbarian magic. He'd seen battle only once, when a party of barbarians had tried to raid an area that his troop patrolled. He'd exchanged sword blows with several of their warriors, and though they were very strong, they hadn't been impossible to fight. Fiddle had knocked their smaller horses out of his way, and they'd bled when his sword got through their guards.

And they could be killed, for he'd seen their bodies on the ground when the battle was over. Not many bodies, not nearly as many as his troop had left there, but they weren't immortal. His commander said that the sheer screaming frenzy with which they fought protected them, but knowing what he knew now, Tobin wondered. Did this blood trust really give supernatural powers to the barbarian . . . Duri? . . . warriors?

Tobin had always felt awkward calling them barbarians, but he'd known no other name for them. Now that he did, barbarian sounded like the perfect description.

The trick with the chest worked perfectly. The sun was just rising when Tobin heard the first shouts, and it was the work of seconds to climb into the box and pull the string to bring the spears clattering down on top of him.

It was far harder to lie still, with his heart hammering and sweat pouring off his body. He held his breath when he heard voices coming into the tent, though even the amulet's translation didn't let more than a few words though the muffling wood and the beating of his own pulse in his ears.

He felt the box's lid rise and then slam shut an instant later. Other lids opened and closed. The voices left.

Tobin could have pushed up the false bottom and the lid from inside, but it would have sent spears clattering to the earth. He didn't dare make so much noise in an "empty" tent.

It felt like he spent years in the small, cramped space. But finally someone lifted the lid, then removed the spears quietly, so Tobin knew it was One-Eye long before the false bottom was whisked away.

The slanting sunlight of midmorning was shining through the tent flap.

"Very good!" the old man murmured. "They're searching outside the camp now, and they've sent most of the women out to search nearby, so we've got some time. I even managed to get myself assigned to spread the news of your escape. It's all going perfectly."

Tobin didn't think that having every barbarian in the army searching for him was at all perfect, but he'd already chosen to place his life in this man's hands. And while he'd hidden in that box, waiting, another question had occurred to him.

"What's your name?"

"Vruud," the older man replied. "I wonder if it would be safer to dye your hair and change your clothes in here. I'd planned to do it in the woods, outside of camp, but I didn't expect the place to be this deserted."

"Aren't you going to ask what my name is?" Tobin demanded.

"Softer, I don't care. Did you think I was doing this for your sake? I'll get you back to your Realm, and you'll convince them not to kill me when we get there. That's all that matters to me."

# CHAPTER 3

# Jeriah

"DO YOU HAVE TO LEAVE so soon?" Jeriah's father asked. "You've only been here a few days."

It was very different from the last time his father had come to the stable to see Jeriah off. He'd been banished from the estate then—so even this mild protest against his leaving constituted a vast improvement in their relationship.

Telling his father the truth about what both he and Tobin had been doing over the past six months had been the right thing to do, but there was still strain between them.

"I need to get back to the palace, sir. That's where the goblins will look for me when they get back from the Otherworld. And if Tobin hasn't turned up in another week or so, I'll have to go find out why."

His father nodded, but more slowly than Jeriah had expected. "You mean to go into this Otherworld in search of him? I've no mind to lose both my sons there."

Given that Tobin had always been his father's favorite, and it was Jeriah's fault he'd been trapped in the Otherworld in the first place, that was generous.

"The goblins will bring him back." Jeriah tightened Glory's cinch. "I wouldn't have let them go without me if I wasn't certain. You know that."

"I know." His father sighed. "It's just . . . Never mind. I'll ride with you part of the way."

He went to get his own horse, and Jeriah took a deep breath and tried to be fair. It was because of him that Tobin had gotten involved with the sorceress—although she was the one who'd dragged his brother into the Otherworld! And their father had broken his own honor trying to get Tobin off for Jeriah's crime. The fact that Jeriah hadn't asked—or wanted!—either of them to do either of those things meant nothing.

*I think we've all learned an important lesson about telling each other the truth,* his mother had said. As if she wasn't the biggest liar among them!

Still, she had a point. Telling the truth, most of it, had created a tattered peace between him and his father, and riding together through the sprouting fields wasn't nearly as awkward as it had been. Jeriah resolved to be more truthful in the future. As soon as he finished just one small deception.

"The crops . . . everything looks good."

His father snorted. "Do you even know what's planted in that field?"

Jeriah looked at the rows of ruffled leaves. If it had been late summer, when the plants were bigger, he'd have had a better chance. "Beets?"

"It's lettuce." But his father's face held wry humor, instead of the grim patience that would have been there only a few weeks ago, and Jeriah laughed.

"I'll never make a farmer. You might as well give up on me."

"I think I will," said his father. "Oh, not give up on *you*. Beets and lettuce are very different, but I plant both of them, because both have their place."

And was he lettuce, Jeriah wondered, or a beet? "Thank you, sir. Soon Tobin will be home, so you won't have to do without either beets or . . . What's going on with the dike? I thought you'd decided not to repair it."

Most of the goblins who'd found a home in the flooded village had followed Cogswhallop into the Otherworld, but not all of them.

"Don't worry about your friends," his father said. "After what you've told me, they're welcome to make their homes anywhere on my land. And our people are already putting out goblin bowls, if they ever really stopped, no matter what the priests said."

"Yes, but you told me rebuilding the dike was too much work, since we'll just have to pack up and move to the north in a few years anyway."

"But you said the Hierarch doesn't favor the relocation," his father pointed out. "Now that he's no longer being drugged—I can hardly believe a priest would dare to drug the Bright Gods' Chosen one! But now that he's recovering, will the relocation go forward at all?"

It was exactly what Koryn had feared.

"The reason for it still exists," said Jeriah uneasily. "The barbarian army is still there, no matter what's been happening to the Hierarch. If anyone's figured out how to drive them back across the desert to their own lands, I haven't heard about it."

"Yes, but the relocation was Master Lazur's idea. Now that he's dead, perhaps some means to deal with them can be found." This from a man who was more inclined to cautious pessimism than most! "In any case, I've got some idle hands now that the planting's finished. If we can repair the dike and drain the fields before midsummer, the houses might dry out before irreparable damage is done to their structure. But I sent Alan to explain all this to your goblins, including my offer to help them build their own homes, before we ever started work on the dike. He said he felt silly, rowing out to the middle of that deserted square and shouting at empty houses, but they've heard my message. I won't leave them homeless, I promise you."

Now, that was the least of Jeriah's worries.

Could his father be right?

Koryn had told him that in bringing down Master Lazur, Jeriah had stopped the relocation as well. She'd cursed him for destroying the whole Realm, condemning everyone in it to death with that one act. And he knew that whatever else had passed between them, she'd never forgive him for that. He didn't need her forgiveness!

Besides, surely she might be wrong, and his father might be right?

She had slapped his face. Of course he'd wanted Mistress Koryn to slap him. A misplaced flirtation had been the best excuse he could come up with to abandon her in that ravine, where her crippled leg would trap her while he exposed Master Lazur's treachery. She'd been working for the priest, and Master Lazur was plotting against the Hierarch himself! It was only when Jeriah remembered how slender, how frail she'd looked in the moonlight . . . He snorted. Her leg might be crippled, but Koryn was tougher than he was, in every way that mattered.

He didn't miss her, either. It was only guilt—completely misplaced guilt!—that kept the last thing she'd said to him hovering in his mind, like a wasp he didn't dare ignore or crush.

But . . . could she have been right?

Glory's springy walk carried him rapidly down the road that led to Brindleford. From there Jeriah could turn either north, to the City of Steps, or south. Looking at the orderly fields he passed, the tidy farms, Jeriah's worry deepened. The command to relocate had never been rescinded, but would people be repairing fences and barns that they'd have to abandon soon?

And if they were planning to resist, were they wrong? Koryn and Master Lazur had believed that the Realm couldn't stop the barbarian army anywhere in the wide spread of the Realm's South- and Midlands. Bright Gods knew the Southlanders and the army had been trying! Master Lazur had believed that their only hope to hold back the barbarian army was the ancient wall that spanned the narrow neck of land that joined the Realm to the great northern woods. Jeriah's old commander had agreed with them.

But Master Lazur had also been drugging the Hierarch into imbecility, so he could control the council himself. Commander Sower had spent half a dozen years trying to stop the barbarian army as it pressed farther and farther into the Southlands. And Koryn's whole family had been slaughtered by barbarian warriors. So their judgments might well have been unduly influenced.

Were they right? Did the relocation really have to go forward, or was there another way?

Jeriah had wanted, desperately, to go into the Otherworld and bring Tobin back himself. It had been clear from the start that the sorceress had seduced his brother. Having watched his mother use her own dark beauty, Jeriah understood how much influence a beautiful girl could wield. But once she realized that the Otherworld would kill Tobin, surely the sorceress would let him go. And Jeriah had come to know the goblins. When they made a bargain, or thought they owed you, they kept at it till the debt was paid. Cogswhallop would bring Tobin back any day. They might be back already!

If Jeriah really had put the Realm at risk to save his brother, then he had to set it right. And for the first time in years, he wasn't assigned to anyone's service. Nevin had reclaimed his old post as the Hierarch's body squire, and although Master Zachiros had promised to find Jeriah "something to do, I'm sure," he currently had no job at all. No one was expecting his arrival. Leaving Jeriah free to go south to the border, and see for himself if the relocation really was necessary. Because if the barbarians couldn't be stopped, then it was up to him to set the relocation in motion once more.

When Jeriah had first ridden to the Southlands, to join his older brother fighting the barbarians, the journey had taken three weeks. He was familiar with the way the land grew drier and the weather hotter, with each day he traveled. He hadn't expected to be stopped in Marvele, a full three days' ride from where he'd stopped the last time.

"You don't want to go south of here, lad," a grizzled trooper told him. "Not unless you want to see bits of your liver being picked out of some barbarian's teeth."

"I'd heard they'd made a push," Jeriah said. "But I didn't realize . . . They took over a quarter of the Southlands!"

"About that," the soldier agreed. "They've been resting up since then, recovering. Bets are running high on whether they'll wait out the summer, like they used to, or make another big push soon. Now that they're camped in the Southlands and don't have to cross the desert to fight us, the smart money's on another summer attack."

"Your money?" Jeriah guessed.

The trooper grinned. "All I've got to do is survive to collect, and I'll be rich enough to live like a lord behind the great wall."

So the South, or at least the soldiers posted there, assumed the relocation was going forward as planned. Did their officers?

"Where's Commander Sower these days?" Jeriah asked.

The trooper didn't know. It took Jeriah several hours to learn that Commander Sower was currently posted out of Grayven, and most of the next day's ride to get there.

During the journey, Jeriah rode alongside enough patrols to learn that despite the familiar red tabards, with the church's golden sun gleaming on their breasts, the army had changed. Last year most of the soldiers had possessed the lighter skin and hair of men from the center and north of the Realm. Now, almost two-thirds of them had the dark hair and swarthy skin of Southlanders. Refugees? Almost certainly, which explained why the mood of the army had changed too.

When Jeriah had been here before, most of the soldiers were men sent by their landholders, who owed the Hierarch a levy of men to defend the Realm. Those men had been more interested in going home than in fighting anyone—and many of the injustices Jeriah objected to had sprung from that. He understood that the commanders couldn't simply release any man who wanted to go, but flogging a man half to death for trying to return home to be with his wife when their first child was born was too harsh.

The subcommander who'd ordered that punishment had soon found his tent swarming with ants—Jeriah, by dint of several childhood experiments, knew that ants would follow a honey trail for an amazing distance. The next inspection of the subcommander's troop had been so disastrous that Jeriah still grinned at the memory . . . and the subcommander had been reduced to a common trooper.

Jeriah had also used practical jokes to cover more serious activities, carrying messages for the conspirators who had sought to overthrow the cadre that controlled the council, to reform abusive laws, both in the army and in the Realm at large. Which probably explained the sour expression on Commander Sower's face when Jeriah was shown into his office.

"What are you doing here?" he demanded. "I thought you were bedeviling, ah, serving the Hierarch now."

If Sower knew he'd come here on his own, he would send Jeriah away.

"Yes, sir," said Jeriah smoothly. "As you seem to have heard, I was honored with an appointment as one of the Hierarch's body squires."

And that appointment hadn't been taken away from him—only the job had—so technically . . .

"Then what are you doing here?" Commander Sower repeated.

There was a time when you either had to press forward or yield. And Jeriah had never been good at yielding.

"I don't know how much else you might have heard about the Hierarch," Jeriah began carefully. "Lately, that is."

Sower's brows drew down. "I've heard some rumors. I also received an official report that Master Lazur was hanged for treason. Couldn't believe it. The man was the architect of the relocation and the army's best advocate in council. And they say he tried to poison the Hierarch? Nonsense!"

"I'm afraid that part's true," said Jeriah. And he hoped this man never learned how much he'd had to do with that truth being uncovered. "Oh, not poison. But he did try to give the Hierarch a drug that would make him . . . compliant."

In fact, Master Lazur had been giving the Hierarch that drug for seven years, but that was something no one was allowed to know.

"Well," said Sower blankly. "What a demonish mess."

"Exactly so, sir. And that's why I'm here. Everything Master Lazur had a hand in is now considered suspect, including the reports he made about conditions here on the border. There will be an official inquiry, of course—"

"They're already here," Sower told him. "In Helverian, last I heard, some twenty miles from the border. They show no signs of moving closer."

Jeriah made a mental note to avoid the official inquiry at all costs.

"I think the Hierarch suspected that kind of thing might happen," he improvised. "That's why he sent me, and a few others, to gain a . . . less formal impression of what's really going on."

"You're here to spy on the army?" Anger began to dawn in Sower's expression.

"If I was here to spy, I wouldn't have told you," Jeriah said drily. "All I'm here for is to gather some unofficial information to compare with the official reports."

"So the Hierarch knows what kind of self-serving scum the council sent," said Sower. "That's the first encouraging news I've heard in weeks."

"Well, sir, you know what official inspections are like."

Sower nodded. "But what am I supposed to do with you?"

"Assign me to a commander on the border," Jeriah told him. "Someone who's seen some action and can tell me the truth about the barbarians and what it will take to stop them."

Sower sighed. "I'm not sure it's possible to stop them. Just slowing them down is hard enough! Yes, it would be a very good idea to give the Hierarch a clear picture of what's going on down here. I'll assign you, as an aide, to Commander Malveese. Tell him it's temporary, so you won't dislocate his command structure when you depart."

He was already looking for a blank sheet of paper. A few minutes later Jeriah left the office, orders in hand, which would perfectly position him to learn what he'd come here to learn.

Of course, his resolve to tell the truth was in pieces—again. Though nothing he'd said was technically a lie, except for the part about the Hierarch sending him. And if Jeriah reported whatever he discovered to the Hierarch, he could make that part true in spirit, if not in fact, so it wasn't a lie either. Technically.

Commander Malveese had the typical Southlander's dark coloring and stocky build, the Southlands' soft accent—and perhaps a bit of the Southlands' laziness as well. He assigned Jeriah to a troop without seeming to think much about it, which suited Jeriah just fine.

Three-quarters of Jeriah's troop were also refugee Southlanders, and their iron-clad hatred of the barbarians reminded him of Mistress Koryn. If determination alone could defeat their army, the barbarians were done for. But under the soldiers' hatred lurked a deep depression.

Over the next few days, as Jeriah's troop patrolled the border, he heard many tales of battles—both won and lost—against howling madmen with supernatural strength, who never tired and had personal demons that guarded them from death. Maybe that accounted for the fact that all the soldiers wore their full accoutrement of chain mail and metal plates, though most of the men in Jeriah's previous patrol had found full armor too hot and cumbersome for the warm Southlands.

Jeriah dismissed the wilder stories. Koryn had said

something about barbarian magic, but she'd been maddeningly vague about what it was. Jeriah had never fought the barbarians himself, but he'd seen their bodies carried back to camp for burial, so he knew they could be slain. And the Southlanders really wanted to slay them, so their persistent belief that the barbarians couldn't be beaten seemed strange.

Jeriah decided to ask Malveese about it, so on the next border patrol that the commander led, he pulled his horse up to the front of the loose column.

"You've seen something?" Malveese asked, scanning the brushy slope intently.

The Southlanders took patrolling much more seriously than the troop Jeriah had served with last year—these men had lost their homes to the barbarians' last major attack. But that had been in the summer, when it was well known that the barbarians never attacked, so the army's strength had been much reduced. Now they were kept at full strength all year round, and the barbarians hadn't launched a major offensive since. Which made his comrades' constant alertness a bit tiresome.

"No, sir," Jeriah replied. "Nothing to report. I just have a few questions."

"Finally." The commander sighed. "I was beginning to think you'd never get around to it."

"To what, sir?"

"To your spying for the Hierarch, of course," said Malveese. "Did you think I wouldn't check up on you?"

"Ah . . ." That was exactly what Jeriah had thought.

"It was no secret that you were dismissed from the army to take up a post in the palace," Malveese went on. "And it took very little for me to learn what post you achieved. Commander Sower didn't say much, but the subcommander you served under bragged about you at quite unnecessary length."

Jeriah blinked. The subcommander had detested him, and as for the rest of it . . .

"I was given a post in the palace because my mother once served the previous Hierarch's mother," Jeriah said. "Not much to brag about. As for being appointed as the Hierarch's body squire, well, I was there and available when the job became vacant."

"And now you are here to spy on the army for him," Commander Malveese concluded. "Oh, don't protest— I think it an excellent idea. Besides, there was something else I heard about you. Not from the officers, but from the common soldiers. They say Jeriah Rovan has no stomach for injustice."

"Ah . . . ," said Jeriah blankly. He hadn't thought anyone had noticed that his pranks were aimed at people who deserved them.

"There's a great injustice here," the commander said soberly. "Will you take it to the Hierarch and make sure he knows of it? The other Southland landholders, they say no one is listening."

"If I can," said Jeriah cautiously. It was one thing to pretend he was going to report on the condition of the army. It would be another entirely to do it. "But anything I say will be weighed against all the official reports."

"And unofficial ones too, no doubt," said the commander. "But you have the Hierarch's ear, correct?"

The Hierarch liked Jeriah and would remember him kindly. He could get a minute with the man and say whatever he needed to. "I suppose so."

"It's the land," said Commander Malveese. "Or rather, the lack of it. Only a landholder can appear and speak in council, so in the last barbarian attack many Southland lords lost not only their homes and friends, but their voice in the Realm as well."

His face twisted, and Jeriah suddenly realized that Commander Malveese might be one of those men.

"But surely . . . they didn't strip landholders of their titles just because the barbarians conquered their lands?"

"They did," the commander confirmed. "The law decrees that the title comes from the land itself. Though some of us see a difference between losing your land through gambling and bad management and losing it to enemy attack."

"But that's—that's wrong!" Jeriah protested.

"So I think, and so do many Southland lords whose estates are still within their grasp. They see that their time will come. But with the loss of almost a third of our number in the council, the Southland lords are a small minority, and the others . . . The land a man is granted in the north is to be based, as a percentage, on the land he owned before the relocation. So the fewer landholders there are when the relocation officially takes place, the more land there will be for the rest. There are some Southland lords who think that way too." Cold anger lit his face at the thought of his neighbors' betrayal. "They are sabotaging our efforts to obtain justice for those who bore the brunt of the first attack."

"I've been gone for a while," said Jeriah. "But I don't think the Hierarch knows anything about this. Lord Brallorscourt is the one who controls the largest faction on the council—"

"Lord Brallorscourt knows all about it," said Commander Malveese. "But he's one of those who is perfectly content to seize more land for himself. Will you help—"

A man screamed. Jeriah spun just in time to see one of their soldiers topple from the saddle with an arrow in his side. Then the brush around them erupted with screaming, white-painted bodies, and Jeriah had no time to notice anything.

He was still fumbling for his sword hilt when one of the barbarians rushed him. The clay-covered face, surrounded by spikes of stiffened hair, was set in a wild grimace. He was close enough for Jeriah to see his eyes brighten as he realized that his surprised opponent wouldn't be able to get his blade free in time, and Jeriah felt a flash of piercing despair. Then Commander Malveese's blade flashed out, raking the barbarian's face, and blood welled from a deep gash across his cheekbone.

The barbarian screamed in pain instead of battle frenzy, and Glory leaped aside.

Jeriah yanked his blade from its sheath and turned Glory back to the wounded barbarian, but the man had vanished in the chaotic sea of struggling forms, and two more barbarians were closing in on the commander.

With a battle yell of his own, Jeriah kicked Glory forward, and one of the barbarians turned to him, raising his sword.

The clash of steel on steel numbed Jeriah's wrist, but he'd practiced often enough with Tobin, and with his father's master of arms, that going on to the next parry, then the next, was automatic. Glory, better trained for battle than he was, circled to keep anyone from coming up behind them.

Jeriah was so focused on trying to break through his opponent's guard—and on keeping the barbarian from doing the same to him—that he didn't even see the Southlander who crept up behind his enemy until the barbarian's face froze in a sudden rictus. The man tore his gaze from Jeriah's face and looked down.

His leather breast plate was being pushed away from his chest from the inside, and Jeriah looked behind him in time to see the Southlander pull back a blood-covered sword.

More blood flooded from under the leather, dripping to the ground, and the barbarian collapsed. The sword must have cut right through his heart, Jeriah realized. But it was an absent, almost distant thought, for Jeriah was already whirling Glory to look for a comrade who needed his aid.

The fighting had spread out over the slope, and Jeriah

saw that the Southlanders outnumbered the barbarians by maybe a third. He wondered that the barbarians had dared attack them at all!

Was that why so many called them madmen? Even though they'd taken down several Southlanders with that first flight of arrows, it was still easy for Jeriah to ride up behind one of them who was already engaged in the fight. Jeriah soon discovered that if he yelled as he drew near, the younger barbarians would often turn toward him, and the Southlander they'd been fighting could launch whatever blow he wished at his enemy's back.

The older barbarians disengaged from their duels and fled when they heard Jeriah approach, but those close to his own age died—too caught up in the fight, too inexperienced, to know how to break off a combat and withdraw. Jeriah wasn't sure he could have managed that himself. He made a note to learn how as soon as possible.

He was roasting in his armor, sweat running down his body, but when an arrow raked Glory's shoulder and pinged off his thigh guard, Jeriah was profoundly grateful that the Southland troopers hadn't let him leave off even one piece.

More arrows fell, and the remaining barbarians broke off their fights and ran down the hillside. A few minutes later they were galloping out of the small canyon at the bottom.

For a moment Jeriah wanted to follow, but the Southlanders were already stringing their bows and he'd only get in their way. Then exhaustion struck like a lance. Jeriah slid out of

Glory's saddle and opened his breast plate, letting the fresh air rush over his heated skin. He wanted water with a desperate thirst, but his arms were too tired, his fingers too stiff, to reach up and untie the skin from his saddle.

And it wouldn't be nearly enough. He needed a river that he could plunge into, cooling his whole body while he drank and drank.

Dark spots were dancing in front of his vision when a hand grasped his shoulder and pressed him down.

"Fighting in the heat," a voice with a Southland accent said. "It takes Northers like that, for a while. Just sit here and sip on this. You'll recover soon enough."

A waterskin was thrust into Jeriah's hands, and he took a sip before he found the strength to murmur, "I'm from the Midlands."

His stomach was rebelling, but Jeriah refused to be sick after his first battle.

*He'd just fought a battle.* But that realization was distant too, compared to the urgent stresses of his body.

If the Southlander said anything else, Jeriah didn't hear it. Eventually the whirling chaos in his stomach and head subsided, and he was able to sit and watch the aftermath of the fight—though he didn't feel like helping yet.

He had just fought in his first battle, and though he hadn't killed anyone, he'd helped several other men do so. He shivered, suddenly glad that his own sword, though it had picked up several nicks, wasn't coated in blood.

The Southland troops were gathering the corpses, both the barbarians' and those of their own men—the barbarians' to be buried now, in a trench grave, and their men to be carried back to camp and buried with proper reverence. Though only four Southlanders had been slain, there were at least half a dozen barbarian bodies.

*We should get their amulets.* The church had forbidden the Realm's soldiers to wear them, since their making involved human sacrifice. But they did collect them and allow them to be worn by the insanely brave men who scouted behind enemy lines.

And Jeriah had sent most of the Realm's supply of amulets into the Otherworld with the goblins, so he'd better make sure that these were gathered up.

He stood slowly, and after one lazy spin the world steadied under his feet, and he approached a man who was dragging one of the enemy corpses over to the place where the others had begun to dig.

"Are you taking their amulets?" he asked.

"What for? The priests won't let us wear them, and the few who tried it anyway found they didn't exactly work like the stories said."

"What do you mean?" Jeriah asked. "I thought the barbarians wouldn't fight a man who was wearing one of those amulets. That's why scouts and spies are allowed to wear them."

"That's what they said," the man told him. "But I've seen barbarians attack men wearing those amulets just like anyone else. In fact, they seemed to go for the soldiers who wore them more than those who didn't."

"But I thought . . . I've heard of scouts and spies who survived because of those amulets," Jeriah said.

The soldier shrugged. "Maybe it's different for them, somehow. If you want any amulets, they're yours for the taking.

He dropped the corpse he was dragging near the rest and walked away.

Jeriah fought down a surge of revulsion. He'd helped kill these men. You could call them barbarians all you wanted, but they were still men. Men who were trying to conquer his Realm and slaughter its citizens. And then eat them.

Jeriah took a deep breath and knelt to lift the dead man's head and remove the amulet from around his neck. He tried not to look at the man's face. He couldn't help but look.

Jeriah froze, his hand clenching in the clay-stiffened hair. It was the barbarian who had first attacked him, the one from whom Commander Malveese had saved him, cutting open the man's cheek.

There was blood on the dead face, staining the white clay, washing some of it away . . . but the skin beneath it was whole. The cut was gone, leaving not even a scar behind. Completely healed.

"Yes, they heal themselves," Commander Malveese confirmed. "Almost instantly, in the midst of combat. And it's not those amulets you gathered that causes it. We've done some experiments, despite the priests' orders."

He reached out and added another log to the fire, keeping his eyes on the blaze. Jeriah had waited, storing up question after question, till they'd returned to camp and he could talk to the commander alone.

"They also don't tire the way we do," the commander went on. "I've seen battles in which the numbers were even to start with, where we were forced to withdraw simply because our people were exhausted, and they fought on and on like . . . like an incoming tide. But I've killed enough of them to know they're flesh and blood. Any stroke that kills too swiftly for their healing power to act will slay them. But that's the only way to do it, and that's why we can't win."

He looked up, for the first time, and met Jeriah's eyes. "The official inspectors, safe in Helverian, they say that's impossible, that we're making up wild tales to excuse our failures. But look at today. We outnumbered them by a third, and that let us kill seven of them to the four men I lost. But I have two more so badly injured they may never fight again, and another eight who will take weeks or months to mend their wounds—which makes it fourteen of ours to six of theirs, at least for a time. And numbers like that," he finished grimly, "is how they're taking the Southlands."

"But what can we do?" Jeriah asked. "If they always heal like that . . ." He'd seen it himself, and he still had trouble believing it.

"The first thing is to get the Hierarch and the council

to listen to what we tell them," said Commander Malveese. "That the barbarians cannot be stopped. Myself, I think they'll take the whole of the Southlands in the next year, and the rest of the Realm within five. And the only reason it will take them that long is that there aren't more of them. Will you go to the Hierarch for us, Jeriah Rovan? And convince him and the council that no matter what else Master Lazur did, he was right about one thing: The relocation *must* go forward. Every month, every day it is delayed will cost more lives."

Jeriah thought about his father, rebuilding the dike because "now some other solution may be found." About the countryside he'd ridden through, where as far as he could tell all plans for relocating had simply been abandoned. As if all over the Realm, people had made up their minds that now Master Lazur was dead, it didn't have to happen.

"I'll try," he said. "No, I'll do it."

Because Koryn had been right. In exposing Master Lazur, in bringing him down, Jeriah himself had single-handedly stopped the relocation in its tracks. If he couldn't get it back in motion, the barbarian conquest of the Realm would be entirely his fault.

"I'll do it," Jeriah repeated. "I have to."

# CHAPTER 4

# Makenna

TWO WEEKS AFTER THEY SENT Tobin back to the real world, Makenna cut off her hair.

She woke from a nightmare, sitting up with a jolt, gasping for breath. But the familiar ceiling of the tent looked just as it always did in the dim moonlight. It wasn't buried in drifting sand, summoned by the howling wind to smother her, as she had dreamed.

The wind was real. It had been blowing since the night after they'd trapped the water spirit, leaving everyone edgy and tense. The spirit had kept her promise not to harm the humans herself. She'd made no promise about her friends.

Makenna reached up to run her fingers through her sweaty hair, and they stuck in snarls right next to her scalp. She swore. The last time—in fact, the last four times this had happened—it had taken her and her goblin helpers hours to comb out the long, dark red-mass. And Makenna wasn't the only one. Several of the goblin women who slept alone had received visits from the same taunting spirit, and one little girl, Onny, had been particularly troubled. If they didn't tangle your dreams at the same time, it wouldn't be so bad.

Makenna was tired of being the spirits' victim. Tired of food that now rotted only hours after it was picked, and tents sinking in mud puddles that hadn't been there when they were set up that evening.

Enough! Kneeling on her bedroll, Makenna drew her knife, its copper blade honed almost as sharp as steel by the goblin smiths. She cut the hair a scant inch from her scalp, so the tangles fell in long, matted hanks onto her blankets. She had to feel her way carefully at the back of her head, to keep from cutting herself, but soon she could run her fingers through the short pelt without catching a single knot. Her head felt as if it was floating on her shoulders. Her heart, also, was oddly light. Unencumbered, ready for the next phase of the fight. Dark One take the spirits! It was time to go on the offense, and let them defend for a while.

Cogswhallop found her over an hour later, sitting in the remains of her shorn hair, with a spell book in her hands.

There hadn't been much in the priest's books about spirits, particularly about catching them or getting them to leave you alone.

The few references Makenna did find made tantalizing comments about something called the Great Outcasting. Had the priests once driven all the spirits out of the Realm, as they'd later tried to drive the goblins out? If so, it must have been a long time ago. None of Makenna's mother's teaching had even mentioned them.

In fact, the only hint she'd found that might be useful was something one of the hedgewitches Master Lazur had abandoned here to die had told him: that spells worked best against the spirits "when I put myself into them."

To Master Lazur, that had meant a rune that represented you worked into the casting. But Makenna knew more about hedgewitches than he had.

He'd been a cold man, all in all. Reading his books and notes had given her more insight into him than fighting against him for her life. She'd once told Tobin's brother that she pitied the man, so lost in his obsession that he'd lost his humanity. Reading about some of the things he'd done had shrunk that pity to the vanishing point—but his mind had been keen.

Makenna felt as if this trap—using her own interpretation of a clue he'd missed—was a way of fighting against him as well as the spirits.

"It looks complicated enough," said Cogswhallop, eyeing the mass of chalked runes and the fragile cat's cradle of silver and copper chains. Every goblin woman in the camp had sacrificed bits of jewelry for this. Makenna hoped she'd be able to return it.

"I'll admit," the goblin went on, "if we were still fighting settlers in the wood, and they set up something like this, I'd make it a target."

"The more reason for us to be watching it, then," said Makenna with a confidence that was only half feigned.

Her magic had been so much weaker than her mother's, weaker than the magic of the goblins she lived with, that Makenna hadn't realized how much a part of her it was till the Otherworld had drained it to the dregs. Those amulets were all that prevented their power from being leached away right now. But they were preventing it, and Makenna felt like her power had come back even stronger, in this magic-rich world. Her will to fight had returned with it.

It made the first stage, which was to go quietly off to bed, harder than anything she'd done for a long time. At least she didn't have to sleep. Makenna lay awake, her clothing concealed under a blanket, tossing through the passing hours. She heard the first shift of goblin guards trade off with the younger, less reliable-looking shift that Miggy led. His confidence had grown since he'd left the wood, and she had no doubts about putting him in charge of this second, vital step. The departing shift warned the youngsters not to forget to wet down all the chains when the moon was high. It was nonsense, of course, but it looked like magic, and that was all she needed. It also gave her helpers a chance to mingle and chat for a bit before they separated to their stations and drifted into feigned sleep. If it wasn't feigned, she'd have their hides off!

The first sign that the trap had been sprung was a crash that shook the earth beneath her. Makenna had bounded out of her blankets, then out of her tent, before the guards began to shout.

The moon was half full, enough light for her to see the goblins converging on the fragile web of chains. Chains that had been sundered like cobwebs by the strange being who crouched in the middle of the circle, trying to shake off the snare ropes that Miggy's brigade had snubbed around nearby trees. It growled, its voice echoing even through the wind.

Makenna decided there was no need to run and strolled over to the shattered spellworks. They had looked so magical and fragile, and had taken so many hours for her to set up and inscribe, that she knew some spirit was bound to try to smash them.

The creature straightened at her approach, glaring. She thought this one was male, though it was hard to be sure. It was clearly a tree spirit, with a sturdy trunklike torso, gnarled features, and rough, barklike skin. It had far too many limbs to call them arms, and they moved stiffly and seemed to be jointed in the wrong places.

"What is this rope?" it said, in a voice that held the hollow boom of wood striking wood. "It *burns*."

"Burns" was probably the ultimate curse to a tree spirit, but it didn't seem to be in too much pain—and right now, Makenna found it hard to care.

"It's made of clothing we brought with us and pulled apart for the threads," Makenna told it. The rope was mostly wool from Tobin's cloak, which they hadn't had time to send with him—and a good thing, too. The goblins' garments were too small to contain much thread, and Makenna had little to spare.

"It's also full of my own hair," she went on. "So it's me that bound you. And finally"—she touched the amulet around her neck—"it's woven through with these. They have an adverse effect on your folk, I've noticed."

"Death bringer!" This time the voice was a hiss of whispering leaves.

"Now that's not fair," Makenna said. "I may have killed, but I've brought no death to this world. I've not even threatened it. Though I have to say, you folk are tempting me."

"*That* is death." He gestured to her amulet. "And whatever the water woman did, I will not bargain with one who carries it."

"If you want us to go so badly," Makenna said, "all you have to do is stop the magic drain long enough for us to cast a gate, and we'll leave your precious world. Taking our death amulets with us. If the water spirit had given us just a bit more of that water that stopped the draining effect, we'd have been gone long ago."

For a moment, she thought she saw temptation sweep over those rough features. She'd told the truth. With their magic fully restored, and some practice behind them, Makenna was fairly certain she could hold a gate long enough for all the goblins to escape. She'd cast the gate that had brought them here and the gate she'd used to get Tobin out—and since then, she'd had time to study Master Lazur's spell books thoroughly. Getting herself out might be trickier. Before, the magic stored in the great wall had sustained the gate while she passed through. Makenna had no idea what would happen to a gate when its principle caster went into it. But she was willing to take the chance—if she could only find a way to stop the substance of the Otherworld from sucking down every rune she placed on it.

"No," said the spirit. Its toes dug into the ground, and rock cracked as if a real tree had rooted there. "I'm not a traitor. I will not bargain with you, death-human."

Makenna sighed. "Not even to get rid of us, once and for all?"

The creature shook, not its head, but its limbs. "You would only return, bringing the hunters with you—and then there will be no world free of them."

This was new information. "Humans have hunted you?"

The glare that answered that was so contemptuous, it needed no words.

"Those were other humans," Makenna said. "Not me. And have you ever been hunted by goblins?"

"No," the spirit admitted. "Their kind have never done us harm. But they ally with humans!"

Cogswhallop had joined her some time ago. Now he snorted. "You've not been paying attention, barky. The humans have taken to hunting us too."

"The old bond is there," the spirit said. "Or you wouldn't be standing at her side."

Makenna eyed those rootlike toes that had so easily broken solid rock. "If we let you go, will you agree not to harm us in the future? Not in any way, not even by rotting the wood we cut?"

It hesitated, and she added, "If you don't promise, there's no way I can let you go."

"Hey!" Miggy protested. "We had a hard time catching this one!"

"You did well," Makenna told him. "But even if it refuses to help us, we've still no right to kill it. It's doing nothing but defending its home against those who hunted it, just as we defended the wood against those who hunted us."

Miggy's mouth closed with a snap. Clearly he hadn't thought of it that way.

It was also clear that Cogswhallop had. "Get its promise first," he reminded her. "That one's strong enough, and angry enough, to give stomping us into the ground a good try."

"All right," the spirit yielded. "I give wood oath I'll not harm you or your goblins in the future, not even to rip up your puny tents or rot the wood if you try to build."

"And your friends?" Makenna asked. "Will you keep them from harming us?"

The spirits reminded her of goblins, in their insistence that promises be kept. And they probably also shared the goblins' tendency to interpret promises in a very literal way, when that was to their benefit.

"I can't speak for the others," the spirit said. "Even if I gave an oath, it wouldn't bind them."

"That's honest," said Makenna. "Though if we've got to capture every spirit in this world and get their oaths one at a time, it's going to be a long process. Tell your lads to let him go, Miggy."

The goblin cast her a dubious look, but he obeyed. With goblin hands helping, the tree spirit soon waddled off into the night.

"Was that wise, Gen'ral?" Cogswhallop asked softly. "It goes against my grain as well, harming a creature that did no worse than we were doing ourselves, not so long ago. But they're going to get harder to catch."

"With any luck," said Makenna, "we won't need to capture another. This one told me all I need to know without saying a single word. If I'm right, we'll be out of here before the next one can do worse than tangle up our hair."

In fact, it took most of another week for Makenna to figure it out. First experiments with the amulets, because she'd finally realized that if they negated so much of a spirit's power and stopped the magic drain in both human and goblin flesh, they might stop the drain on her spell runes as well.

Makenna's mother would have figured it out days ago, and that sharp priest would probably have seen it immediately. But Makenna lacked her mother's instinctive understanding of the forces that worked on the world. There was less pain in memories of her mother now, as if the magic that hummed in her blood in this strange world had somehow drawn them closer.

Makenna would probably lose that magic in the real world—but for peace and safety, it was a better than even trade!

The spirits stepped up their harassment when she started experimenting with the amulets, but Makenna soon learned how large a piece of ground could be protected from the magic drain.

With trees she had to embed the medallions in the bark to make her runes stable, but an amulet buried under only a thin covering of earth would stabilize a circle about three feet wide. In the end, Makenna had the smiths link the amulets together, like a spider's web.

Fortunately, that web didn't have to be too large. Tobin's irresponsible brother had sent all the amulets he could lay his hands on, St. Keshrah be praised. But even with the patron of responsible experimentation on their side, a score of goblins had been forced to give up their amulets to create the web, and to shield Makenna and the goblins she'd need to help her cast the spell.

Makenna then fastened the amulets on the trees that formed the gate structure to the earth web. She'd given her word to two spirits that she and the goblins would take the death amulets away with them—and her mother would never have forgiven her for leaving behind something Makenna suspected could poison the very fabric of this world.

While she worked out the details of casting a *stable* gate, Cogswhallop and Erebus organized the exodus. Makenna could hear their angry voices clear across the camp, arguing about whether each goblin through the gate had to be checked off the Bookeries' list or if they could just line up and be counted.

Finally the time came.

The sky was barely gray with the approach of sunrise, the air cool and damp. Makenna had chosen dawn hoping that a time of transition might aid the transition from one place to another.

Her team of casters spread out the ground web, covering the amulets and their chains lightly in the earth of this world. Those who carved fresh holes in the tree bark and stuck the amulets into the sap wrapped them in threads of fiber from the real world—the home to which they hoped to return.

Makenna herself drew the runes, runes describing this world scratched in the earth—where the children had been warned not to trample, on pain of being sent to their tents for the rest of their lives.

The goblin parents kept a tight grip on their wayward offspring, as they gathered into lines to be checked off the Bookeries' lists.

Makenna ignored the arguments about whether or not someone would be allowed to go back and hunt for a lost basket, or the pretty stone they'd meant to pick up. Cogswhallop and his troop would sort that out.

The runes of the real world went onto the trees, to lead them from this world into theirs as surely as the trees sprang from the soil into the air. Or that was Makenna's symbol, anyway. The priests' magic worked almost entirely with power in the abstract—which was fine, if you had so much you could afford to waste it. Hedgewitches, like Makenna's mother, needed symbols to guide and focus what small power they possessed. And they'd done well enough with those small powers that when the church planned to do something wildly unpopular, it had perceived them as a threat.

But the priest who'd been behind all that was dead, Cogswhallop had told her. It was safe to go home.

And to guide them, each goblin carried a token from the real world, something that came from there and represented home in their own hearts.

Makenna had brought little besides her mother's spell notes into the Otherworld, so she had chosen a handful of thread left from the unraveling of Tobin's cloak for her token.

It was made of wool from sheep that grazed on real-world grass. It had been spun by a woman breathing real-world air. And it had been worn by a young knight who was there right now, waiting for her to join him. Symbol enough.

When all the amulets were buried, the runes drawn, the goblins who'd volunteered to lend her power formed a circle around the edge of the web, holding hands.

Makenna ran her eyes down the long lines of waiting goblins. They stood quietly, gazing back at her with a trust this disastrous exile to the Otherworld should have destroyed. But it hadn't.

She looked at Erebus, who nodded confirmation. Everyone she'd led into this mess was here, along with the brave fools who'd come with Cogswhallop to rescue them. She looked at Cogswhallop, who nodded as well. Everyone was ready.

Makenna laid her hand on one of the trees, on the amulet set into its bark, and felt two small hands pressing against her knees. She began to chant, and power, even stronger than when they'd practiced this, flowed through the goblins' hands, through her hands, and down the amulets' linked chains.

The runes sprang to life as if the rising sun shone through them.

*Power.* Was this how the priests felt, casting their spells? She was so full of power, it felt as if she could take the world into her grasp, molding it like clay.

The gap between the trees filled with a pane of glowing light, and through that light Makenna saw a forest glade. Once she would have seen no difference between it and the glade they stood in. Now the trees of the northern woods were instantly identifiable, compared to the forests of this alien world.

She checked all the runes once more—no flickering. Even

the rune of stability glowed as cool and steady as moonlight. Makenna nodded to Cogswhallop, and the goblins in the first line picked up their packs and jogged through the gate in an orderly file.

It was a far cry from their desperate escape from their own world, with Makenna clumsily casting the spell as she read it, and goblins searching frantically for friends and family as the soldiers who would have killed them all thundered toward them.

The first line went through and the second line followed, without so much as a gap between them. Makenna felt a deep surge of gratitude for both her competent lieutenants.

Even the power that was theirs in the Otherworld began to diminish as the third line went through. The first time Makenna had cast a gate, she had drained the reserve of power that scores of ancient priests had sunk into the great wall. Now, though the gate was much smaller, the power came from her and her goblin assistants, and she felt the drag of it in blood and bone.

The chanting around the circle took on a determined note, and more power flowed down the goblins' linked hands.

Makenna was vaguely aware of Cogswhallop's voice shouting at the fourth line to run "Faster, faster, blast you!"

The last of the fourth line ran though the glowing gap, Cogswhallop on their heels, and now it was the spell casters' turn. They had rehearsed this, sending the weakest through first, speculating about what would happen.

It was less drastic than they'd feared, but that didn't make it good. As each caster passed through the gate, his strength vanished from the circle, leaving it weaker and weaker.

The last of them, an old Flamer called Mogarty, cast Makenna a worried look before she leaped through—but someone had to be last. Makenna had flatly refused the others' offers to try to take that part. She was the caster, the anchor who held it all in place.

The spell was sucking power from her body now, fast and hard. Makenna's temples throbbed, and her bones felt as if they were turning to sand. She had to go now.

She stepped to the far end of the linked chains and wrapped the loose chain they'd made ready for her around her wrist. She had no idea if this would work either, but she had to try.

She took a deep breath and poured every scrap of power she had left into the spell. The runes brightened—it was the most she'd get.

Makenna raced for the gate, amulets bursting from the earth in showers of grit and dead leaves. The last few feet yanked the remaining amulets out of the trees, and she threw herself into flickering gate like a diver.

The flash behind her was so bright, it looked like lightning, but no thunder followed.

Makenna fell to her hands and knees, aching as if she'd been beaten, but from the earth beneath her palms, from the very air around her, she felt the gentle seep of real-world magic. It wasn't as powerful as that of the Otherworld, water compared to wine, but it felt better; cleaner and more honest.

In the Otherworld, toward the end, she'd felt that she had almost become the powerful sorceress her enemies had named her.

She wouldn't miss it.

She lay down, rolling to face the sky, wondering where the goblins were. A moment later she heard human voices approaching—coming to investigate the soundless lightning, no doubt. The goblins would appear once they were gone.

There was a time when Makenna too would have dragged herself into the nearest bush and hidden, but her head still ached, and according to Cogswhallop the Decree of Bright Magic had been rescinded. She could deal with humans now. Maybe even live with them, part of the time.

"It's a girl! Are you all right, lass? What happened here?"

The speaker was a middle-aged man, who helped her sit up, concern in his broad face. His rough clothes might have suited a number of tasks, but a scent of fresh-cut wood surrounded not only him but the two younger men who'd accompanied him. Lumber men. She'd driven a number of them out of the Goblin Wood—or even let them cut there, if they left the goblins alone.

Were they in the Goblin Wood now? In some other northern forest? She would ask, eventually, but more important . . .

"What happened is a long story." She smiled at them all. It felt odd, smiling at humans. "But I'm well enough. I don't suppose you've heard of a young man, Tobin Rovan, arriving sometime in the last few weeks like I just did?"

They stared at her, the older woodsman with a worried frown that was echoed on the face of one of the younger men.

The last man's jaw had dropped. "I know her!" His astonished expression turned to fury in a heartbeat. "She's the sorceress of the Goblin Wood! The one who killed all those folk! Arrest her!"

Looking at him, Makenna recognized one of the settlers Master Lazur had brought north to colonize the wood. They'd all gotten a good look at her, chained to a log as bait for the goblins, before Tobin had set her free.

The rough hands that seized her now were all too familiar, and so were the expressions of anger, doubt, and disgust.

So much for living with humans.

She made no protest as they hauled her off to jail.

## CHAPTER 5

# Tobin

WHEN VRUUD SAID THEY'D TELL the other Duri camps to watch for an escaped prisoner, Tobin hadn't realized it would be more than two weeks before they returned.

Vruud had produced a pot of oily black sludge and told Tobin to work it into his hair. He went out again while Tobin obeyed, and came back soon with a pile of worn, drab clothing.

The shirt wasn't too different from Tobin's. The long trousers that gathered at the ankle were looser than his britches and felt strange, though they weren't uncomfortable. A leather vest with pockets completed the outfit, along with a pair of sandals. The sandals were uncomfortable, their soles pressed into the shape of someone else's feet, but a horseman's boots under the clothing of a chanduri servant would be a dead giveaway. And, Vruud told Tobin, "dead" wasn't a figure of speech.

When Tobin was dressed, Vruud tipped a polished shield toward him. "What do you think?"

Tobin gazed thoughtfully at his distorted reflection. "I look like me with black hair. A lot of those warriors got a good look at me. This won't work."

"Those young louts have the brains, and attention span, of flies," Vruud told him. "And it will be a while before they see you again."

But it wasn't until after they'd crept out of the quiet camp, Vruud riding a mule and Tobin leading a pack mule behind him, that they came to the top of a low rise, and Tobin realized how long it might be before they returned.

The sun had risen. The endless clusters of round barbarian tents spread over the plain, out and out till distance alone shrank them to invisibility. And in the clear air of the Southlands, that was a long way.

It was a sight to strike dismay in any Realm knight's heart. "How many men do you have here?"

"There's no precise count," Vruud told Tobin. "No way to make one, really. But there are eight greater clans and three lesser. A greater clan will have about fifty to sixty camps like ours, and we field about eighty warriors. The lesser clans aren't that much smaller—say, ten thousand men among the three of them. I'd put the total at around fifty thousand Duri."

The Duri were their warriors. Fifty *thousand* warriors. Tobin didn't know the exact count of the Realm's army, but he thought it was around thirty thousand.

He swallowed, trying to fight down rising panic. This was

why the Realm was relocating, after all. Using the great wall to the north as a barrier, a much smaller army could hold off any number of enemies. As long as the relocation went forward, the Realm would survive. But for Tobin himself, the odds were worse than he'd thought.

"How far are we from the border? Are there camps like this the whole way?"

If there were, he'd never make it, even with Vruud's help. And after the man's frank declaration of indifference, Tobin wasn't sure he could trust the storyteller. Or rather, he was certain he *couldn't* trust him, to do anything except look out for himself. If Vruud hadn't needed him, he'd have sacrificed Tobin in a heartbeat. At least he'd been honest about it.

"No," the storyteller answered his question. "There's about twenty miles of disputed ground between your camps and ours. Both sides patrol their own borders—and for a week or so, ours will be thick with people looking for you. We'd better get going. I need to set that search into motion."

"Isn't it crazy to tell your Duri to go looking for me?" Tobin demanded. "With me standing right there?"

"Ah, but I'm telling them to look for an escaped Softer knight," said Vruud. "It's my servant who's standing there. Or better yet, tending the mules, arranging for my dinner, and laying out my bedroll in the guest tent."

Tobin foresaw dozens of problems with this scenario, not least that while the amulets translated what was said in the listener's mind, they did nothing to change the words that reached the ears.

But Vruud was right. As Tobin later learned, each of the eight greater clans had a completely different language base, and even within the clans many camps had their own dialect. Some of them were so different that warriors within the same clan often found it hard to communicate. They were all so accustomed to letting their amulets translate for them that they paid no attention to the actual spoken language.

Further, the idea that the escaped knight might be traveling with the storyteller who was spreading word of his escape was so ridiculous that no one thought of it.

The clans, and even some camps within the clans, had different customs too. No one found it odd that the storyteller's servant wasn't sure where the mules should be tethered, or which tent housed travelers, or whose cooking pot he should go to for their meals.

And while servants in their own camps weren't allowed to wear amulets, a servant traveling from one camp to another had to have one if he was to be of any use at all, so both Tobin and Vruud wore their amulets openly despite being chan. If a chanduri in his own camp needed to communicate with Tobin— "Don't lead your mules past that cage; the Kabasi camp owns a hunting leopard"—he'd simply lay a hand on Tobin's amulet so he could understand what Tobin said.

Despite some difficulty with the leopard, whose scent made the mules nervous even from a distance, no one even blinked at Tobin's many mistakes. After the third camp he began to relax into his role—although the Duris' reaction to news of an escaped Softer was far from reassuring.

As Tobin soon figured out from the comments around him, the camp that had so carelessly allowed him to escape had forfeited half their right to his sacrifice. If a different camp captured him, a complicated negotiation would take place to determine how many warriors from which camp would reap the benefit of his death. The only reason they reported his escape at all was that if Tobin was recaptured by a camp that *hadn't* been alerted to look for him, that camp would have complete ownership of Tobin's blood death. The camp that had found him in the first place would have no rights at all.

"If you think that's complicated," Vruud told him cynically, "wait till you see what happens when someone locates a spirit. There are strict laws/traditions for possession of an area where an uncaptured spirit lives. After all, you can always find someone so old, or a servant so lazy, that you can afford to give them up. Spirits are a lot harder to come by."

Despite his own disgust at their customs, Tobin had wondered at Vruud's willingness to betray his own people. He wasn't surprised by it now. The Duri generally weren't bad masters, but the chanduris' knowledge that the Duri would slaughter them the moment it became expedient colored every aspect of their lives. Many of the servants quietly hated their superiors—especially those who'd seen a loved one's veins laid open by the sacrificial knife. But few tried to run, for the Duri were skilled at tracking them down. In almost every camp there were one or two chanduri so badly scarred from the beatings the Duri gave to those "blood traitors" that they were almost crippled. And those who were useless were next in line for the knife.

Yes, Tobin understood Vruud's determination to escape. But that didn't mean the storyteller's nebulous plan to observe the next battle—"so I can make the bravery of the Morovda camp a legend for the ages"—and thus get them closer to the border before they made a run for it, would work.

"Because even if your chief . . . Morovda, was it? Even if he agrees to let you ride with the Duri, and take your servant along with you, we can't simply start running from your side of the battlefield to the Realm's. Because first the Duri will shoot us full of arrows, and then the Realm knights will take us for attacking warriors and kill us before we can identify ourselves."

They were traveling down the dusty road to Vruud's home camp when he brought up the subject. The open road was the only place Tobin could be certain no one could overhear them.

"It's not perfect," Vruud conceded. "But we'd only have to cross a few hundred yards, in the midst of the chaos of battle, instead of twenty miles of open territory with every patrol on the alert. And when the time nears, something might occur to give us an opportunity."

Tobin was dubious about that, but he had to admit that Vruud's mad scheme had worked so far. His steps still began to drag as they mounted the rise and the Morovda camp appeared below them. After spending the last few weeks touring Duri camps, Tobin realized how small and isolated it was. Morovda had quarreled with a couple of other chiefs on the Heron Clan council and had chosen to set his camp apart from the others.

"Did I mention how many of the Duri got a good look at me?" Tobin said nervously. He was walking beside his "master" now and had to look up to see his face. The mule Vruud rode had been named Mouse, not only for his gray hide but because he was remarkably timid for a creature who was almost as tall as a horse.

"You've been around the Duri for weeks," Vruud told him. "You know they never look at a chanduri's face. And there's no reason for anyone to look twice at a servant I hired from another camp."

That was true. The Duri regarded the chanduri like a farmer regards livestock he knows will be slaughtered—he might treat them kindly, but he'd never allow himself to form an emotional attachment. And, like livestock, servants were traded from one clan to another.

Along with their daughters. The Duri were careful not to become too inbred, lest it weaken the warrior lines. In fact, Vruud told him, in some clans it was forbidden for a woman to marry a man of the camp in which she was born. In others it was frowned on, and young women were expected to go to men from another camp, but they weren't exiled if they didn't. In yet another clan all girls were fostered to different camps at the age of thirteen, and returned to their childhood homes only to visit.

The Realm was much bigger than the Duri army, and its population was scattered across a large area, but it had a common language, common customs and laws. Had the Seven Bright Gods given them this gift when the church was founded? If so, Tobin owed them more prayers than he usually offered.

Despite his nerves, and despite the fact that he recognized half a dozen of the Duri, when Tobin entered the Morovda camp and Vruud introduced him as "a servant I picked up from a Bear Clan camp to tend the mules," no one looked at him twice.

He knew without asking that Bear would be one of the clans with a very different language base. Vruud might not be his friend, but Tobin never underestimated the man's intelligence.

In a way, he thought, as another chanduri showed him the horse line and gave him instructions about where to go for grain, he was grateful to the storyteller for keeping their relationship on a remote, aid-traded-for-aid level. He would take the one-eyed man with him if he could, but Vruud wasn't Tobin's first consideration any more than Tobin was his. For once there was no younger brother, no Realm, no goblin children whose safety Tobin had to put before his own. This time it was simple—Tobin would save himself, and save Vruud only if it wouldn't damage his own chances. Which meant that he might actually survive after all.

Acting as Vruud's servant was trickier in the storyteller's own camp, because Tobin was supposed to make himself useful to the camp as well as caring for his master. He helped the woman who cooked for Vruud, chopping vegetables and cleaning fish and fowl. He carried horse and mule dung to the midden and fetched water from the burned-out village's well.

None of these tasks was mysterious to someone who'd been raised on a country estate, and Tobin had been traveling among the Duri camps long enough that he made few mistakes. He'd begun to think that Vruud was going to be right yet again . . . when he looked up from the pool where he was washing Vruud's clothes and met the startled gaze of the woman who'd brought food and water to his cage.

Her expression left no doubt that she'd recognized him, astonishment giving way to fear. She opened her mouth and drew in a breath to scream.

"Please," said Tobin. "Please don't."

She couldn't understand him, but she didn't scream. By sheer chance they were the only ones working at the series of shallow, stone-lined pools the chanduri had created to do their washing. The woman dropped the bundle of cloth she carried and backed away, one step, then another.

It was barely possible that Tobin could leap to his feet and knock her unconscious, but then what? Run, with every Duri in camp on his trail? Even if he could bring himself to kill her, his masquerade would never survive a murder investigation—particularly in a camp where he was the only stranger.

Tobin slowly pulled the amulet from under his shirt and held it out to her, his palm open, his posture as unthreatening as he could make it with every nerve in his body shrieking for action.

She stopped backing away and watched him warily, but she hadn't turned to run. She wasn't screaming.

"Please," Tobin repeated, trying to summon a reassuring smile. "I'm sure we can reach some understanding."

He wasn't sure, but since she couldn't understand what he said, it didn't matter. Vruud had told him a chanduri was expected to learn the language of a new camp, and surrender the amulet he'd no right to wear, within a year of his arrival. He'd started to give Tobin lessons, but Tobin didn't plan to stay for the summer, much less a year, and he hadn't paid attention. Now he wished he had.

"Vruud took you in," the woman said thoughtfully. "He's hiding you. He must have been the one who got you out of that cage. You didn't find the cracked bar by accident."

"I hope you didn't get in trouble for it," Tobin said.

She grimaced incomprehension and looked with distaste at the amulet he held out. "I don't want to come that close to you."

The only words of this camp's Heron Clan language Tobin had learned so far were "no," "yes," and "I don't speak Marshok." For a miracle, one of those phrases fit the situation.

"I don't speak Marshok," Tobin said in that tongue.

Humor ghosted over her tense face. "You certainly don't."

He lifted the amulet once more, in silent plea. Even if he could promise her safety, with all the eloquence that panic and the amulet could lend him, there was no reason for her to trust his word. Except . . .

"Vruud," said Tobin urgently. "Vruud, yes?"

She snorted. "You mean that Vruud spared you, so I should too? That arrogant old weasel would do anything that . . ." Her voice trailed off. She stared at Tobin in furious speculation. "Anything that served his own purpose. What could you do for Vruud?"

Tobin lifted the amulet once more. "Yes?"

She cast the amulet a look of loathing that gave Tobin some hope, then stalked forward and laid her hand on it.

"Talk," she commanded.

He had only to close his hand and yank her down as he raised his left fist. And then what?

Tobin seated himself cross-legged, so he was even less threatening, and told her what had passed between him and the one-eyed storyteller after he'd freed Tobin from the cage. Tobin tried to keep back some of the details, like Vruud's whole escape plan, but she saw the gaps in his story and refused to let him gloss over them.

"You talk, Softer. Or I'll talk to the others."

In the end, it was a relief to reveal all of it, including his doubts. "Because you're right," Tobin concluded. "Vruud's only looking out for himself. I don't even know how much of what he told me is true."

He'd picked up some confirmation listening to the chanduri in other camps—but since they couldn't understand him unless they were touching his amulet, it was hard to casually bring the conversation around to the hunt for the missing Softer, the nature of blood magic, or any of the things about which Tobin desperately needed assurance.

"Oh, he told the truth," the woman said now. "If you wear that blood trust outside one of the camps, the patrols will sense magic moving alone, just as they'd sense a spirit or some other magical creature. They'd track you down with ease. But I'm not sure his plan to accompany the Duri into battle so he can make a story about them will work. Nine-tenths of his tales are lies anyway. Why shouldn't this one be? And why would he need his servant there?"

"He didn't say he was certain it would work," Tobin admitted. "But it was the best idea he had. He's really only interested in his own escape. If he didn't know that he'll need me when he reaches my side of the lines, I'd still be in that cage. He made no pretense of anything else."

"Maybe I can think of something better," the woman said. "Since I'll be going with you."

Tobin's jaw dropped. He'd been about to propose that the storyteller would pay lots of money to keep her quiet.

"Vruud will never agree to that," Tobin told her. "He's going to be furious that I told you about this at all. He'd never jeopardize his chance by taking someone else with us. If he didn't need me to keep him alive when he reaches the Realm, he wouldn't take me!"

"And you think Vruud's the only one prepared to be ruthless?"

Her expressive face was closed now, but Tobin could see thoughts moving behind it.

"My mother was slain to make a few dozen of those amulets, just three years ago," the woman said. "That's why I didn't want to touch it. I've no way to know, but it might be her very blood and death that we're using to talk right now."

"It's the only way I can speak to you," said Tobin apologetically. "But my own people, our church, declared them unholy when they found out how they were made. They forbid anyone to use them, except in cases of dire necessity."

"Like going to spy on the enemy?" she asked.

"Spies are one of the exceptions," Tobin admitted. "But I didn't come to spy. I really am here by accident."

How had Makenna managed to get past the magic drain and create the gate they'd shoved him through? Had she made others? Had she too been captured, and were she and Regg and Onny, all his goblin friends, being held in some other camp's captive cage?

If they were, there was nothing Tobin could do about it. His job was to get himself and Vruud to safety . . . and perhaps one other?

"I don't know if Vruud will agree," Tobin said honestly. "I don't even know how I can get myself to our lines, much less you and Vruud. But if you don't tell the Duri about me, I'm willing to try."

"What about Vruud?" the woman asked. "Will he try as well?"

"What choice does he have? If you open your mouth, it condemns him too."

"It would be many years," she said slowly, "before I need to fear the knife myself. If I ever did. Most of the chanduri die of age or illness, just as we used to."

*Used to?* Had there been a time when the Duri didn't practice their sacrifices? What had changed?

"But in those years I stayed alive, how many of my friends, my loved ones, would I see screaming their way to death?" the woman finished. "I want out, young . . . I can't call you Softer, not if we're working together."

"Vruud does," said Tobin. "But I'd guessed it was an insult."

"Only mildly contemptuous," she told him. "Not much worse than chan. But I don't want to insult my partner. What's your name?"

106

"It's Tobin." Ridiculously, his eyes stung. "What's yours?"

"Hesida. Now let's wash our clothes, and see if we can come up with a more sensible plan for getting three people who have no business on a battlefield right up to the enemy lines."

But hard as they thought, no plan emerged. The best advice Hesida had was for Tobin to get himself taken along as one of the grooms who tended the Duris' remounts. It was a better excuse for him to approach a battlefield than any he'd have as Vruud's servant. Perhaps she could get herself included as one of the chanduri who prepared food in the lulls between battles?

It sounded incredibly tenuous to Tobin, and as he'd predicted, Vruud was furious to learn that someone else had been added to their escape plan. Though as Tobin pointed out, they had no choice. Their lives depended on Hesida's silence.

Vruud pointed out in turn that every person they added doubled the chance that their escape would fail. Getting himself and Tobin across a battlefield would be hard enough. Adding a woman, adding anyone, could easily end in catastrophe.

Tobin knew that the storyteller was right, but he'd promised. He had to try.

Tobin began working more with the grooms who tended the Duris' horses, helping lead them down to the stream when he watered Vruud's mules, currying their coats and cleaning their hooves. Within a few days he was tacking them up for the Duri who went on patrol and taking care of them when the patrols returned.

He no longer feared the Duri would recognize him. Even if they remembered the escaped Softer's features, they now knew him too well as Vruud's servant for any other identity to occur to them. And they really didn't look at the faces of their chanduri servants.

Nor did they pay attention to what they said in their presence. Tobin kept his head down, and his expression blank, but a careless comment that "the new battle tactics will crumple up those Softer knights like paper" set his ears twitching.

*What new battle tactics?*

Of course, the talk then turned to a wrestling match between them and a nearby camp, and there was no further discussion of the things Tobin wanted to hear.

*What new tactics?*

Later that night Tobin lay on his bedroll listening to Vruud snore—but for once, it wasn't the noise that kept him awake.

Over several years of warfare, captured blood amulets had allowed Realm knights to spy on the barbarians. A handful of them had even returned alive. But no spy had ever gotten as deeply into the Duri camps as Tobin had.

If they did have some new battle plan, something that might make a difference in their next fight against the Realm, wasn't it his duty to find out what it was?

Yes. No matter how many excuses he came up with, if Tobin could make the barbarians' next big push into the Southlands fail, he had to try. The black skeleton of the burned-out village was a grim reminder of how many lives he might be able to save.

He'd been accepted here, and no one suspected him. It shouldn't be *too* hard to learn something about the new battle plans.

But his simple escape was getting a lot more complicated.

# CHAPTER 6

# Jeriah

JERIAH WAS HALF A DAY'S ride from the City of Steps. He'd considered pressing on to the city last night. The palace gates would have been closed, but he could have found a room in town. However, urgent as it was to get the relocation back on track, Jeriah knew it wouldn't happen instantly. Not for weeks, maybe months, even if all went well. Commander Sower had given him a dispatch, signed by all the army commanders, begging the Hierarch to send more troops and expedite moving the Southland civilians north. Weighing against that was the fact that every town Jeriah passed outside the Southlands—and even a few Southland towns—had abandoned all preparations for the relocation.

Would Koryn forgive him when she saw that he was trying to get the relocation back on track? Would she speak to him long enough for him to tell her what he was doing?

Misty gray eyes that were never anything as soft as "misty." Bright with enthusiasm, sharp with thought, blazing with fury . . .

*. . . I hope you do get your precious brother back. I hope his*

*presence consoles you when a barbarian spear goes through your father's heart, and your sisters are hacked to bloody rags. . . .*

In the end, despair had washed even the anger out of her eyes.

*You're a fool.*

Jeriah pulled Glory's saddle off the log that had kept it out of the dew-wet grass and slung it onto the saddle blanket on her back. He would get the relocation back on track—no matter what Koryn thought of him!

Although, given the resistance everyone outside the Southland felt toward the whole idea of relocating, Jeriah was amazed that even Master Lazur had managed to take the plan as far as he had. There was an old saying that if you cut off a snake's head, the body would die. Of course, that was true of any living creature—but Jeriah was beginning to fear it was even more true of political causes. Hanging its leader had certainly killed—

"Good morning, hero. You're a hard man to find."

Jeriah jumped, but he'd given up complaining about the goblins sneaking up on him.

"Cogswhallop! What are you . . . You're out! Where's Tobin? Is he all right?"

The goblin shrugged. "He was alive last I saw him, and there's no reason to assume that's changed. But I have to tell you, he was very ill. If we'd been a week later getting him out, it would have been his corpse we brought back with us."

"Is he recovering now?" Jeriah asked anxiously.

"I've no reason to think otherwise," said Cogswhallop.

"I'm here because the gen'ral's run into trouble. You remember the things we heard about gates not always coming out where you'd expect?"

Jeriah nodded. Master Lazur had told him you could cast two gates, minutes apart, in the exact same place, and they could come out hundreds of miles apart in the Otherworld.

"Well, the gate we came out through, by sheer bad luck, was on the edge of the northern wood," Cogswhallop went on. "And one of the humans who came to investigate recognized the gen'ral. The sorceress of the Goblin Wood, no less."

"But the Decree of Bright Magic was rescinded," said Jeriah. "Just as I promised."

"Aye," Cogswhallop drawled. "Unfortunately, both you and I forgot about a couple of writs for murder they'd laid on the lass. They've dropped all charges of sorcery, but the murder charges stand. The judge seems inclined to fairness when it comes to trial—but about half the town is prepared to build a scaffold right now and skip the formalities."

"She did kill people," Jeriah said reasonably. "She probably should be tried for it." And if she hanged, he wouldn't have to worry about her getting his brother into even more trouble.

Fury flashed in the goblin's eyes. "If she killed, it was because she had no choice! As your own brother recognized when he threw in with her!"

"They've arrested Tobin too?" Dread clutched at Jeriah's

heart. "Why didn't you tell me?" No wonder Tobin hadn't come home yet!

Cogswhallop hesitated a moment. "The soldier was her accomplice. Shouldn't he be tried for it?"

"We don't have time for sarcasm! Why don't you just break them out of jail?" Jeriah knew they could do it.

"This near the Goblin Wood, they know enough about us to be holding her in chains of charmed iron. We can't touch 'em. The last time they held her so, it took your brother to free her. And now . . ."

"Now he's imprisoned too," said Jeriah resignedly. "I thought *I* was the one who was always landing myself in trouble!"

Getting involved with the sorceress had driven Jeriah's sensible brother mad—that was the only explanation. He'd have to separate them, talk some sense into Tobin. But first Jeriah had to get him free.

"At least in jail he'll be safe and get the nursing he needs," Jeriah said. "How long before this trial takes place?"

"That's the only good news," said Cogswhallop. "The judge wants to wait till the mood in town has settled a bit. He's set a tentative trial date for two weeks from today."

"Two *weeks?* And this town's in the north of the Realm?"

Cogswhallop nodded. His usually sardonic expression was inscrutable, but Jeriah, deep in travel calculations, took no notice.

"She's in jail in Brackenlee," the goblin went on. "It's just north of—"

"I've been there," Jeriah said. "I'll have to keep switching between Glory and Fiddle, and they'll both be exhausted, but if we have two weeks, I'll get there in time."

"You'll have them," Cogswhallop promised. "I've got to go see that fool Hispontic. He says there's trouble with the library. As if that matters now! But I left orders that if the town seems to be calming down, the lads there are to work a bit of mischief and stir things up again. The gen'ral's known to be our leader, so she'll be blamed for anything we do."

"Which is fine," said Jeriah, "unless they stir up too much trouble, and the judge decides to hang her just to put an end to it."

He finished tightening Glory's girth as he spoke and swung into the saddle. If they convicted the girl, his brother's conviction as her accomplice would soon follow. The Realm would have to look out for itself for a while—Jeriah had a brother to save. At least, thank the Bright Gods, this should be the last time it was necessary!

The Hierarch would have to wait.

And Koryn . . . She probably wasn't waiting for him now. Jeriah was surprised to realize how much that bothered him.

Twelve days later Jeriah rode into Brackenlee, almost as exhausted as the horses he'd been riding.

The town was gray and drab, with rain dripping from the thin wooden shingles and running in surly streams down the gutters. He'd forgotten how miserably cold and wet the Northlands could be, even in early summer. But Jeriah was going to see his brother again, and until that happened, he could ignore the worst kind of weather. Exhaustion and misery as well. Once he had Tobin safe, nothing else would matter.

Cogswhallop had promised to meet Jeriah in the town, after he dealt with Master Hispontic's problem. Goblins could travel faster than humans, though they never explained how. Jeriah had spent the journey thinking and had decided that the simplest way to free Tobin would be to get the sorceress released into his custody, and just bring his brother along with her.

If it was up to him, he'd leave her there! But Tobin, who'd been firmly convinced of her innocence, would never leave her behind to hang. Jeriah wasn't convinced, but if Tobin wanted her free so badly, it would be more efficient to rescue both of them at the same time.

So even though he longed to see Tobin, Jeriah went to an inn, stabled his horses, and changed, not into his court clothes, but into traveling gear that wasn't so worn. The soft leather and subdued embroidery had the richness that a provincial judge would associate with a servant of the Hierarch.

He then went to the town hall and politely requested a few minutes with the magistrate in charge . . . in the Hierarch's name.

He had to wait for only fifteen minutes, which he took to be a good sign. But the shrewd-eyed man who sat behind a paper-strewn desk in his shirtsleeves didn't look as easy to impress as his clerk had been.

"Aren't you a bit young to be representing the Hierarch?"

"I'm his body squire," said Jeriah, almost truthfully. "One of them, anyway." If this man could confirm that Jeriah was the Hierarch's personal squire, then the rest of his preposterous tale would seem a lot more plausible.

"Hmm." The judge looked him up and down. "You're a long way from the Hierarch's body, sir squire."

"I was sent to the Northlands as a courier," Jeriah said. "There was information the Hierarch needed—not urgent, but he wanted it carried by someone he trusted. So when news of the sorceress's capture reached him, I was the nearest person who could execute his will in this matter."

"The *Hierarch* is interested in that hard young wench?" the judge asked.

"She was Master Lazur's enemy for a number of years," Jeriah pointed out, also truthfully. "A powerful sorceress might have ways of spying on that renegade priest, even from a distance. Now that Master Lazur's treachery has been revealed, the Hierarch needs to learn all he can about any plots the man had a hand in. And since this girl might know something about that, he wants me to convey her back to the City of Steps, where her case will be dealt with properly."

It sounded outrageous to his own ears, but Jeriah'd had a lot of practice over the last few months in controlling his breathing and expression. The rapid beat of his heart would be invisible to the judge, who was now eyeing him skeptically.

"So the Hierarch wants me to turn my prisoner—a prisoner who's charged with several murders—over to you? Where's the order for her release?"

This was the hard part. Jeriah spread his hands in a helpless shrug. "Unfortunately, the messenger who was sent to inform me of the Hierarch's will was robbed by a band of those Southland brigands who have been so prevalent lately, and his orders were destroyed. But he did give me the Hierarch's verbal instructions, and since we knew she might face trial soon, we didn't dare wait for another set of orders to be sent."

He hated speaking ill of the Southlanders, but it wasn't slander. Some of the refugees, having lost their homes and wealth in the last barbarian push, had taken to robbery. It was more common in the South- and Midlands, but the problem was known to every magistrate in the Realm.

The judge watched Jeriah closely, rubbing his chin with one thick thumb. "Do you have any evidence at all, then? Because I'm afraid . . ."

"Only this." Jeriah hauled out the dispatch Commander Sower had given him. Addressed to the Hierarch and marked with an official seal, it was exactly the kind of document Jeriah would be carrying if his story was true. The judge's frown deepened.

"I need to think about this. Do you want to see the prisoner?"

There was only one prisoner Jeriah wanted to see, and

it wasn't the sorceress—but Tobin was probably in the cell next to hers. He considered asking, but if this man would let him take custody of the girl, he should have no trouble getting his brother thrown in.

"I should identify her," Jeriah said. "To be certain she really is the sorceress of the Goblin Wood. I was Master Lazur's assistant before I went into the Hierarch's service, and I was present when she was first captured, so I can confirm her identity."

"She admitted her identity," said the judge. "But by all means, confirm it."

He summoned a guard to show Jeriah to the cells. The town hall's cellar wasn't as grim as Jeriah had expected, being mostly used for records storage. But the only source of heat was a brazier at the head of the corridor, where another guard was stationed.

Jeriah tried to peer through the small, barred windows in the wooden doors he passed, but without making a show of stopping to look, he couldn't see anything. The guard led him halfway down the hall and opened a door with one of the keys in his jingling ring.

The girl sat on a cot, wrapped in several blankets against the damp chill. Her hair had been hacked off close to her head, so untidily it looked as if she'd done it herself without comb or mirror. If the townsfolk were so angry they'd done that before she even went to trial, then she needed to be rescued! But Jeriah couldn't see any bruises.

She showed no surprise at the sight of him, her expression closed and sardonic.

"Stand up," the guard ordered. "Let me see those chains."

She stood, letting the blankets fall away. She was wearing britches and a button-covered vest, and her shirt was dirty. The chains, clamped to both wrists and one ankle, clanked as she lifted her arms.

The guard went so far as to make sure they were locked, though he looked a bit embarrassed when he saw Jeriah's quizzical expression.

"We've had trouble from the goblins since we took her. This is charmed iron, and the local priest swears they can't touch it, but better safe than sorry, eh?"

"Certainly," said Jeriah. "I commend your caution. But since you know she's securely bound, could I converse with her alone? This woman may have information the Hierarch needs. The sooner I can establish that, one way or the other, the better for all of us."

The guard glanced at the girl uneasily. "I promise not to bite him," she said. "Or turn him into a rat. Though if he does go missing, you might be careful what you put into your stew."

"Sass does you no good," the guard told her. "Call me when you want out, young sir." He locked the door behind him, and they waited in silence till the sound of his footsteps faded.

"You made good time," she murmured, beating Jeriah into

speech by half a breath. "Cogswhallop didn't expect you for another day. What could I possibly know that the Hierarch would be interested in?"

"Things about Master Lazur," Jeriah told her. "The Hierarch is trying to find out about everything Master Lazur was involved in, so it makes sense. Where's—"

"It makes nonsense." Her voice was low, but the words cut. "The priest was my enemy, Jeriah Rovan. I know far less about him than, say, one of his loyal aides."

There were at least two insults buried in that speech, and maybe more.

"*Smart* people spy on their enemies," Jeriah said. "If you didn't, you'll have to fake it till I get you out of here. Where's—"

"Hero!" Cogswhallop's face appeared in the window. "That was a grand tale you told the old man, but he's sent clerks flying to check on this and that, so I hope it's true. If not, you'll likely end up in the cell next to this one."

"All the parts he can confirm are true," Jeriah said. "And the rest can't be checked on because I traveled so fast. Is Tobin in the next—"

"Where is Tobin?" the sorceress asked. "I half expected him to be with you. It would be a foolish risk, but no one ever called him the cautious sort."

A core of ice formed around Jeriah's heart.

"What do you mean, 'Where's Tobin?' He went into the Otherworld with you. I thought . . . You didn't leave him there!"

His voice had risen.

"Shh!" Girl and goblin hissed the word together.

"He was with me," she went on, "but he sickened quickly, so I gated him out as soon as those amulets reached us. That was over three weeks ago! No matter where he came out, he should have gotten home by now. Or word from him, if he was too weak to travel."

"No word's reached his family," said Cogswhallop. "Nor him neither. I keep in touch with those still on his father's land."

The ice began to spread. "I thought he was with you," said Jeriah. "Cogswhallop told me . . ."

Fragments of remembered conversation flashed through his brain. If Cogswhallop had never actually *said* that Tobin was imprisoned with the sorceress, he'd certainly implied it. As far as Jeriah was concerned . . .

"You lied to me," he told the goblin coldly.

He expected the creature to deny it. Technically . . .

"Aye, I lied," Cogswhallop admitted. "I needed you to get the gen'ral out, not go haring about looking for your brother. So I—"

"Wait a minute." The girl was standing now, her sardonic expression melting into concern. "If Tobin's not with your family, and he's not with me, where in the Dark One's name is he?"

"I don't know," said Jeriah grimly. "But I'm going to find out. Guard!"

Cogswhallop argued in a fierce whisper right up till the

guard's key clicked in the lock, but Jeriah ignored him. If the goblin had endangered Tobin in his haste to get his cursed general freed, Jeriah would never forgive him.

He'd thought the goblins were his friends. Hah!

Jeriah was prepared to leave the girl to rot—or hang! But when the guard led him up the stairs to the hall, he found the judge waiting for him with a woman whose face was vaguely familiar.

"That's Jeriah Rovan, sir," she confirmed. "He traveled all the way to the wood with us, working as Master Lazur's aide. And he carried messages back and forth on the journey."

Jeriah's boiling fury stilled. If he suddenly abandoned his "mission," he might still end up in a cell—and that would do Tobin no good, wherever he was. Besides, if he left the girl to hang, his brother would never get over it.

"I take it my identity has been sufficiently established?" Jeriah asked the judge. It came out with more anger than he'd intended, and the judge smiled placatingly.

"I had to make certain. Particularly in the absence of written orders. But since your identity has been established, and our local priest was able to confirm that you were appointed as the Hierarch's squire, I believe I'm justified in releasing the girl into your custody."

"Ah," said Jeriah. "I don't want you to bend your own rules, sir. If you'd like to keep her here, unharmed, until orders could be sent . . ."

"No, no," the judge assured him. "In truth, I'm glad to see her go. Many of those who were driven out of the wood by the goblins came here. And even though a settlement was established after the goblins were gone, their memories are bitter. I'd not have allowed her less than a fair trial. But I'll admit, young sir, I wasn't sure how to bring it about! I'm delighted to turn her over to legitimate authority."

And if he didn't continue to act like legitimate authority, Jeriah realized, he would become a suspicious character himself. One who had to be held, pending further instructions.

"Very well, sir," said Jeriah. "I'll take her off your hands. But leave those chains on her, if you please! I've no mind to find myself bedeviled by every goblin between here and the City of Steps."

They had traveled away from Brackenlee, mostly in silence, when Cogswhallop dropped out of a tree and onto the back of Glory's saddle. Fortunately she was accustomed to the goblins and only shied a little. Jeriah could remember a time when Cogswhallop would have stayed in the tree, beyond human reach. If this was a sign of trust, it was misplaced.

"Well done," Cogswhallop told him. "As neat a jailbreak as ever I've seen! There's a bend up ahead where you can ride into the woods and take off those chains."

"What for?" Jeriah asked.

"Why, because . . ." The goblin's voice trailed off.

The glint in the girl's eyes deepened. "Been training him to bargain, have you?"

"Daroo." Cogswhallop sighed. "He was determined to

civilize him. I warned the lad it would come to no good, but does he listen to his parents? I must say, hero, I'm surprised to see you bargain over doing what's right."

"Why shouldn't I? You goblins made me pay every time you helped me. And now you've reneged on the payment. You promised, at least by implication, that my brother would be here if I freed your general. Until I get him back, she won't go free."

"I've been too busy keeping track of this situation to put much effort into finding him," Cogswhallop admitted. "Not to mention what that fool Bookerie has been up to! But now she's safe, I'll spread the word. Finders have a limited range, but there's nowhere in the Realm he can be hidden from our folk. Not for long."

"Then I suggest you start," said Jeriah. "Because until I'm standing in his presence, you owe me."

"Oh, he'll be finding Tobin anyway," said Makenna. "That's now his first priority, by my order. I mean it, Cogswhallop. No arguing."

"And I'll do it," said the goblin. "So why not take her chains off now?"

"Because he's got something in mind." The girl spoke before Jeriah could. "I've been watching him forming up some scheme ever since we left the town hall. It looked like hard work, for him."

Jeriah was finding it very easy to keep Makenna in chains.

"This situation might do some good," he told them. "What

I said to that judge, about the Hierarch wanting to know everything about Master Lazur's plans, that wasn't nonsense. Even if you didn't have the wit to spy on your enemy, I can still use the fact that you *were* his enemy. If I present you to the Hierarch as one of Master Lazur's victims, and he can thwart the man by freeing you, maybe it will . . ."

Maybe it would lessen the Hierarch's fear, give him a sufficient sense of power and control that he could listen when Jeriah explained that not everything Master Lazur had done was wrong. Or at least that the reason he'd wronged so many, including the Hierarch, was a good one. Necessary.

Because if the relocation didn't go forward, if the Realm didn't get to a defensible position while it still had a large enough army to man the wall, soon none of this would matter to any of them.

Two pairs of eyes were staring at him inimically.

"You mean to turn the gen'ral over to the Hierarch?" Cogswhallop demanded. "As a prisoner? We'll not permit that, human. Be warned."

Jeriah had seen what the goblins could do, and he didn't take that warning lightly.

"I've got three lengths of charmed chain. If I use one to chain her to myself and a tree, and put one around each horse and their gear, what can you do?"

"You'll find out," the goblin growled. The threat seemed a bit incongruous, since he was riding behind Jeriah, in easy reach of the human's much stronger arms. But Cogswhallop meant what he said. It might not be war to the death, but it would still be—

"No." The note of command in her voice transformed the girl into the general. "It makes no sense for either of us to waste time and strength fighting each other. Cogswhallop, you'll leave him alone, all of you, till you find Tobin. Then bring him to us, or if he's still too weak to travel, get word to us so we can go to him."

To Jeriah's amazement, the goblin's head bent in obedience even as he protested.

"But Gen'ral, if he turns you over as a prisoner, in those chains . . . What if they find against you? You might be hanging yet!"

"The Hierarch will never hang one of Master Lazur's enemies," Jeriah put in. "No matter what they've done. That's part of the problem. I'm hoping that if the Hierarch can spare one of the priest's enemies, he'll be more able to think about the relocation instead of just reacting against it."

"I think the kind of fear and hate you're describing won't be appeased by a sop," said the girl. "But I should be safe enough, and we don't know if Tobin's safe or not. You've got your orders, Cogswhallop."

The goblin sighed, and the slight weight on the back of Jeriah's saddle vanished. When he looked around, the goblin was gone.

They reached an agreement, Jeriah and the sorceress. She could ride free of chains if she promised not to escape. And to Jeriah's surprise, she kept her word. Which probably meant she had some reason of her own for traveling south, at least for a while.

She thought his plan to give the Hierarch some sense of victory over Master Lazur by freeing one of the priest's enemies was ridiculous. "You're trying to convince the old man to do just what Lazur wanted. You're not going to do that by tearing down the priest's influence."

But Jeriah knew the Hierarch better than she did, knew that if he could get the Sunlord past his irrational fear of the priest, he might be able to look at the things Lazur had tried to accomplish more rationally. Or at least it might work that way, and trying risked nothing that mattered—not to Jeriah.

It wasn't that he and the sorceress weren't speaking to each other all the way to the City of Steps, but whenever they spoke, they ended up quarreling. Despite that, she learned a lot about what had happened last spring, and all about Jeriah's concern for the relocation, and the threat presented by the barbarian army.

He saw no need to bring Mistress Koryn into the tale. His fight with her was his own business.

Jeriah learned almost nothing about the sorceress. But he'd come to know her well enough to interpret her expression when they rode over a low rise and the City of Steps came into view.

It was early summer here in the Midlands, and the city's hill was a mass of blooming trees, sculpted into flowing layers by the seven great walls. She pulled Fiddle to a stop, staring, and Jeriah stopped Glory beside her.

"You've never seen it?"

"It's beautiful," she whispered. "How can a place where so many humans . . . I expected . . ."

"It's beautiful inside too," Jeriah told her. "In a different way on each tier. The low town, where most people live and work—it doesn't have so many gardens and fountains, but it brims with life. Tobin always worried because I liked it."

A smile flickered in her eyes. They both knew how Tobin worried.

But the thought of his brother banished any inclination to smile back. Cogswhallop had turned up several times during their journey, both to check on his general and to report, and Tobin hadn't been found.

Makenna and the goblin thought he must be in a city somewhere, since fewer goblins lived in cities and towns. But Finders in the towns were searching too, and there was still no sign of his brother.

Makenna had told him about casting a clumsy gate and thrusting his brother out of the Otherworld. Her description of the wavering spell had horrified Jeriah, but she'd seen Tobin reach the other side intact, near a crowberry bush on a dusty road. So unless there was another world with crowberry bushes, Tobin had to be somewhere.

The carved wooden gate into the low town wasn't guarded.

The girl seemed subdued by the teeming crowds and flinched at a sudden burst of shouting, but Jeriah ignored both the crowd and her nerves. He did stop at the comb-and-scissors sign that indicated a barber shop, wondering if it might be worth a few copper bits to have someone trim her ragged hair. After looking at her closely, he decided that it made her look more pathetic as it was—and nothing could dim her staggering beauty.

Jeriah was handsome himself; he knew exactly how to use it, and how little it really mattered. Koryn wasn't even pretty, though he'd come to see a kind of beauty in her fey angular face, in the thin awkward body that was far too slight to hold a hero's spirit. He'd see her soon. . . .

Jeriah shook off the thought. First he had deal to with the girl who rode beside him, this strange, half-wild girl commander who didn't even seem to know she was beautiful. Perhaps it came from spending most of her life among goblins, but her utter indifference to her looks was more effective than the way most girls tried to flaunt whatever beauty they possessed.

He didn't think the Hierarch would harm her, but just in case . . .

"I'm not going to put your chains back on," said Jeriah. "But if I'm presenting you as a prisoner, and Master Lazur's victim, it might be better if I tied your hands."

He did so just before they reached the fourth gate, which admitted them to the palace grounds. The look she gave him before she turned her back and extended her wrists for the rope made Jeriah very aware that she was submitting to this of her own free will—he was not in charge.

It didn't give him much confidence as he pulled her up the steps to the third-level terrace, which was the lowest level of the palace itself, and asked a clerk where Master Zachiros might be found.

It turned out that the secretary was attending the Hierarch, who was meeting with several councillors in a closed session on important Realm business.

"The Hierarch's meeting with the council?" Jeriah tried not to sound incredulous. The Hierarch he had served had been incapable of meeting with anyone "on business." The drugs Master Lazur had given him had befuddled his mind so thoroughly that the secret could be kept only by shrouding him in layer after layer of formality. He must have recovered far more swiftly than Chardane had expected.

"Yes," said the clerk. "The Hierarch frequently meets with the council now. I think he decided to take more control over secular matters after that priest betrayed him. We've had to send most of the personal petitioners back to the lower courts, and the wait for a hearing with the Hierarch himself is backed up for weeks. Are you certain the lower court can't help you?"

The Hierarch had recovered! He must have recovered completely, or almost completely, and a great burden lifted from Jeriah's heart.

"Let me talk to Master Zachiros," he said. "He'll determine whether I should see the Hierarch or not. Can you let him know I'm here when they take their next break?"

The clerk admitted that they were due for a break soon, and he went off to inform the secretary's assistant.

Makenna was watching Jeriah, speculation in her dark eyes. "If he's meeting in closed session with the landholders, that means his mind has cleared, doesn't it?"

"How do you know . . . Oh."

"Aye, Cogswhallop told me everything as soon as he'd a moment to spare," she said. "But he said that your herb-healer priest, Chardane? He said she wasn't certain if the Hierarch would recover, or how fast."

"Yes, but the fact that he'd been drugged for the last seven years is a state secret that . . . that . . . It's a really big secret!" Jeriah told her. "You mustn't mention it to anyone, under any circumstances, ever!"

The girl snorted. Given that she and her goblins had been fighting the Realm for the last five years, she probably didn't care about their secrets.

"It would break people's trust in the Hierarch, in the church itself, to learn that their ruler had been so badly incapacitated, and that we, ah . . ."

"Faked it," said Makenna cheerfully. "I must admit, I was impressed by the tale."

"Keep your voice down," Jeriah snapped. "Even in the palace, only a handful of people know the truth."

Fortunately the clerk came bustling back and told Jeriah

that Master Zachiros would meet with him and his prisoner, in his own office, in five minutes. The clerk also sent a guard with them, even though he knew that Jeriah knew the way.

The secretary stood in his office doorway, watching for them, and greeted Jeriah with a beaming smile. "Come in, dear boy, come in. How was your stay with your parents? It must have been wonderful, since you were gone so long. We've been so busy here, I hardly noticed the time passing—though we could have used you, indeed we could!"

Looking from the spectacles that slid down his long nose to the floppy slippers on his feet, Makenna's mouth quirked contemptuously. Jeriah noted the warning directness in the secretary's bright gaze and answered cautiously.

"I didn't spend all that time with my family, sir. I've got a lot to tell you."

"Oh, I can see that," said Master Zachiros cheerfully. "But perhaps we can discuss it in private. You and your, ah, companion?"

"I have orders to stay with the prisoner, sir," the guard put in. "Until the others arrive."

"Others?" Jeriah asked.

"Whose orders?" said Master Zachiros.

"Wait," said the girl. "I want to speak to the Hierarch myself. That's why I came. To talk to him or whoever's in charge."

"Lord Brallorscourt's orders," said the guard. "He . . . Here they come now."

Jeriah turned. Four more guards marched down the

corridor and came to a stop before Master Zachiros.

"Is this the sorceress of the Goblin Wood?" their leader demanded.

"Why do you care?" Jeriah asked. This wasn't going the way he'd planned.

"Yes," said Master Zachiros calmly. "And as you can see"—he gestured to the girl's bound wrists—"she's my prisoner."

A frown creased the guardsman's brow. "Lord Brallorscourt put out the order that if she ever showed up, we were to take her prisoner. His prisoner."

"Then I've beaten him to punch!" Master Zachiros said. "Jathan, take this young woman down to the palace dungeon. No need to be rough about it. She won't make it necessary. Will you, my dear?"

"But I want to talk to the Hierarch!" Makenna protested. "I've got to—"

"You've got to go with Jathan now," said the secretary calmly. "Or you'll never get your chance."

"Lord Brallorscourt said we were to take her to his town house," Jathan protested.

"And if she was his prisoner, you no doubt would," Master Zachiros said. "But since she's my prisoner, she'll be housed where I say. I'm sure when you explain it to him, Lord Brallorscourt will understand."

This was clearly a matter above Jathan's rank. "Whatever you say, sir."

"As for you, my girl," Zachiros went on, "I'm afraid you

have to go with this nice guard, who's going to show you to a comfortable cell. And Jathan? She's not to speak to anyone along the way, and she's not to have any visitors. Not unless I personally approve them."

"But—" Makenna began.

"Come along, mistress," Jathan said, taking her arm and leading her down the corridor. "I've orders to see to your comfort and treat you with proper respect—as long as you cooperate."

"But—"

Next time she wouldn't underestimate the mild-looking secretary. Jeriah bit down a smirk as Master Zachiros ushered him into the office, and the older man's foolish cheer dropped away. "She knows about the drugs? Given who your helpers were, I thought she must, but it's a great pity. We don't dare allow her to reveal that to anyone."

"Well, I didn't tell her," said Jeriah. "And without my helpers, the Hierarch might still be drugged and none of us would know the truth. But what in two worlds is going on with Brallorscourt? Why would he want to take her prisoner? I didn't think he knew she existed."

"I have no idea. But she's safe in my custody, and I'll soon find out what Brallorscourt's interest is. In fact, he'll probably be hammering on the door and telling me all about it as soon as he learns I have her." The secretary shuffled to a chair and lifted his sore feet onto a stool, while Jeriah found another chair for himself. He'd once burgled the desk in this office, but he now felt amazingly at home. And the secretary's foolishness was an act; Jeriah knew he was both kind and just, and had the Realm's best interests at heart.

"I'm more concerned about what *she* knows," the kind and just man went on. "This is a girl who once went to war against all humanity. If she's still so inclined, she could do the Realm a great deal of harm simply by revealing our secret."

"I don't think she'll do that," said Jeriah slowly. "I think there's something else she wants. The goblins didn't try to free her, all the way here from the northern woods, and that has to have been on her orders."

"So she's up to something," Master Zachiros summed up neatly. "But you don't know what it is."

"That's true," Jeriah admitted. "But if you ask her, she might tell you. She doesn't like me, but she's not much of a schemer. Oh, she can plan out a battle or a raid, but she's really very straightforward."

"Unlike the two of us," said the secretary. "But you don't have to dissemble with me. What *were* you doing on the border?"

Jeriah thought he was straightforward, though given how many lies he'd told lately . . . He told Master Zachiros everything he'd learned about the barbarians and handed over the army commander's dispatch.

The frown in the bespectacled eyes deepened. "This is tricky. And the Bright Gods know it's important, but I'm afraid it may do little good right now."

"But his mind has cleared, hasn't it?" Jeriah asked. "I mean, if he's meeting with the council . . ."

"Oh, his mind has almost entirely cleared," said Master Zachiros. "It's his spirit that concerns me. There are days, my boy, when I think it's not safe to ask the Bright Gods for anything."

This was the man, Jeriah remembered, who had prayed for the Hierarch to survive a terrible fever, only to see him do so with his mind—supposedly—destroyed. He must have prayed for the Hierarch to recover from the drugs too.

"Can I see him?" Jeriah asked. "I promised to deliver this report, and I have to try—"

"Oh, you'll certainly do that!" said Master Zachiros. "In fact, your arrival is very timely. The council has been discussing these matters, and its break is about to end. Come along, dear boy."

For a man with sore feet he moved swiftly, whisking Jeriah through the maze of marble corridors and down a servants' stair to the big chamber where the Landholders' Council met.

Jeriah had wanted to talk to Koryn, to get another intelligent view of what was going on in the palace, before he approached the Hierarch. Frankly, he'd planned to use that as an excuse to convince her to speak to him. To let him explain . . .

But Master Zachiros was right. This opportunity was too good to miss.

A number of men were milling about—influential land-holders, clerks, courtiers, servants. Jeriah knew many of them by name. Even Nevin's scowl, as he looked up and saw Jeriah approaching, was familiar.

But it was the man beside whose chair Nevin stood who commanded Jeriah's attention. As he stepped forward and knelt before the Hierarch, sky blue eyes focused on his face. And recognized it.

"Jeriah! Jeriah . . . Rovan, isn't it? I thought you were visiting your family."

"Yes, lord," Jeriah said. "I'm sorry I was gone so long."

The Hierarch's broad hand waved dismissively. It was covered with rings that Jeriah had placed on those fingers and later removed, as if their owner was a child. "I'm sure your leave was well earned, and I remember your kindness during my illness."

*My illness.* They'd had to admit that Master Lazur had tried to drug the Hierarch, in order to bring him to trial for it, but they'd concealed the fact that he'd succeeded in doing it for seven years. Jeriah knew that Master Lazur himself had never revealed that truth, in all the long days of his trial. It would have harmed the Realm. Even when that Realm was about to hang him, that had still been the priest's paramount concern. Now, it seemed, drugs were no longer even being mentioned. Jeriah fought down a shiver. The Hierarch remembered his "kindness," so perhaps . . .

"I've done more than just visit my parents," said Jeriah.

"In fact, I've gone from one end of the Realm to the other since I was here last. On your business, Sunlord."

After that, they could hardly help but ask why.

Master Lazur had suppressed the information that the barbarians could heal themselves. The fact that the barbarians possessed magic that the Bright Gods' priests couldn't defeat undermined the very foundations of church theology. Having seen the situation on the border, Jeriah didn't give a tinker's curse about church theology.

He told the Hierarch and the council the full story of all he'd heard and seen during the barbarian attack, and also about the report from the army commanders he'd given to Master Zachiros.

"But you can read what they have to say for yourself, sir. And the council should also know exactly what our army is facing."

"That the enemy uses black sorcery is hardly surprising," said the Hierarch. "The Bright Gods will no doubt show us how to defeat them in due course. Though your report does raise some questions we should consider."

"Helping the army overcome its challenges is the proper business of both the Hierarch and the council," Lord Brallorscourt interposed smoothly. "Your assistance is appreciated, Rovanscourt, but I'm not sure it was necessary."

A snicker ran through the room, and Jeriah flushed.

"It's Rovan," he said. "My brother's still alive. You were wrong about that, just as you were wrong about—"

"My squire's intention was to protect me, the Realm, and the church," the Hierarch interrupted firmly. "He shall be given credit for that."

Jeriah hadn't been going to say anything indiscreet. But if the Hierarch decided to silence him . . .

"I've brought you more than information, my lord," said Jeriah hastily. "Though that information comes directly from commanders who are fighting the barbarians on the border of our Realm. A border the barbarians have already pushed back once. As you would hear from the Southland lords, if they hadn't lost so many of their numbers."

The Hierarch frowned. "That does seem unjust. Perhaps—"

"The rule that to be a landholder a man must hold the land is the tenet on which the council was founded," Lord Brallorscourt said. "I put it to you, Sunlord, that only a few weeks recovered from a devastating illness is not the time to change a law that's been in place for over a thousand years!"

The Hierarch's uncertainty deepened, and Jeriah's heart sank.

"But as I said, I have more than mere information," he went on swiftly. "I was summoned north to identify one of Master Lazur's enemies who was recently captured. Since I feared she wouldn't receive true justice there, I brought her back to the City of Steps for your judgment, lord."

And your judgment is just fine, whatever Brallorscourt implies!

Several councillors glared at him, and Master Zachiros stepped forward. "I think young Rovanscourt . . . ah, Rovan is right. She might not have received justice anywhere in the north. Our prisoner is the sorceress who led the goblins behind the great wall, driving out so many settlers that Master Lazur himself was forced to go and deal with her. And then she escaped from him as well."

Only someone who was watching the man closely would have seen Lord Brallorscourt stiffen.

"A sorceress?" The Hierarch clearly knew nothing about it; he'd been drugged while the girl was fighting her war. "If she practices dark magics—"

"She doesn't," said Jeriah. "Sorceress is what her enemies called her, but she's only a simple hedgewitch."

Or so she claimed.

"In truth, it's a tragic story," said Master Zachiros. "And a tricky case. I found many notes regarding her in Master Lazur's papers, so I know something about it. Her mother was a hedgewitch too, drowned by their village priest in the first year after the Decree of Bright Magic passed, when this girl was just ten years old."

Jeriah, who hadn't known that, blinked.

The Hierarch's brows rose. "Then she's only . . . fifteen years old? How much trouble could a girl that age have caused?"

"Plenty." Master Zachiros said drily. "She organized the goblins who were fleeing the decree and fought off the settlers, and even the army, so effectively that she brought the relocation to a standstill."

"But the Decree of Bright Magic was rescinded," said the Hierarch. "Those who practice the small magics, and those magical creatures that do no harm, are no longer under sentence of death. Why should we prosecute this girl? Especially if her mother was slain, I think she can be forgiven for resisting an unjust law. A new unjust law," he added, with a pointed look at his chief councillor.

Brallorscourt nodded reluctantly.

"Unfortunately," said Master Zachiros, "her resistance wasn't passive. She, or the goblins under her command, killed several men."

"Then try her for murder," said Nevin. "And be done with it. There's no need for you to be bothered with this, Sunlord."

"But was it murder?" Master Zachiros asked. "If you claim that the conflict between those of lesser magic and the church was war—and the law's original phrasing called for 'war against all who serve the power of darkness'—then in fighting back, she did no more than any soldier. And now that peace has been made, she can't be prosecuted for it. On the other hand, if you rule that the Decree was simply a law, not a declaration of war, killing those who tried to enforce that law is murder. Though even then, I think extenuating circumstances might be considered."

The Hierarch looked at Brallorscourt for guidance, and

Jeriah's blood ran cold. He'd been wondering whether he should mention the charmed iron chains, still in his saddle-bags in the stable. He decided not to.

Lord Brallorscourt shrugged. "A tricky case indeed. Just the kind of case the judges of the lower courts are most fitted to—"

"Speak with her yourself, Sunlord," Jeriah said urgently. "Hear her side of the story before you make any decisions."

"I shall," said the Hierarch. "But not today. This is a complex matter, which will require both more information and careful consideration on my part. But if she managed to delay that accursed relocation, she certainly can't be all bad. Right, my friends?"

The answer was a cheer that rocked the rafters.

Jeriah always knew where to find Koryn. The library table where she sat was crowded with books, notebooks, and scrolls, as always—but today the books were closed and the stopper was still in the ink pot beside her. Curly, dark Southlander hair formed a shadowy halo around her face, and her wide, pale eyes were fixed on the middle distance.

He didn't think he'd ever seen her doing nothing before. She had a restless energy that was always driving her, mind and body. It might have been her obsession with destroying the barbarians, but Jeriah suspected it was just the way she was.

He dropped into the chair opposite her, but several

moments passed before Koryn's gaze turned to him. Had she lost weight? She'd always been too thin, but he didn't remember her bones standing out that starkly.

"I hear you failed," she said. "Again. Unless your goal was to sink the relocation further than you already have."

He clearly hadn't been forgiven yet. On the other hand, the last time they'd spoken, she'd cursed him with white-hot fury, so this grim depression was probably an improvement. Jeriah didn't ask how she'd learned about the council session so quickly—if it had to do with the relocation, Koryn made it her business to know.

"I'm trying to get the relocation back on track," he told her. "I'd hoped that freeing one of Master Lazur's enemies might make the Hierarch a little less frightened of the man. It still might!"

"If you think that's all it will take, you're dreaming," Koryn told him. "If you'd thought for five minutes before making this mess in the first place, we wouldn't—"

"At least I'm doing something," Jeriah retorted, stung. "Now the Hierarch, the whole council, knows why the barbarians are such a threat! You and your precious Master Lazur were keeping it secret. Now that he knows—"

"You think he's going to do anything differently? The Hierarch doesn't care about anything except escaping the clutches of a man who's already dead! The barbarians aren't even real to—"

"It's more progress than you've made," Jeriah said.

"You've spent over a year digging through those books, and how much have you accomplished? In less than a month, I've given him something that might lessen his fear, and I've brought new facts to light. Facts the council might listen to, even if he . . . You're not listening to me."

"You're right," Koryn murmured. "That's just what I've been thinking."

"What?"

She got up and limped out of the room without replying, which was just like her, Jeriah reflected irritably. Talking to Koryn only depressed him. He didn't know why he'd bothered to seek her out.

The next day he learned that Koryn had left a note for her uncle and departed for the Southlands.

# CHAPTER 7

# Makenna

MAKENNA HAD BEEN EXPECTING THE face that appeared at the grate set into the floor of her cell. That it had popped up behind the sewer grate was . . .

"Isn't there some other way out?" Makenna asked.

"What, you want us to lead you past two guard stations and up the main stair?" Cogswhallop asked impatiently. "It's not so bad as you think. And you're not fool enough to care, even if it was."

Makenna frowned, and the goblin added persuasively, "The hero did it twice, and he hardly whined at all." Having silenced any further complaints on her part, Cogswhallop went on, "We'll have you out of this in a bit, Gen'ral. Just give the Stoners a chance to take the grate out."

"What if I don't want to go?" Makenna demanded. "I came here to talk to the Hierarch himself. I can't see how running will accomplish that. And your escape route's not exactly appealing—though I like the idea of Jeriah doing it."

In truth, she didn't care what she had to crawl through in

order to escape. But if she could talk to the Hierarch herself, then maybe she could accomplish something for her goblins. Rescinding the Decree of Bright Magic meant they were no longer under death sentence, but that didn't give them a safe place to live. If she'd been allowed to speak to the Hierarch—who certainly should be feeling grateful!—she'd intended to ask him to deed the woodland north of the great wall to the goblins. Or some other place where they could build their villages openly, without having to hide from humans.

"You'll not reach him." Cogswhallop wiggled through the sewer grate as he spoke. He was muddy—at least, she preferred to think of it as mud—but he didn't smell as bad as she'd expected.

"Lord Brallorscourt will do whatever he must to stop you, and he's got a long reach. You wouldn't be safe here if Zachiros hadn't put you under his protection. And I can't swear how long that will last, so you'd best be going—whatever you think of the route!"

"Why would Brallorscourt want to stop me from talking to the Hierarch?" Makenna asked. "Why would he care about me at all? I've never had a thing to do with the man!"

"You haven't," Cogswhallop admitted. "But the same can't be said of your minions."

"My what?"

"Your minions. The vast goblin army that runs about spying on everyone for you. At least, that's Brallorscourt's take on it, and you can't entirely blame the man. Given the conversations he's been having with Master Hispontic and all."

A horrible foreboding seized Makenna. The Bookeries' leader had been left behind in this world. Ordinarily, the goblin was reasonable and cautious . . . except in pursuit of knowledge, when no Bookerie was ever cautious.

"Why has Master Hispontic been dealing with Lord Brallorscourt? With any human?"

Cogswhallop sighed. "Well, the short version of the story is that the hero granted Hispontic and his lot the run of all the papers in the palace. Brallorscourt, who keeps a close eye on his secrets, found out about it and tried to get the priests to cast 'em out. Hispontic took this as the breaking of a human promise and got back at Brallorscourt by giving his papers particular attention . . . and learned that Brallorscourt knew that Master Lazur was drugging the Hierarch, almost from the start. Which explains how he came by so much of the power he's throwing around these days. Not that the Hierarch can't stand up to him, if he sees his way clear. He's too fearful of being controlled again to allow anyone to run him. But the old man was wandering in his wits for seven years—he has to rely on someone's advice. And I'm afraid he's picked the wrong man."

"Who is Lord Brallorscourt? I mean—"

"Head of the Landholders' Council," said the goblin. "Which makes Hispontic crossing him even more idiotic than it sounds. Because Hispontic went and blackmailed

Brallorscourt with the secret, demanding he leave the Bookeries alone, and Brallorscourt had to agree. But in the course of that conversation, Brallorscourt asked Hispontic who his human master was—not even thinking that the want-wit might be acting on his own—and the only human Master Hispontic, or any goblin, serves . . ."

"Is me." She'd seen it coming, but she still winced. "So Brallorscourt's under the impression that I've been spying on him, and blackmailing him, and he probably thinks that I want to talk to the Hierarch to expose his secret. And get him hanged. No wonder he set the guard to watch for me!"

"And he'll be sending assassins to these cells as soon as he can arrange it."

With a soft *crack*, the sewer grate came free. Makenna peered into the shaft. "I can't get through that. It's too narrow."

"Leave that to the Stoners," said Cogswhallop calmly. "It'll soon be bigger."

She knew he was right. She had to go. But . . .

"How am I going to get to the Hierarch if I run? I still need to talk to him!" Though given what Jeriah told her about the barbarians, the relocation would have to go forward after all, and there would be no land beyond the wall for goblins to inhabit. So where could her goblins go, with or without the Hierarch's consent?

Unless, of course, the humans chose to dither around till the barbarians wiped out the lot of them.

No. There was a time Makenna might have wished for that, but she no longer did. Even when she was fighting for the Wood, the only men she'd ordered slain had killed her goblins—and had been about to kill more! Her troops were usually too clever to be cornered, but trapped they were no match for a human sword. Of course, the humans who wielded those swords weren't immune to goblin arrows, so it all worked out.

The only death she regretted was the babe a pregnant woman had lost, after Makenna had driven her and her husband out. The traps the young couple had set for the goblins had been lethal, so Makenna didn't even care for the parents' grief. Only the babe hadn't deserved to die.

There were humans who didn't kill, but she'd found precious few of them. Barbarians all.

"Maybe the hero could help," Cogswhallop suggested. "He's already been to see Hierarch. Though the meeting didn't go exactly as he hoped."

"That's 'cause he's a bumbler," said Makenna. "Or at best a dreaming fool."

Cogswhallop, who seemed to have developed a soft spot for Tobin's disastrous brother, scowled. "I think he's right— the old man would free you if it was up to him. Young Jeriah didn't know what Brallorscourt and Hispontic have been up to. And he didn't warn the guards to put those chains on you, though he knows how easily we can work down here. You can hardly blame the lad for losing Tobin, Gen'ral. He never had him in the first place!"

Cogswhallop knew her too cursed well. "Have you heard anything about—"

"Still no word," said Cogswhallop. "It's a big Realm. It takes time, even for Finders, to search every corner of it."

If Tobin was well and free, he should have contacted his family by now.

But there was no reason to think he was dead, and if he wasn't free, or well, there was nothing she could do about it.

So put your mind to what you can do.

"How dangerous will this be?" Makenna asked, gesturing toward the hole in the floor. The scraping sounds that emerged were too soft to call the attention of the guards—she could barely hear them from where she sat. A human who didn't know the Stoners would never believe how quickly and quietly they could work.

"At this point? About as dangerous as a stroll in the park," Cogswhallop told her. "In fact, getting you through the palace park and into the city will be more dangerous than bringing you out of the palace itself. Since the Bookeries had permission to copy the library, they've made themselves right at home. There's a whole network of goblin tunnels through the palace now. Getting a human out is a bit harder, but not much."

The gleam in his eyes hinted that he wanted to surprise her, so Makenna obediently changed the subject. "Is that how you know what went on at the Hierarch's meeting?"

"Aye. There's not much in the palace we can't look in on now. Least, nothing that takes place in a room with books or documents in it." It was warmly familiar, being briefed by Cogswhallop.

A round, lumpy face emerged from the sewer shaft. "Big," the Stoner announced, and held out a hand to Makenna.

Stoners weren't much for talking, but Makenna valued them nonetheless. She had to search among her remaining buttons to find one made of rock. The Stoners were willing to be paid in tokens, a symbol of the larger trade between her and all the goblins she defended, but they had no interest in wood or bone or copper.

She finally found one, carved from mottled jasper, and the Stoner nodded approval as she handed it over.

The shaft was four feet long, and large enough for her to wiggle through, though Cogswhallop had her take off her button vest before she did so. Makenna discovered why when she slithered through the ceiling of a largish culvert and fell onto her back in the stream of cold water that flowed down its bottom. At least the . . . mud, she told herself firmly, that lay beneath the shallow current kept her from bruising.

Cogswhallop dropped neatly onto her stomach and then leaped to the drier stone above the water level before she could roll over.

"There, that's kept your vest clean," he said, and grinned at her snarl.

The culvert ended in a round room whose ceiling was lost

in the darkness above. Makenna was more interested in a pool of clear water in the center, into which a chain of buckets splashed and then rose, dripping, to carry water up to the palace.

The drier part of the room was filled with a small mob of smiling goblins.

"You can wash up here," Miggy told her. "We've got clean clothes for you, and the Stoners have already widened their access to the main tunnel. We're getting good at this!"

"What main tunnel?" Makenna asked, shedding her muddy clothes. Most of the male goblins turned their backs, but they'd fought together too long for any of them to pay much heed to modesty.

"The Hierarch's escape tunnel," Miggy told her proudly. "It's supposed to be this big secret, but it was on the builder's drawings, and half the servants know there's supposed to be one, though they don't know where it is. The Bookeries paid the Stoners to open a shaft into it from this room. They've been using it to get in and out of the palace for over a month now."

He didn't bother to add that the humans didn't have a clue what was going on under their noses; they never did.

The boy's shirt and britches were more ragged than those she'd shed, but dry and clean. They were cut like the garments she'd seen on some of the laborers, as she'd ridden through the teeming streets of the low town behind Tobin's brother.

Raised in a small village, then exiled to the emptiness of the great northern woods, Makenna hadn't dreamed so many humans could be crushed together in one place. It wasn't as if she'd never been in a town before—though she'd been so young at the time, all she really remembered was looking up at the big clock tower. Riding into the greatest city in the Realm, she had found the noise, the looming buildings, the stench of so many people sweating and working and pissing in one place, horrifying. The cramped cell hadn't been much better.

Emerging from the stone-lined tunnel into the quiet woods of the palace park was like balm to her battered soul. The setting sun gleamed red and orange beneath a dense scatter of clouds, and Makenna blinked at the brilliant light. Somehow she'd expected darkness, though it had been morning when they'd arrived and she hadn't been locked up long.

"Won't those who bring my dinner raise the alarm?" A polite woman had brought her bread, cheese, and soup soon after the cell door had been locked behind her, and later returned for the tray.

"They likely will," Cogswhallop said. "But by the time they finish searching the palace, we should have you out of the park. By the time they've searched the park, you should be well out of the city. Assuming we can get you off this tier before the alarm is raised."

This tier held not only the tame woods and gardens that

surrounded the palace, but also the army barracks and several great halls of government—which were now releasing a number of clerks, who had worked through dinner and wanted to get home before the sun set.

The goblins brought her a worn leather satchel, the kind messengers carried, and a short cloak with a hood that wouldn't look out of place on a chilly evening. Its folds helped to conceal the fact that Cogswhallop's small body filled the satchel almost to overflowing.

"I'm too old for this," he grumbled, trying to arrange the satchel's flap so he could look out without being seen.

"Then let Miggy come with me." Makenna was watching the crowd of clerks heading toward the great gate.

"That loon! He couldn't possibly guide you."

"Should I change my face?" she asked. "There's a spell I could try—"

Cogswhallop frowned. "How long would it take? And how sure of the spell are you?"

"Only a few minutes to cast," said Makenna. "But I haven't tried it since I was a child." And then it had usually failed.

"They don't have any description of you," Cogswhallop said. "Or a reason to be looking, so likely we're best off doing this fast. Unless you want to stand around gabbing till all that changes?"

For the first few minutes of her escape, Makenna didn't need guidance. It was simple to step out of the trees onto the path, and no one gave her a sideways glance. Of course, that was what the guards at the gate were there for.

"Why not over the wall?" she murmured to Cogswhallop. The guards appeared to be paying more attention to their conversation than to the clerks who streamed past them— several of whom, Makenna noted, had already raised their hoods. "Or under it?"

"The wall around the palace is like the great wall in the north," Cogswhallop murmured back. "Or rather, like the great wall used to be. The priests who created it poured it chock-full of magic, and since this wall surrounds their church, the priests maintained their spells. The Stoners can't damage it, trees tend not to grow near it—and if one does, it's cut down right quick. If anything bigger than a fox tries to burrow under, the guards seem to know about it. We haven't tried to put anything bigger than a cat over it, but I expect the same thing would happen. Some sort of warning spell, near as I can figure. Mind, only the wall around the palace grounds is spelled like that, just as this is the only gate that's both locked and guarded at night. But for a human . . ."

They were nearing that gate now, and the guards didn't look very alert. If Makenna's goblin sentries had been that careless, she'd have had sharp words for them at the least! The thought gave her courage, and she lifted her head and strolled through the gate as if she had every right to be there. The guards didn't even notice her.

". . . for a human, the gates are easier," Cogswhallop

finished. "Especially with guards who're such great ninnies!"

"It would be different if the alarm had been raised."

The light was dimming, and Makenna picked up her pace, as many others on the street were doing. The high town, which held the wealthier citizens' homes and a few expensive shops, didn't assault her senses as the low town had, but it still held too many humans to suit her. On the plus side, the fact that her satchel was talking to her was lost in the general hubbub. The bad side was that the high town was built on steeper slopes, and its roads and stairways formed a twisting maze.

"Take this street to the left," said Cogswhallop. "I think. Why they didn't put their gates in a line, with a straight road up to the palace, I'll never understand."

An old history lesson came back to her. "The streets and gates were offset deliberately, to slow down any army—like the barbarians—who might be trying to reach the palace."

"And that hasn't happened for how many centuries?" Cogswhallop demanded. "Seems to me they should have got round to fixing it. Go down those stairs on the right, Gen'ral."

They missed several turns and had to retrace their steps, but without Cogswhallop's directions she wouldn't have reached the next gate before dawn. Jeriah had led her through those tangled streets so swiftly and easily, Makenna hadn't realized how tricky it was. Or maybe the young knight had known a quicker route. He'd spent some time in the city, assigned to the army here and later serving the Hierarch. Evidently he'd had time to learn his way about.

But Cogswhallop had the essentials down. There were no guards posted at the gate between the high and low city tiers—and though it might be locked later, it wasn't even closed now, despite the fact that darkness had fallen.

The moon was almost full, but it only emerged from the clouds at irregular intervals. The streets of the high town had been well lit, with lanterns beside most of the doors and gates. In the low town, only an occasional torch illuminated a tavern sign. And the bursts of conversation and laughter coming from those doors would have identified them anyway.

An encounter with a drunken human was the last thing Makenna needed, so she crossed to the other side of the street whenever she spotted one. There were still people moving through the streets despite the darkness, but they hurried about their business, eager to get home behind locked doors.

The streets here were broader, running over gentler slopes, easier to navigate. Still, Makenna felt she'd been walking for miles when Cogswhallop's whispered directions brought her in sight of the last gate.

Makenna had started toward it, trying to convince herself that running would look too suspicious, when a small shape emerged from under a step and raced over the cobbles toward her feet.

At first she took it for a rat, though country rats never

ran at people like that. She was backing away, ready to kick, when the moon made one of its fickle appearances and she saw that it was Daroo.

She knew the young goblin too well to think he'd expose himself in the open street for a prank. She swooped down and tucked him into her cloak, even as his father hissed in alarm.

"You young whelp! I told you and your mother to wait outside the city. What are you—"

The tiny body trembled against her arm, lungs heaving for breath.

"You can scold him later," Makenna told her lieutenant crisply. "Daroo, report."

"The gate's guarded!" Daroo gasped. "They've orders to look for you, mistress. A good description of all you're wearing. Well, of your button vest, and they know your hair's cut short and you're dressed like a boy. They're stopping anyone who goes near that gate, just to take no chances."

It was too late even to take off the distinctive vest. Turning around and heading in the other direction would look suspicious too, so Makenna kept walking down the street, but now she drifted toward the shadowy shops on the other side.

"How do you know this?"

"Jeriah," the goblin boy replied. "About being in the city, Fa, Mam decided—"

"That would be the same Jeriah I told you not to go near?" his father asked grimly. "And you promised you wouldn't involve yourself in any more of his schemes?"

"What did Jeriah say?" Makenna asked. She was almost opposite the gate, but there were still handfuls of people about. No reason for the guards to pick her out, as long as she didn't try to go through.

The guards had concealed themselves in the shadows of the great arch. She would never have spotted them in time.

"When they found you gone, they sent for Jeriah," Daroo told her. His breathing had slowed, but his light body still quivered with tension. "He acted all surprised that they hadn't thought to put charmed iron around your cell. Master Zachiros, he said you'd lived in the country all your life, and that you'd get out of the city as fast as you could. Brallorscourt, he wanted to search the palace, but Master Zachiros sent guards straight to all the gates with a good description of what you look like. And he only saw you for a moment! He's got keen eyes, that one."

"And you were listening to this," said his father, "even after I forbade you to meddle in human schemes, because . . . ?"

"I'd just gone to visit him," said Daroo. "I wasn't spying. Though if I had been, I wouldn't have had to run so hard. He had to tell me all about it, and then tell me how to get to this gate fast enough to warn you off."

These guards must have reached their posts in the time it had taken Makenna to go from that last gate to this one, or she'd have been intercepted an hour ago. But their only orders were to arrest someone trying to pass the gate. If she didn't stare, didn't do anything to call attention to herself . . .

"Hey, boy! You in the cloak. Let's have a word with you!"

Everyone else on the street turned to look at the guard who'd shouted. Makenna took to her heels without a backward glance.

Country living was good for something. She might not be able to navigate the city streets, but she easily kept her distance from the running footsteps. Within a few blocks she heard the guard's breath start to wheeze, and the distance between them increased.

Darting left and right at random, praying she wouldn't find herself in a dead end, Makenna noticed that only one set of footsteps ran after her. So even if she could circle back to the gate, it would do her no good. It appeared that not all the sunsguards were ninnies, and she cursed under her heaving breath and followed Daroo's directions without hesitation—even when he hissed, "Left now!" and sent her into a slot between two shops that was so narrow, she had to turn sideways and couldn't possibly run.

The guard's footsteps grew louder and she froze, deep in the shadows, as he whisked past the gap. A moment later the footsteps slowed, followed by a muffled curse.

"Farther in." Daroo's voice was so soft Makenna barely heard it—and he didn't have to warn her to be silent. Placing each foot with careful deliberation, Makenna crept to the back of the gap and emerged into a wider space between several buildings. She turned, still moving quietly, and pressed her back against the wall, listening to the erratic footfalls as the guard searched along his back trail, trying to determine where she'd gone.

She thought he paused at the gap between the buildings, but they'd passed several such gaps and this one was narrower than most. The footsteps moved on, and Makenna let the tension drain from her back and neck.

The moon was shining for the moment. At one time, the space in which she stood had probably been a yard behind one of the buildings that now formed its walls. A rotting shed that might once have held tools or gardening implements leaned precariously in one corner. But at some point in the city's history the surrounding buildings had extended themselves into the old yard, which was now little more than a tall shaft. Judging by the mound of trash heaped in the center, these days people mostly used the yard for rubbish thrown down from their windows.

At least they hadn't used it as a midden, for it smelled no worse than the rest of the city. But Makenna was accustomed to the country, where scrap lumber was either stacked in tidy piles for reuse or burned for heat, and even broken crockery might be smashed to gravel a path. She found the heap of abandoned objects distasteful.

"How long should we wait?" she whispered to Daroo and Cogswhallop.

"Depends how fast we can get you away safely," Cogswhallop admitted.

"And that'll be a while," Daroo added. "If they don't stop you at one of the gates, they plan to send out troops to scour the countryside. Jeriah said you'd be safer in the city."

"Unless he decides it'd be better for the Realm to tell them where I'm hiding," Makenna said.

"He wouldn't!" Daroo protested. "Tell her, Fa."

Cogswhallop shrugged. "Turned her over to 'em just now, didn't he?"

"Aye, but with those chains off, he knew we'd get her free," said Daroo. "And he sent me to warn you the moment he realized you might be caught. And we weren't caught, so he was right!"

"I'm not so sure I want to leave this city," Makenna told them. "I came here to talk to the Hierarch. I can't do that if run."

"You can't do that if you stay, either," Cogswhallop said. "Getting you out of the palace was one thing. Getting you past the Hierarch's guard, into his presence, is something else entirely. In fact, suicide comes to mind."

"You can hide here," said Daroo. "Mam decided several weeks ago that we'd be safer in the city with our friends, so we're already here. You could stay too, if they'll let you."

"Who are . . . ?"

Several pair of eyes gleamed amid the rubbish. Looking at it with goblins in mind, Makenna could see that it was really a goblin cottage disguised as a trash pile, though most humans would never have picked up the subtle signs.

Seeing that she'd spotted them, three goblins emerged to perch warily on the rubbish. They were thinner than most goblins she'd known and bore no obvious mark of whatever gift they possessed—but that was true of many whose gift was crafting some material.

"So you'd be this 'mistress' they're all talking about." The tallest goblin spoke up boldly. "Queen of the goblins, you are."

His city accent was thicker than those of the humans she passed in the street.

"I'm queen of no one," Makenna told him. "Nor mistress either, though I've traded for my services as a battle commander with a fair few."

She waited as he thought this over. A female goblin—his wife?—was frowning, but the third goblin, a girl a bit older than Daroo, crept up a jagged beam till she could peer into Makenna's face.

"She means it, Pa," the girl said. "She rules no one, and she's no mind to do so."

"I'd be bad at it too," Makenna said. She wished Brallorscourt could have heard that statement—not that he'd have believed it.

"Noggat and Simmi." Daroo gestured to the older pair. "They call themselves Ferrets, though their gift seems very like Finding to me. They can locate things of value, things humans have lost or discarded, and they're skilled menders too. Etta, she's their daughter, she can tell if a person's telling truth or not."

This was a goblin magic Makenna had never heard of, and she studied the girl with interest. "Does your gift breed true?" If there were other Truth Detectors among the city goblins, she could certainly use their gift in her forces.

The girl grinned suddenly, her angular face becoming sharper. "No way to know, just yet. But I'm interested to meet you, Mistress Makenna."

"Makenna will do." She seated herself on the ground so she wouldn't loom over them. "Would you be willing to hide me here for a while?" She still needed to talk to the Hierarch, but it would probably take some time to arrange it. "Cogswhallop, Daroo, and Etta here as well, they can tell you that I'd never betray you to the humans."

Etta nodded, then cocked her head curiously. "You say humans as if you weren't one of them."

"I may have been born to them," said Makenna. "But they haven't been my people for a long time. There's one I owe some loyalty, but that's all."

And where was Tobin, and why hadn't Cogswhallop been able to find him?

Master Noggat looked her up and down. "You might fit into the shed. It may not look like much, but the roof don't leak and we can clear out our storage. But what for?"

This stopped Makenna. These goblins owed her nothing. They'd want a fair trade, not the tokens she exchanged with her own troops.

"I've only the clothes on my back," she admitted. "If

there's something heavy to be lifted, I might manage that."

Simmi shook her head. "We can lift anything we wish, with a few pulleys and a bit of rope. You've no money? You'll not last long in the human world without it. Feeding you is a different matter than hiding, and you can't even pay for that!"

"Simmi's a great builder," Daroo put in. "What were you calling it? Engee . . ."

"Engineer, you lummox," said Etta. But there was no heat in the goblin girl's voice. "You got a messenger's satchel," she added, turning to Makenna. "Why not work as a messenger?"

"Because, sass box," Daroo told her, "the whole point is to keep her out of human hands! They're looking to arrest her. Or hadn't you noticed that small problem?"

"Aye," Cogswhallop said slowly. "But there might be a way around that. The hero's proved a time or two that bold fakery can work right well. You said you could change your appearance, Gen'ral?"

"I think I can," said Makenna—though without her mother's spell books, she had some doubts. "But I can't pass as a city messenger. I don't even know what they do. In the country a messenger will carry documents for miles, or days. I don't even have a horse."

"Don't need one here," said Etta. "A city messenger does much the same, but over shorter distances. And it's not only documents they deliver, but all manner of things. Finished goods from the seamstress and cobbler, hot bread to the back door of some house where the cooks are slacking off, papers of all sorts. Anything that's not so heavy you need a cart to haul it, a messenger carries. A fair few of them have country accents too. But they're mostly boys, and no one who gets a look at you by daylight . . ."

"Let me try something." Makenna had tried this spell as a child, up to mischief, and it had usually failed. In the Otherworld, trying to make magic with no power at all, she'd realized that she'd become more adept at spell craft over the years. She reached down and picked up a handful of damp earth. On one cheek, she used it to draw the rune of illusion, bending the minds of those around her to see what she willed. She'd used that rune in a hundred ruses and raids, and the power flowed smoothly into it. On her forehead she drew the rune of familiarity, to help folks see what they expected to see. She'd often welded it to the rune of illusion, though it felt strange to draw it by touch on her own face.

Runes might be only symbols, as her mother had said, but symbols could matter.

Finally she gathered more of the gritty dirt and traced the rune of maleness on her other cheek. This was a rune she hadn't used in years, but male and female were universal constants, among the first runes her mother had taught her. She was fairly certain she got it right.

Then Makenna rubbed all the runes into her face, not so much erasing them—though it did that too—as blending and spreading them. She raised her face from her hands, and Daroo gasped.

"You look like a boy!" Etta exclaimed.

"More to the point," said Cogswhallop, "you don't look like yourself. Shed that button vest, and no guard who's been told to watch for a lass dressed like a boy will give you a second look. So why not get out of here right now, tonight?"

"I'm not ready to leave just yet," Makenna told him. "But I'm not sure about this messenger business. How can I deliver anything if I don't know the streets? If I have to stop and ask directions every ten paces, someone will get suspicious no matter what I look like."

"That's no problem." Etta crept forward and touched Makenna's face. "How long will it last?"

"Until I wash my face, or the magic fails," Makenna told her. "I'd give it most of a day, though I can renew the spell again."

"This is true magic," the girl said. "Isn't it?"

"No more than finding what you need by thinking on it," Makenna told her. "And less magical than knowing truth from lie, in my opinion."

Etta knew it for the truth. "I can help you find your way about the city," she said. "I'll do it for half of what you make as a messenger."

Cogswhallop snorted. "Seems to me that half's a bit much, considering the gen'ral will be doing all the carrying."

"Seems to me that half's not much at all," said Noggat,

"considering she couldn't deliver a single load without Etta telling her where to go. And half of Mistress Makenna's half isn't so much to ask for lodging, when you note that we'll be hiding her as well."

"Three-quarters of her wage to your family, for a few directions and a leaky shed? That's robbery!"

Makenna ignored them, her gaze on Etta's face. "Do you speak the truth, as well as sense it?"

The goblin girl shrugged. "Most often. I'm not obliged to, though."

"Then tell me true, won't being among humans all day be dangerous for you?"

Etta's sharp face softened amazingly when she laughed. "Not for me, mistress. Nor for you, not looking like that. No matter who's after you."

"That's the first thing I'm going to fix," Makenna told her. "If I'm about to start work as a messenger, I'm going to write Lord Brallorscourt a letter."

Makenna spent most of the next morning composing her letter, on the cheap paper provided at a public message board near the goblins' home. Its delivery would be her first job as a messenger, and Etta crouched in her satchel to guide her through the convoluted streets.

There were guards today at the gate that separated the low city from the area where the rich lived. They looked closely at all the girls near Makenna's age who passed through—and didn't give a ragged boy more than a glance.

Makenna was feeling confident as she approached the rambling stone-and-timber manor Etta said was the Brallorscourt town residence. But as she took in the jumbled wings and the reflection off hundreds of panes of expensive glass, her steps slowed.

"You should go to the servant's entrance to deliver a letter," Etta told her. "Around to the back of the house. What are you stopping here for?"

"Money is power," Makenna told the goblin girl. "I hadn't realized how much of it Brallorscourt has. But you're right—that means nothing to a lad with a letter in hand."

As she approached the back entrance, Makenna let all the interest and curiosity she felt show on her face. It was a natural reaction for a poor boy in such a grand setting, and her heart was beating faster than it should.

The manservant who answered her knock wore a blue-and-black tunic that looked like a house uniform to Makenna. Not as grand as the red and gold of the sunsguard, but close.

"I got a letter for Lord Brallorscourt," she said, trying to mimic Etta's accent. "Three copper bits owed."

The manservant frowned. "Who's it from?"

"I dunno. Some lady gave it to me, but she didn't put a sender's name on the outside. Just the receiver. And she only paid half up front."

The servant sighed. "Wait here." He came back in moments

with three copper bits, for which Makenna exchanged the letter. Then he shut the door in her face.

Makenna walked back to the street, excitement singing in her blood as if battle had been joined instead of a simple message delivered.

"What did you say to him, anyway?" Etta asked from the satchel under Makenna's arm.

"I told him the truth. That I'm not interested in anything he did in the past, and that Hispontic wasn't working for me when he got that information and used it. I told him I wanted to speak to the Hierarch about goblin affairs that were nothing to do with him . . . as long as he gets out of my way."

"You think he'll believe it?" Etta sounded skeptical. "And how's he supposed to answer you?"

"It told him to post his reply on the message board outside the Pregnant Pig," Makenna said. "As for the rest of it . . . we'll see."

She waited till early evening to visit the message board. Etta said that messengers visited the public boards all the time, but there was a fair chance that the servant who had received the letter might be sent to post the reply. Makenna didn't want him to see her again. He might wonder, and having anyone even begin to suspect her disguise could be fatal in an all too literal sense.

As it turned out, waiting did her no good. Half a dozen men in the blue-and-black Brallorscourt tunic hovered in different places around the street. They were trying to be inconspicuous, but there were too many of them, and the street was too small. Makenna wasn't the only one who stared.

Etta took one look, ducked down into the satchel, and held still. "Go up to the board," she whispered. "Look for messages someone might pay to get a bit sooner; goods for pickup, a job offered, that kind of thing. Copy down anything that sounds promising, and who the message is for. We might as well get a bit of coin out of this."

Makenna did as the girl suggested, simply reading Brallorscourt's message along with the rest.

When she left the board, none of Brallorscourt's men paid her any attention at all.

"They're looking for you around the town as well," Master Noggat told Makenna later. "Asking in the taverns if anyone has seen you and promising 'a significant reward' for information. It's a good thing you're no longer a girl with dark-red hair and a button-covered vest, lass . . . ah, mistress."

"Lass is fine," Makenna told him. "I just wish Brallorscourt didn't take me for a fool."

"That note is practically an insult," Daroo agreed. "Asking you to meet with him so you can 'discuss the matter in private.' He might as well have told you to meet him alone, in a deserted alley, at midnight!"

"He thinks of traps before he thinks about negotiating,"

said Makenna. "That's something worth knowing about an enemy."

"Well, the hunt's up in the city now," Noggat said. "At least, Brallorscourt's men are hunting in the city. The suns-guards who're after you have mostly moved out into the countryside. But between the two of them, I'd advise you to stay a boy a bit longer."

"It seems I must," Makenna said. "At least till the hunt dies down. After that, I'll have some thinking to do."

Without Etta's help, working as a city messenger would have been impossible. But the goblin girl's guidance made it easy, and to her own astonishment, Makenna began to enjoy it. She grew accustomed to the smells, and the people weren't unkind, busy and noisy as they might be.

Etta was also right about there being little danger to her-self. If Makenna's satchel was too full for her to ride there, she tucked her legs through the back of Makenna's belt and rode beneath the loose woolen vest that had replaced the one Makenna had covered with buttons.

Neither of these hiding places was secure, and people sometimes caught a glimpse of the goblin girl—but they didn't care.

"Why should I object to your small friend?" said the plump woman who owned the crockery shop. Makenna had delivered a teapot, to match a set that had already been sold when the customer's son had bumped into the stand at just the wrong moment. The mother was willing to pay for the breakage, but she wanted to purchase a complete set and refused to buy till she could see for herself that the new pot was a good match.

It wasn't terribly fragile, but Makenna had carried the well-wrapped bundle through the bustling streets in her hands instead of the satchel. She'd reached the shop without incident, handed it over to the shopkeeper . . . and watched the lid slither out of the straw as the shopkeeper unpacked it. It would have fallen and broken if Etta hadn't leaned precariously out of the satchel and snatched it up before it had a chance to hit the floor.

"Aye?" Makenna watched the woman warily, though she seemed more interested in whether the new pot matched the set than in hauling Etta off to the nearest priest. "But I thought city folks didn't hold with goblins. It was in the city that the Decree of Bright Magic was first enforced."

"Of course it was," said the woman. "With the church sitting right on top of us. But that's not to say the townsfolk favored it. Oh, there were some who didn't care—which was very short-sighted of them, for my herb-healer did better by my sick headaches than the priests, and she charged less. Which was likely why they passed it in the first place, curse them. My friend Margy, who grows flowers for the street sellers, she started having all kinds of problems in her flower beds after the goblin family that lived there left. Moles! I had no idea how much damage one mole could do, and neither did she till her Greeners were forced to flee. Her profits are down almost twenty percent! And I think she misses seeing them about. Your friend just saved me having to pay for another lid—and if it didn't match, we'd be back to square one again! Why should I object to her?"

"You don't think that goblins and hedgewitches serve the Dark One?"

The woman laughed. "Boy, that's a country superstition. We in the city . . . Well, by your accent you come from the country, so I shouldn't talk. But have you ever seen the Dark One appear in his cloud of flame and shadow, to reap men's souls with his great scythe? Or met anyone who cast dark magics in his name? Or known anyone who knew anyone who did?"

Makenna, who'd long since figured out that the Dark One was nothing but some priest's tale, was a bit indignant on behalf of the countryside. "The priests all say it's so, and it's hard for folk not to believe 'em. Or don't you believe in the Bright Gods and the saints, either?"

"Me? I believe there are good people." The woman unlocked her cash box for Makenna's fee. "Whatever inspires them to do good is all right by me. I also believe there are people who do bad things—even a few who just are bad—and some of them use magic to work their will. Maybe it is because some dark god corrupts their souls, but more likely they simply allowed their own selfishness, greed, or fear to get the better of them. So your goblin friend has nothing to fear from me. That's three copper bits for the delivery?"

She threw in an extra copper for Etta, for saving the lid, and the goblin girl refused to count it as part of their wages when they divided their take at the end of the day.

After that conversation, Makenna became curious about the city dwellers' attitude toward goblins, magic, and the church. She stopped eating lunch alone, purchasing a hot pastry or a sandwich from a stall and sitting near enough to some group that she could eavesdrop. For the most part they discussed their own business or gossiped about friends and family, just as the country folk did. But this was a city built around the church of the Seven Bright Gods, and gossip about the Hierarch, his court, and his council was as common as country folk gossiping about the local landholder.

"How can he be all that divine, if a traitor can use a drug to fuddle his wits?" a burly stonemason demanded. "Shouldn't the Bright Gods have protected their Chosen? If he can be poisoned like a man, he can be wrong like a man."

"You could argue that his guards discovering so swiftly that his illness wasn't natural was a matter of divine intervention," a carter pointed out. "Who's to say the Bright Gods don't work through us? That's what my district priest said."

"Assuming they did discover it early," a clerk put in. "Anyone who supported that ridiculous relocation for seven years wasn't all there to begin with, if you ask me!"

The murmur of agreement was subdued, but no one disagreed. The only reason the relocation had been accepted at all was because, as an apothecary drily put it, "An idea as crazy as that almost had to be divinely inspired."

The relocation's abandonment, coming on the heels of the news that a treacherous priest had poisoned the Hierarch with a drug that induced symptoms akin to a brain seizure for "several days," had shaken whatever faith these cynical town dwellers had.

Makenna remembered Jeriah's tales of barbarian warriors who were not only stronger than their adversaries but healed a deep gash in a handful of minutes. She hoped the young knight had exaggerated, because having gone back on the relocation once, there was no way the Hierarch could convince the city people that divine will was guiding him in that direction again.

And remembering Jeriah's steady, haunted eyes as he talked about the barbarian threat, she didn't think he'd been exaggerating.

But fighting off the barbarian army—Dahlia, saint of lost causes be thanked—wasn't her job. Makenna was becoming ever more certain that her chosen task was the right one.

If she could only reach the Hierarch, Brallorscourt wouldn't dare act against her. But to do that, she had to not only get past Brallorscourt's men, which her disguise might have allowed—she had to get an appointment to see the Hierarch himself. And her disguise would make that impossible! Makenna had once thought she might use the evidence Master Hispontic had uncovered to make Brallorscourt himself let her in, but Brallorscourt had proved even less trustworthy than most humans. She needed some other human's help. Someone who had access to the Hierarch, who could influence people in the palace who had the power to protect her from Brallorscourt, and who might listen to her. And she knew only one person who fit that description.

"Daroo," she asked as they sat at dinner outside Noggat's well-disguised home. "Can you get me into the palace to see Jeriah?"

Daroo put down his small bowl, his eyes thoughtful.

Simmi had to prepare a whole extra kettle of stew to feed Makenna along with her family and Cogswhallop's. Natter, Daroo, and Nuffet were living in a lumber merchant's loft a few doors down, but they ate with Noggat's family. Cogswhallop himself—having negotiated a hot dinner and a breakfast into the price of Makenna's lodging—had gone to supervise the hunt for Tobin.

Makenna had expected him back over a week ago, and Natter was beginning to worry.

"Aye," Cogswhallop's son told her now. "Wearing that face, you could stroll through the fourth gate in broad daylight. Messengers go to the record halls all the time, and they'll never think to look for their escaped prisoner going back in. Into the woods, then into the tunnel. You'd have to wait there till everyone's asleep before we could take you to Jeriah's room. He's on the third level, so you can go up the ladder and not risk getting caught on the stairs. But why?"

*Why,* Makenna noted, not *What do I get for it?* It seemed the civilizing process went both ways.

"I need to talk to him," Makenna said. Daroo considered the human a friend. He might not approve of what she intended—but Jeriah had turned her over to the authorities once, and Makenna wasn't going to let that happen again.

Breaking into the palace was much easier than getting out. It helped that the goblins had access to the Hierarch's "secret" escape tunnel, but still! Her goblin camps had had better security.

Of course Makenna was only trying to reach a lowly squire, not the Hierarch himself. That was what she needed the squire for.

Back in the room with the pool, she washed off the dirt and her magical disguise. Simmi had trimmed up her ragged hair, muttering about "nightmare," though Makenna didn't know if that referred to the task or her appearance. But the squire would likely be startled enough, even if his unexpected visitor wasn't disguised. She didn't want to create more confusion than she had to.

The long, iron-runged ladder ended in a small room with a narrow door. It was only an access to the shaft that held the bucket chain, but it gave her a place to hide while Daroo and his Bookerie friends made sure the corridors between her and Jeriah's room were clear.

It felt strange and dangerous to walk through the sleeping

palace wearing her own face. Makenna's palms were sweating when Daroo hustled her through the door to Jeriah's room and closed it silently behind her.

She'd heard so much about the richness of the Sunlord's palace that this spartan room surprised her. It held two beds, for Jeriah supposedly shared it with a tax clerk, though he was almost always gone. Daroo had established that he was gone tonight before he'd led Makenna onto the palace grounds.

There was no window in this inner room; the only light source was the glow beneath the door from the corridor's night lamps. Even Makenna's dark-adapted eyes could barely make out the shape of the young knight sprawled across one of the beds. She needed to see his face.

She went out into the corridor, ignoring Daroo's warning hiss, and kindled a candle stub she'd had the sense to bring with her. Back in Jeriah's room, she lit the lamp on his nightstand. The light didn't even make him stir. A sound sleeper, was he?

Makenna grinned, sat down on the bed beside him, and laid her knife against his throat. "Wake up, traitor. It's time to pay for what you did."

Even then, he took some time yawning his way to wakefulness—though he stiffened when he finally noticed the knife.

"Excuse me, would you mind repeating that?" he asked.

Makenna blinked. "I said it's time for you to pay for

turning me over to the noose."

"That's what I thought," said Jeriah resignedly. "You don't look hanged to me. And I should warn you, Daroo is about to hit you with the fire poker."

He did it so well that Makenna had started to turn, and his hand had started to shoot for her wrist, before Daroo gasped, "I'm not!"

She spun back to Jeriah, pressing down on the blade, and his hand fell away.

"Though if I'd known you were going to be so unfriendly," the young goblin went on, "I'd have warned him we were coming. He helped you escape! What are you doing, mistress?"

"He helped me escape, after he got me jailed in the first place," Makenna said. "So I'm making sure he doesn't call for the guards, not till I've had a chance to warn him that if he ever again turns me over to anyone, for any reason, your fa'll never tell him what happened to Tobin."

Jeriah jerked, and a red line appeared on the skin of his throat. "What's happened to Tobin? Do you know where he is?"

Her order would weigh more with Cogswhallop than anything the goblin might owe Jeriah, and Jeriah clearly knew it. Makenna withdrew her knife and sheathed it.

"Cogswhallop hasn't found him yet. Or if he has, he hasn't come back to tell me about it."

The young knight sat up in bed but made no move to seize

her, clasping his hands around his knees instead. "It's been too long, hasn't it?"

Her own worst fears echoed in his voice.

"Aye, it's too long. Something must have happened to him. And my goblins are your best bet to find out what it is, so you'd best do as I ask!"

"That depends on what you want." The tone was still polite, but there was a stubborn set to his mouth. Young he might be, and worried about his brother, but he wouldn't strike a bargain blindly.

Makenna sighed. "I need to talk to the Hierarch. Alone— or at least, without that vulture Brallorscourt hovering. I need him to attend to what I say and not arrest me at the end of it. If you can arrange that, Jeriah Rovan, you'll get Cogswhallop's report right after I do. And if you can't arrange it, then you'd best start looking for your brother on your own, for you'll never hear word of him from any goblin who owes loyalty to me."

# CHAPTER 8

# Tobin

TOBIN CONTINUED TO WORK WITH the Duris' horses, hoping to learn more about their battle plans. But as the days dragged past, he heard nothing but complaints about how much territory they were expected to cover, boasts about their wrestling prowess, and a few arguments over women. That first mention of their new tactics had been a fluke—he could eavesdrop on their casual conversations for years without hearing anything that mattered.

So when a Duri warrior from another camp rode in and demanded to meet with the battle commanders, Tobin waited till they'd settled in one of the large gathering tents, picked up a halter that needed some work, and sat down in the shade behind the tent to mend it.

The rumble of voices, clearly translated by his amulet, was only slightly muted by the leather wall.

". . . prove excellent news for both our camps." Tobin thought it was the stranger speaking, though he couldn't be sure. "But it must be dealt with properly, in strict accordance with our law/tradition, or we risk—"

A blow to the side of his head sent Tobin sprawling. He stared dazedly up at one of the Duri who'd accompanied the stranger.

"What are you doing here?" the man . . . no, the guard . . . demanded.

No chanduri protested any treatment the Duri meted out, for fear they might be labeled troublesome.

"Nothing, master." Tobin fumbled for the halter and held up the worn strap. "I was just—"

"Well, you don't do it here, not when there's a war council in session. Take yourself off."

Aware of the danger, Tobin rolled with the kick and managed to collect his gear and scramble away before he earned another.

Were there always guards on this tent when the council met? If so, they would thwart any chance he had to learn about those "new battle tactics."

He watched, unobtrusively, from the door of Vruud's tent, where he'd taken his mending. The two guards kept only a casual eye on the camp, but they never left the tent, and they walked around it every few minutes. Tobin decided he had gotten off lightly. If they'd become suspicious, he could have been badly beaten, which might have brought a few of the camp's own warriors out. And they might have become suspicious enough to look at him closely and see more than the storyteller's Bear Clan servant.

Despite his realization that he'd lucked out, the left side of his face ached and throbbed. Vruud exclaimed in shock when he rode in from his trip to instruct the young story-teller he feared was training to take his place.

"What did you get yourself into?"

Tobin took Mouse's reins, shrugging the bruise aside. "I was mending a halter, and some Duri who came in with a messenger took exception to where I was doing it. Nothing's broken."

It pulsed pain with every beat of his heart, and he didn't know how he was going to eat with his jaw so sore, but nothing was broken.

"Trying to spy on the council?" Vruud's voice had dropped, but he didn't sound surprised. "I could have warned you not to do that, if you'd asked."

Tobin lowered his voice too. "Vruud, do you know anything about some new battle tactic that's supposed to be very effective against the Realm?"

Why hadn't he ever thought to ask? He knew Vruud had no loyalty to the Duri.

"I don't know much." The storyteller's single eye regarded Tobin shrewdly. "Take care of Mouse, then meet me in my tent. We can talk while I do something about that bruise."

Tobin unsaddled, groomed, and watered the mule, then made his way to his master's tent. Vruud put down a hollow reed he'd been carving into a flute—he played when his audience tired of stories—and dug into his chest for a pot of salve he handed to Tobin.

"Rub it in thoroughly, but don't use too much. Since the Duri heal themselves by magic, there's not a lot of salve made."

"I'd rather hurt than be healed by magic made with someone else's death." Tobin had plunged a finger into the greasy stuff before it occurred to him. . . . "This isn't made with death magic, is it?"

Vruud snorted. "Herbs and goose grease. No magic for the chan, young Softer."

Tobin put the finger he'd yanked away back into the pot and smeared a thin layer over his bruised skin. "Do you know anything about these new battle tactics?"

"I've heard them mentioned," the storyteller admitted. "It worries me. Because if the Duri succeed in wiping out the Softer army . . ."

". . . you'll die soon after," Tobin finished for him.

"If I knew, I'd tell you," Vruud went on. "But I didn't think trying to learn about them was worth risking our escape. I still don't."

Tobin took a deep breath. "Well, I do. And since you can't stop me, you might as well help. If I can't listen in on the war council, where else would they be talking about it? In the men's tent?"

The single men of the camp gathered in one of the large tents every third or fourth night, mostly to drink, as far as Tobin could tell. Vruud often performed for them, but since the warriors who comprised his audience were the people Tobin most wanted to avoid, he hadn't accompanied his master.

"I've considered that," Vruud said. "When I tell stories or play, I can't hear what people are saying. No one would think it odd if my servant joined the others who bring food and beer. It's a little odd that you haven't done so, but since I'm chanduri myself, no one cares enough to notice how I'm served."

It would be dangerous, Tobin realized. It might jeopardize their whole plan. On the other hand . . .

"When can I start?"

The young warriors decided it was time to "listen to the glory of our history again" two nights later.

Tobin's face was still bruised, but his bruises had given him an excuse to grow a bit of stubble. And when he saw how much the young warriors drank, his fears of discovery subsided. Of course, his chances of hearing a coherent account of their new battle tactics dropped along with their sobriety.

He did learn a lot about Duri history and culture that night and in the nights that followed. In the first part of the evening, Vruud told stirring tales of ancient times. The audience's favorite story was the early war with the spirits, when the Duri shamans had learned how to "strongly seize" the magic of their dying enemies—though Tobin thought steal, or maybe rape, was a better description. The story of the later war wasn't often told, for it hadn't gone so well. The short version was that as the spirits had gradually been driven off the land, they'd destroyed it rather than leave it for their conquerors. The Duris' war with the spirits had lasted for centuries, and the destruction it had left behind was what had finally forced the Duri to cross the desert and attack the Realm.

When they were too drunk to listen, Vruud got out his flute, and Tobin was able to eavesdrop on the Duris' conversation. It was when they reached that part of the evening, a few days later, that Tobin finally learned what the stranger had told the war council.

A spirit had been sensed, somewhere between the Morovda camp's territory and that of another camp. The council elders were still working out who would share in its death, under what circumstances.

"Isn't that a problem for us?" Tobin asked Vruud later that night as he prepared his master's bed. "If you're the next one up for sacrifice?"

"I'm not necessarily the next," said Vruud calmly. "One of the ways they keep us from running is to make sure we never know who's next. There are two women and another man from our camp who might go before me. Of course, they're all making the same count and hoping I'm up before them. It also depends on whose shamans capture the spirit. So far they've agreed that rather than fight over the spring—that's where this spirit lives, and it's not clear whose territory it's in. But rather than fight each other, they've decided that whoever doesn't capture the spirit will provide the human half of the trust. Since both camps are small, there will be plenty to go around. And all the shamans in both camps are frantically setting traps, even as we speak."

"What if the other camp's shamans capture it?" Tobin persisted.

Vruud shrugged. "Then I might be in danger. But capturing a spirit is harder than it sounds. It frequently takes weeks, or even months, and sometimes the spirit moves away from its source. Spirits hate to do that, for they're bound to the trees, or rocks, or water they inhabit. But sometimes they disappear. And sometimes it turns out that the careless young fool who thought he sensed one was mistaken. We don't need to panic. Not yet."

As many more days and a few more men's gatherings passed, Tobin learned that Vruud was right. The young warriors discussed the spirit's capture at exhaustive length—far more than they talked about fighting the Softers.

When they grew most inebriated, Tobin would hear long, rambling discussions of the Duris' greatest ambition, which was to invade the Spiritworld itself.

There they would bathe in their enemies' deaths, drawing in power till they were as strong as gods, invincible and immortal.

This was usually the stage when they were drunk enough to draw daggers and cut their own flesh, displaying their will and how quickly even the weak magic they possessed would heal them.

The spurting blood turned Tobin's stomach, but the swiftness with which those wounds healed disturbed him more. He'd patrolled the border long enough to know that for every man who was slain, half a dozen more were taken out by injuries that didn't kill. If the Duri could take out any knight they injured, and the knights had to kill a Duri to remove him from the fight, there was no way the Realm could win—no matter what tactics either side used.

As far as Tobin could see, the Realm's only hope was to get its people behind that great defensible wall, just as Master Lazur had said. Tobin had never liked the priest, but he hoped, passionately, that the man was succeeding in his goals.

Tobin might be able to assist the relocation by returning to the Realm and reporting all he'd learned. If they knew the source of the Duris' power, maybe the priests could do something about it. And if he could only learn what their battle plans were, there might be a way for the Realm's commanders to counteract them!

But as Tobin listened to the warriors complaining about how long it was taking to capture this accursed clever spirit, he realized there was one thing he could do right now.

He set off for the spring soon after nightfall. The moon was full, and so many warriors had gone to the spring by now that their tracks almost formed a trail. Tobin could have followed them even in dimmer light.

After some thought, he'd left his amulet behind. The Duri didn't patrol as much at night as they did by day, but it did happen—and they'd all be using their magic-sensing ability in the area near the spirit's spring. Not to mention how the spirit might react if he showed up wearing a piece of magic made from the death of one of its kin.

It would certainly undercut Tobin's argument that since they shared a common enemy, they might as well help each other.

Tobin had seen only one spirit in the Otherworld, though the goblin children had told him about them until he grew too weak to listen. Was that hellish place, which had drained his life from his very bones, the Spiritworld the Duri spoke of with such deep bloodlust?

It had to be. The Realm priests who'd first opened gates into the Otherworld couldn't have known that the spirits lived there. As far as Tobin knew, the Realm's priests knew nothing about spirits at all. It was the spirits from which the Duris' amulets protected them, not their "gods."

Would approaching this spirit, even without an amulet, put Tobin in danger? Maybe, but if there was anything he could do to prevent the Duri from gaining more power, to stop the creation of more of those filthy blood trusts, he had to try.

The spring was farther than he'd expected. The moon rode high by the time he spotted the patch of blackness that in sunlight would be the dense green foliage that appeared around water in dry country.

Tobin took his time sneaking up on the spring—if he encountered a party of shamans or warriors out here, there'd be no question who would be sacrificed next. The only reason for a chanduri to be this far from camp was that he was trying to run. But Tobin encountered nothing except a startled fox that sprang lightly away through the moonlit scrub.

The scent of water was intense in this dusty land, but only a trickle flowed down the small creek bed. Unable to sense the spirit's presence, Tobin had no idea where it might be, so he followed the tiny stream back to its source, running out from under two huge rocks.

He almost walked into the trap before he saw it, a web of fine wire glinting in the fragile light. It wasn't any kind of snare Tobin recognized, for the wires were tied from bush to stone to one another in no pattern he could detect. The runes, once he spotted them, had been drawn on the rocks and poured onto the dry earth, using some dark substance that smelled like blood.

Tobin smiled grimly. The Duri had finally done him a favor. He'd had no idea how he could prove his good faith to the spirit, but now . . .

Foxes were playful creatures.

He pulled loose almost half the wires and scuffed out most of the runes in the dirt. He only had to make a few fox prints in a patch of sand, and a handful more in the mud near the stream, to make it look plausible. By the time he'd finished, anyone would have concluded that a pair of foxes had blundered into the trap and destroyed it.

Tobin looked around one last time, listening as much as watching. He heard nothing but the rustlings of the Southland night. He saw nothing at all.

He sat down on a rock and took a deep breath. "I don't know if you're listening. I don't really know if you're here at all. But I'm fighting the Duri myself, and I thought we might be able to help each other."

He told the spirit about his need to escape from the Duri and take the information he'd gathered back to the Realm. He paused, waiting.

Nothing but silence.

Tobin went on to warn the spirit about the shamans who were hunting it and what its fate would be if it were captured. He advised it to abandon the spring and flee if it possibly could. Because the shamans were confident that if it stayed, sooner or later they'd succeed.

No spirit rose out of the water to thank him. Tobin was beginning to wonder if it hadn't already moved on. But in case it hadn't . . .

He told it about the war between the Duri and the Realm, making sure that it understood that the Realm had no desire to meddle with spirits or the Spiritworld, despite the recent incursion of Makenna and her goblins.

Was she still there, in that shifting miasma of magic?

Or had she somehow gotten herself and her goblins out, as she'd gotten him out? He asked the spirit about that, but it didn't reply.

His voice was growing hoarse, and judging by the lowering moon, destroying the shamans' snare had taken too much time.

Tobin rose to his feet. "I don't know if you're here or not," he told the empty night. "If you are, I urge you to run—for all our sakes! But mostly for yours. It's a terrible death."

For a moment he thought he felt something, like a breath sighing past him. But although he waited, nothing spoke or appeared. He knew that the spirits could do both those things, so he was probably imagining it.

He had taken too long. The sun rose before he was halfway back to camp, and he had to crouch in the bushes and wait, barely breathing, while two Duri patrols rode past him. If he'd been wearing an amulet, he'd have been caught. Even without it, he now understood why Vruud wanted to be closer to the Realm's lines before they tried to escape—Tobin had had no idea the area was watched so closely.

He was in sight of the camp, and had emerged from hiding to simply walk back in, when he came around a rock and almost ran into a Duri warrior who was tying up his belt. The reek of fresh urine told Tobin what the man was doing away from camp—though why he'd come all this way, instead of using the covered pit, Tobin didn't know. It didn't matter, either. What excuse . . .

The Duri's eyes narrowed. He reached out and closed his fist in the front of Tobin's shirt. "What *abras clahft fa* doing *ress*?"

He wasn't wearing his amulet! Tobin wished, desperately, that he'd had more time to learn the camp's language. He'd been paying more attention to his lessons lately, but he still knew only a few words.

"I'm sorry, master, but I'm not wearing my amulet now." At least the Duri would understand him. "I'm the story-teller's servant. From Bear Clan. I haven't had time to learn your language yet."

Even the Duri weren't so unreasonable as to expect him to learn a language overnight—but not knowing it, Tobin was supposed to wear his amulet at all times.

The man's next question was completely incomprehensible, but his scowl wasn't. What excuse could Tobin make for being out here, without the amulet that would have permitted the Duri to track him down? If he'd had the sense to pick up an armload of firewood on his way in, he probably wouldn't have been stopped, but now it was too late.

The man babbled out another sentence, and Tobin shook his head to show he didn't understand.

The Duri knew that many chanduri would run if they had the chance. Any chanduri caught outside the camp had better have a good reason. And Tobin didn't.

The growing fear must have shown on his face. A sudden

cuff made his ears ring, and the iron grip shifted to his collar as the Duri began dragging him back.

Could Vruud come up with a lie fast enough to save him? If Tobin was beaten—his blood ran cold at the thought— would he be sufficiently recovered when their chance to escape arose? If the Duri decided that Tobin had shed his amulet because he planned to run, the beating he'd get might cripple him for life. *He was going to start gathering firewood, any minute! He'd thought he saw a family of quail he could tell the hunters about. He'd—*

Tobin tripped on a root and fell to his knees. The Duri kicked him to his feet and hauled him on.

No matter what story he told, no one would believe him unless he could think of a reason for taking off his amulet. But there was no reason he would have taken off the amulet except to try to escape.

They were nearing the camp, and many of the chanduri stopped working to stare. Their faces were impassive, but Tobin had been one of them long enough to see fear and pity beneath their closed expressions. None of them would dare . . .

An old woman stalked away from the pot she'd been stirring, spoon in hand. She was one of those Vruud thought might be up for sacrifice instead of him. Tobin didn't know her name.

Her wrinkled face, far from impassive, was full of furious impatience. She burst into a babble of speech and smacked him on the head with her spoon.

"Ow!" She hadn't pulled the blow.

The Duri let go of Tobin's collar, still frowning, and Tobin fell to his hands and knees. The spoon struck his back this time, accompanied by more incomprehensible abuse.

He didn't dare say a word. The old woman drove him back to her cook fire and shoved him down beside a basket full of soft-shelled nuts.

She went on scolding him as Tobin cracked nut after nut, prying out the meats with shaking fingers. Finally the watching Duri shrugged and departed.

The woman kept on scolding, though her voice grew softer. Only when all the nuts were shelled did she allow him to rise, knees still wobbling, to his feet.

"Thank you," Tobin murmured, though he knew she couldn't understand him either.

A flickering wink was his only answer, and he turned and made his way back to Vruud's tent.

He didn't even know her name. He hadn't learned the names of most of the chanduri, because he'd written them off. They were enemies, to be destroyed along with their Duri masters—whether they'd done anything to deserve it or not.

But the chanduri had no choice about being part of the Duris' attack on the Realm. The Duri treated them even worse than they did Realm soldiers.

And the chanduri fought back, whenever they had the

chance. Why hadn't he seen it before? The chan weren't his enemies.

Tobin's heart beat faster, his pulse throbbing in his temples. His head was aching again, from the repeated blows, but his heart ached worse.

He had refused to recognize the plight of the chanduri, even to learn their names, because if he did, he'd have to try to help them. He couldn't leave them at the mercy of their masters, leave them to be sacrificed, any more than he could have betrayed the goblins to Master Lazur's executioners.

Because he couldn't save them, he'd tried to ignore them. But that old woman had risked a beating to save him. She'd almost certainly moved herself to the top of the sacrificial list—and Tobin could no longer ignore her plight, or that of her people.

He had to save all of them. Not just Vruud and Hesida. Not just the old woman and the chanduri in this camp. He had to save every last chanduri from their Duri masters. Duri, who seemed to have no weaknesses at all!

The immensity of it made him dizzy, but Tobin too knew something about wrestling. Strength could be made into a weakness, if your opponent could get the right leverage. And Tobin was beginning to see how he could use the Duris' arrogance and bloodlust to bring them down.

# CHAPTER 9

## Jeriah

JERIAH SAT IN HIS BED and looked at the sorceress. She was still wearing boys' clothes, and sometime in the last week she'd trimmed up her ragged hair, but she looked too tense, too edgy for it to civilize her.

The shallow cut across his throat still stung, so he phrased his answer carefully. "First, tell me *why* you want to talk to the Hierarch."

The girl eyed him warily. Jeriah waited. He wasn't going to promise anything without that knowledge, no matter what she threatened.

"All right. I want him to deed the goblins some land behind the great wall. Somewhere they can build and live openly, where humans aren't even allowed to go without their permission."

"But they're no longer under death sentence," Jeriah protested. "They can go back to their homes now."

"Those whose homes haven't been destroyed," said Makenna. "To live in hiding, on human sufferance. Oh, aye, some humans will welcome them back—but there are some who won't. The goblins need a place of their own, a place that's *theirs*. By law."

The intensity of her vision drove her to her feet, her shadow moving back and forth as she paced. "Since the relocation's dead, the wood behind the great wall will be empty—no reason not to grant it to them, legal like."

Jeriah flinched. "The relocation isn't dead! The barbarian army's still there, and they're not going away. We have to . . ."

It was the grim pity in her expression that stopped him.

"No one's going to agree to move north," she said. "Not country folk or city. Not till the barbarians are burning their towns and fields around them. You know that."

Jeriah did know it, but he still had to try. "Maybe when all the Southlands have been taken, and the Realm is full of refugees, maybe they'll see the danger and start relocating then."

Makenna snorted. "If I know aught of humans, they'll say that now the barbarians have so much land, they'll stop where they are. And they'll go right on saying it till the barbarians roll over them. And who knows? Maybe once they've enough land to settle on and prosper, the barbarians will stop. Your priest said they came here because a drought destroyed their own land. Maybe all they want is a new one, and the Southlands will satisfy them."

That was what his father would say, Jeriah knew, and the

Hierarch and the council as well. And he had no proof they were wrong, except . . . "Master Lazur didn't believe that. And you have to admit he's been right about the barbarians so far."

"As far as I can see, he was right about everything, Bright Gods curse his bones."

Jeriah's brows rose. Master Lazur was behind the Decree of Bright Magic, which had killed her mother and countless goblins as well. And Makenna admitted he was right?

"Oh, not in what he did," the girl said. "But he was right that the relocation would be unpopular enough to turn people away from the church. If they'd had another source of magical healing, even a weaker one, another way to help failing crops and find the right place to dig a well, they'd have been much more likely to resist the move he wanted 'em to make. He was right about that. But that doesn't mean he was right."

The pain was in her voice now, though her face was calm.

"Don't you hate him?" Jeriah asked. "I'd have thought . . ."

"I do, when I happen to think about it," she said. "If he was still alive, I'd hate him like the Dark One himself. But he's dead, so there's not much point in it. I've come to the conclusion, just lately, that hating folks is a waste of time."

Jeriah stared. This was the girl who'd once hated all humans so much, she was willing to slaughter the lot of them! But even if she'd changed her mind, that didn't mean the humans would.

"All right, say I can outmaneuver Brallorscourt and get you an interview with the Hierarch, and even that the Hierarch's willing to grant part of the northern wood to the goblins. Though I still think most of the Realm is going to end up there."

Shattered bands of refugees, running from the barbarian army, tumbling behind the wall without food, shelter, or the tools to produce them. That was the nightmare Master Lazur had designed the relocation to prevent—until Jeriah had stopped him. If that nightmare came to pass, any promises made to the goblins would be broken—and Makenna knew humanity too well not to realize it. Which meant that she too had succumbed to hoping the barbarians would stop short of total conquest. Or that she believed her goblins, entrenched and organized, could fight off whatever starving remnant of the human population escaped over the border. But all that aside . . .

"Even if they grant your request, what's to stop them from hanging you?"

His voice came out harsher than he'd intended, but the girl didn't flinch.

"You needn't worry about Brallorscourt getting in the way. I've already sent a message to Hispontic to bring me some papers that will take care of him. And I think the council will grant my request, sooner or later. Because if the Hierarch isn't willing to show proper gratitude for what my goblins did for him, I'll send them to bedevil the Realm's army so thoroughly that the barbarians will be able to stroll through them like ladies at a garden party. We must have a place. A place of our own, set aside for us, before this Realm erupts in fire and slaughter."

Jeriah sighed. "I was afraid you'd say something like that. What is it with you? Don't you know any way of dealing with people except threats?"

He touched the cut on his throat by way of emphasis, and she blinked.

"What do you think I should say? What else can I do, if the poxy coward hasn't the grace to be grateful?"

This wasn't the time for a lecture on referring to the Sunlord with respect.

"Did it ever occur to you to try bribery? How about offering to have your goblins sabotage the barbarian army, instead of ours? Maybe that way you could get what you want, and they could keep the Realm from erupting in fire and slaughter. Did you even think about that?"

The girl frowned, as if such an idea had indeed never occurred to her. As the moments dragged past, Jeriah could almost see her thoughts turning from negotiation to strategy and logistics.

"The barbarians are as ruthless with any goblin they might catch as they are with Realm soldiers," she said. "I'd be putting them in danger, and it's not their fight."

"Attacking the Realm army would be dangerous too," Jeriah pointed out. "But if the goblins fought the barbarians, maybe the Realm could help them instead."

Her lips twitched. "Given that the Realm's whole army and all its priests can't beat the barbarians, what good do you think my goblins can do?"

"How should I know? You're the general. But Chardane's experimenting with the notion of dumping green vervallen into their water supply, and maybe your goblins could help with that. Or steal all their amulets, or throw their weapons down a well, or . . . stop smirking. Maybe those ideas won't work, but you tied every attempt to settle the woods into knots! There must be some way you could fight the barbarians, to earn that land you're talking about."

She considered this. "Seems to me we've already *earned* it."

Jeriah shrugged. "You know as well as I do that's not going to matter to the council, even if the Hierarch agrees with you. That's done with. You have to offer them something they don't already have to get what you want now."

"And they call goblins greedy!" Makenna's shoulders slumped in acceptance. "All right. There are things we can do to hurt the barbarians. Not enough to beat them, mind, but we could help. I'll give your way a try."

*And if your way doesn't work, we'll try mine.*

The implication was as clear as if she'd spoken it aloud, and Jeriah sighed again. He also noted that dropping the charges against her hadn't been part of the bargain. But while she might be crazy enough not to care whether she hanged at the end of it, his brother would. And Jeriah knew only one person who might be interested in helping him prevent that.

"We need an ally," he said. "But I'm going to talk to her alone first. You'd probably threaten to turn her into a toad, instead of begging for your life like a sane person."

"This is certainly interesting." Chardane's fingers rested lightly on the pile of receipts Master Hispontic had turned over to Jeriah. Receipts that showed Lord Brallorscourt paying the treacherous physician who'd drugged the Hierarch the same amount Master Lazur had paid, whenever the priest was absent from the city for more than a month.

"It's not conclusive," Chardane went on. "Not hanging proof. Though if the Hierarch ever saw these papers, Brallorscourt would have a lot of fast talking to do! However, even if I used them to shut Brallorscourt down, what's to stop another councilman from urging that the girl be hanged? I'm not even certain they'd be wrong. Mistress Makenna and her goblin army killed a number of people and were responsible for the destruction of who knows how much property."

The spicy scents of the herbery eased Jeriah's taut nerves, despite this awkward turn in the conversation. Chardane was now a second-circle priest, the highest ranked member of the church here in the palace, except for the Hierarch himself. She had a big new office and three clerks to help her with the business of governing a large portion of the Realm, but she still spent as much of her time as she could in the familiar herbery. She claimed that the church's primary duty was to heal, and that brewing medicine for headaches kept that goal in her heart far more than sitting behind a paper-filled desk.

"She was a hedgewitch," said Jeriah. "A child whose mother was murdered, who fought to protect others of lesser magic from the Decree. And since *you* led the human resistance against that same Decree, I'd think you'd support her!"

"I was one of several people who tried to help those who practiced the lesser magics," Chardane corrected him. "And we killed no one. This girl was responsible for settlers' deaths."

"You were partly responsible for at least one death," Jeriah said quietly. "Master Lazur would never have gone to the gallows if you hadn't helped me."

Chardane opened her mouth to protest . . . and then closed it.

"She was a commander in a war," Jeriah continued, pressing his advantage. "You sent your people into hiding—she was fighting to defend the refuge where her goblins hid. People die in wars. Her people no less than the settlers. She says some things I'm not sure I believe, but I do believe that the men whose deaths she ordered had goblin blood on their hands."

Chardane shook her head, but her serene expression had given way to doubt. "I still can't approve. She was a hedgewitch, a healer. She knows better than to use magic for harm."

"So using spells to trick an enemy to his death is somehow

worse than sending him to the gallows with lies? You did what she did, Chardane, and you know it. You'd do it again if you had to."

And even knowing how desperately Master Lazur had struggled to save the Realm, Jeriah too would make the same choice.

He stopped, struck by the sudden realization that when Master Lazur had drugged the Hierarch, when he'd passed the Decree of Bright Magic to keep the church strong enough to enforce the relocation, the priest had made those same choices himself! He'd killed more, sacrificed more people—but his cause had been more noble and more necessary than Jeriah's.

Were all of them wrong? All right?

But saving Makenna and her goblins was the right thing to do now. He was certain of it.

*As certain as Master Lazur had been that no sacrifice was too great to ensure the survival of the Realm?*

Jeriah pushed the thought aside. "I'm calling it in."

Chardane had been silent for some time—thinking along the same lines he was? She turned to him now, shaking off the shadows. "What?"

"You once said you owed me a debt for bringing down Master Lazur and getting the Decree rescinded. I'm claiming it now. Get her off, Chardane. Keep Brallorscourt from killing her. And arrange for her to talk with the Hierarch."

Chardane sighed. "The Bright Gods know you're right

about me owing you. Every man, woman, and child in this Realm owes you! Though they'll never know it. . . . Oh, all right! I'll get the girl paroled into my custody, for a start. I can keep her safe, and it won't be hard to find a judge who'd see things your way. I know of a number who were dismissed from office, some even flogged, for refusing to enforce the Decree. They're all back now, so that's no problem. An interview alone with the Hierarch is something else. I can use these papers to muzzle the man, though I'd rather use them for several other things. But the reason Brallorscourt attends so many of the Hierarch's meetings is because the Hierarch wants him there. He relies on the man's advice in secular matters—and young Mistress Makenna is a secular matter, and so's her request. I can silence him, but there's nothing to stop him from setting another councillor to challenge the girl."

"So she might as well face Brallorscourt himself," said Jeriah slowly. "In the Hierarch's presence, where he'll be forced to oppose her openly instead of sneaking behind everyone's backs. I see. And so will she, when it's explained to her. Set it up, Chardane. I'll bring the girl to you, and we'll make sure she's ready."

# CHAPTER 10

## Makenna

THEY MADE HER WEAR A dress. It threw her off, those heavy tangling skirts in which she could neither fight nor run. She supposed the color was good on her, a rich bronze satin that Chardane had found somewhere. It looked almost like a gleaming version of the brown robes worn by the lesser sun priests. And the seamstress who'd fitted it to Makenna had snipped out most of the embroidery that had decorated it, so it was far less fancy than most of the gowns the Hierarch would be accustomed to seeing.

This, Chardane had said firmly, would make her look humble and penitent. She was supposed to act humble and penitent, and right now Makenna felt almost nervous enough to bring it off.

She was used to fighting for what she wanted, not begging for it. But in such unfamiliar territory, Makenna knew she'd better pick her battles. And her weapons. So she didn't haul out the battered messenger's satchel till they were leaving for the hearing, too late for Chardane to object.

The herb mistress flanked her on one side and Jeriah Rovan on the other, as they climbed the flower-lined stairs to the echoing chamber where the Landholders' Council met. Most of the desks were empty now, but a handful of "concerned" landholders had pulled chairs up beside the Hierarch's throne.

Brallorscourt was one of them, and when he saw the satchel hanging over Makenna's shoulder, his scowl could have melted wax. He thought she'd brought Hispontic's evidence—the poor, deluded bastard. He thought he was going to have a voice in this matter, but he was wrong. The Hierarch was the only human who mattered.

The Sunlord wore robes of gold, and the fact that he'd set the glittering gold diadem aside hadn't diminished his power and dignity. That was accomplished well enough by the uncertainty in his eyes. Makenna, despite herself, felt a stir of pity. It strengthened her wobbling knees as she sank into an awkward curtsy before the throne.

"I come to seek the Sunlord's favor." Chardane and Jeriah had been very insistent that she begin with the proper, ancient words. That she maintain a polite and proper demeanor. That she didn't insult or threaten anyone, or refer to humans as another species—and one she held in contempt at that! Or, or, or . . .

"What favor do you seek from me?" the Hierarch replied. The proper answer, which gave her permission to make her plea.

"It's not really a favor I want," said Makenna. "It's justice. The justice you owe everyone who lives in the Bright Gods' Realm, and which has been sadly lacking till now. Though that," she added fairly, "was through no fault of yours."

The lady priest closed her eyes, like someone watching an accident she couldn't prevent, and Jeriah's breath hissed through his teeth. Yet another of the things she wasn't supposed to do was even to hint that she knew the truth of the Hierarch's "illness."

But this man had no responsibility for what Master Lazur had done in his name, and she refused to blame him for it.

The Hierarch regarded her gravely, ignoring the puzzled looks of several of his landholders.

"If it's in my power to provide justice, I will. But as you know, young mistress, even the Bright Gods themselves sometimes disagreed about what was and wasn't just. It's a matter of judgment, and even the judgment of the Chosen isn't divine."

A couple of the councillors murmured in shock. Was his judgment supposed to be divine, or at least, divinely inspired? What fools they were.

"I think I'd trust your judgment," said Makenna. "But I'm not sure"—she gestured to Brallorscourt, who was glaring at the satchel—"that I trust his."

Several of the ninnies actually gasped at this, Jeriah among them, and Brallorscourt hastily rearranged his expression.

"Then you may be in trouble," said the Hierarch. "Because in my judgment, I need this man's advice. I may not always take it, but I will listen."

Was there a twinkle in those bright blue eyes?

"State your case, Mistress Makenna," the Hierarch commanded.

She took a deep breath. "It's the goblins. Who are surely as much the Bright Gods' creatures as you—as humans are."

Jeriah winced.

She told the Hierarch her idea, about setting aside a portion of the great northern wood for goblins alone, a place they could live in safety, and build their homes in the open, without human interference.

"Some will argue that with that accursed Decree rescinded, they're no longer under a death sentence," Makenna finished. "But they've no protection from those who would still drive them out, or wish them ill. It's not enough, Sunlord. They deserve more, after all they've endured at the priests' hands."

*And after what they did for you.* But she didn't have to say it aloud; the thought was clear in his cloudless eyes.

"Goblins had no place of their own before the Decree," Brallorscourt put in. "I must say I see no reason for that to change. The Decree of Bright Magic may have taken things too far, but it should be pointed out that in using magic not sanctioned by the church, the goblins have put themselves outside it—and therefore outside your governance, my lord. They may live in the Realm, on our sufferance, but they aren't part of it."

Makenna hadn't expected him to remain silent. But

it seemed his statement was true—or at least, he thought it was.

"I'm not asking you to make them part of your pox—precious Realm," she said. "All I ask is that you give them a bit of land outside it, and keep your cursed humans from meddling with them."

Chardane had long since resigned herself to disaster and taken a seat off to one side, but Jeriah still stood beside her, and now he stirred.

"There's plenty of unclaimed land north of the great wall, Sunlord. No one would care if it was granted to the goblins."

"Unless more refugees from the barbarian attacks are forced to settle there," Brallorscourt replied smoothly. "As you keep reminding us, Rovanscourt, that land may be needed."

"But you keep telling me that the barbarian army is going to be defeated," Jeriah shot back. "So if you're right, there's no reason not to deed that land to the goblins. And if you're wrong . . . Are you prepared to admit you might be wrong about that, Lord Brallorscourt?"

Makenna considered kicking him, but even if it wouldn't have caused more commotion than it was worth, those cursed skirts would get in her way.

"Besides," said Brallorscourt, "there's another issue to be considered here, Sunlord. This girl herself is still charged with multiple murders, of people who sought to settle peacefully in the same northern woods she now politely asks you to grant to her. Why should she be pardoned for those deaths?"

"So don't pardon me," Makenna said. Her goblins would never allow her to hang, and she was long accustomed to living outside human law. "But you owe the goblins a place they can be safe. And you know it."

Her eyes were on the Hierarch's face, and he nodded slowly, admitting it. But he still hadn't agreed.

"How many men died fighting the goblins?" he asked.

"Four," said Makenna. "Directly. And there was a pregnant woman we drove out, who miscarried her child before they reached the town. Some add that to my tally as well."

She did herself, and it was the one death she regretted.

"Every one of those men had killed several goblins," she added. "And would have killed more if they hadn't been stopped."

"But killing goblins isn't illegal," Brallorscourt said. "Any more than it's illegal to exterminate rats. Killing men is murder."

The old hatred flared, bright and hot and real. But venting it now would do neither her nor her goblins any good.

"That's the exact problem I'm trying to solve." She managed to keep her voice level, but Chardane was the only one who nodded.

The Hierarch's face was troubled. "I had thought more died at your hands," he said. "And these men, they all died in the midst of battle?"

"Four or forty, it will make little difference to the people in the north who fought those goblins themselves, or took in the refugees this girl created," Brallorscourt said sharply. "My lord, I fear that if you pardon her, we may find ourselves facing the same kind of trouble in the Northlands that is only now dying down in the west! We need our troops on the border, fighting the barbarians—not dealing with rebellion elsewhere, and particularly not a rebellion we could easily avoid. Even if Zachiros is right, and she and her goblins were at war with the Realm, that's no excuse. If anything, it's a greater reason to hang her!"

Still true, evidently, for there was no signal from the pouch. But the Hierarch was wavering. He might someday be strong enough to be a just ruler again—if he'd ever been a good ruler in the first place—but he was too weak now.

And Brallorscourt was a man who understood threats.

"If you think rebellion in the north would distract your troops from the barbarians, you might consider what havoc an army of goblins could wreak on your precious forces right there at the border. Goblins can hide, and work, and fight any—"

Jeriah's fingers closed hard on her elbow, and she fell silent. Judging by Brallorscourt's scowl, her point had already been made.

"But if you'd grant my request," Makenna went on, "maybe the goblins could help your army fight the barbarians instead. If they had some stake in the Realm, they'd have reason to defend it. And if they help defend it, then surely they'll have earned the land we're talking about."

She thought they'd already earned it, but the Hierarch's expression brightened. "That seems fair. Let them do penance for their crimes and earn their place by defending the Realm now. And I'll consider past crimes, yours and theirs, settled."

Brallorscourt's scowl deepened. "I hardly think they'd be that useful, my—"

"Lie!" Etta's clear voice rang through the room, and most of the courtiers jumped. Not Jeriah, Makenna noted thoughtfully. He must be more accustomed to goblins than she'd realized.

Etta pushed up the satchel's flap and stood, hanging her arms over the side for balance. Her hair was tousled, her small face flushed. But she didn't seem intimidated by the grand assembly. Not when it came to exercising her gift.

"He's come close to it a time or two." The goblin girl frowned at Brallorscourt. "But that last was an out-and-out lie. He knows right well we could be useful to you. Maybe even make the difference between winning and losing."

The guards stirred uneasily—but what harm could one tiny girl do? A ripple of astonishment ran through the crowd, the humans craning their necks for a better view.

The Hierarch stared at Etta—had he never seen a goblin before? He probably hadn't. They hid themselves so well that humans could go their whole lives without catching a glimpse of them, even if a whole goblin family lived right beside them. And this man would be more sheltered than most.

"This is Etta," Makenna told him. "Her gift is to know when someone's telling the truth. Or not."

"But . . ." Brallorscourt cast the small goblin a horrified glance and fell silent.

The Hierarch gazed at Etta in fascination. "But how do we know this girl is telling the truth, Mistress Makenna? How do we know she's not lying in your service?"

"I wouldn't!" Etta sounded scandalized by the very idea. "That'd be . . . that'd be shoddy workmanship. A bad debt!"

No goblin would cheat on a debt—but humans were different.

"You don't know it," Makenna said truthfully. "You can't know for certain, unless you get a priest you can trust to put a truth spell on her. Though it might be hard to find a priest who has no stake in . . . just about any palace matter, I'd guess."

"It is." The Hierarch's gaze was now very thoughtful.

"My lord!" Brallorscourt's voice was tight with alarm. "This goblin, and her mistress, clearly have a stake in *this* matter. You can't believe a word she . . . ah . . . surely you must consider the possibility that her testimony would be biased."

Etta scowled, then shrugged. Not quite a lie.

"As to truth," Makenna said, "look at the evidence. Lord

Brallorscourt was wondering how useful the goblins might
be in a fight? How much trouble did they cause your settlers
in the north? Master Lazur brought a whole troop against
us, and he couldn't stop us!"

"Um." Etta's voice was hesitant. "That's not entirely—"

"All right," said Makenna hastily. "He did us a lot of damage. But only because he planted a traitor in our midst!"

That same traitor had turned against the priest, risked
his life, and given up the human world entirely to go with
them—and where in the Dark One's name had he dis-
appeared to?

Etta's testimony against Makenna made the Hierarch
chuckle, and he clearly liked hearing that the priest had lost
against them. "It seems to me that Mistress Makenna offers
an interesting bargain. I'll accept on one con—"

"But we won't," said a deep, gruff voice.

Makenna spun, and felt her jaw sag in astonishment as
Cogswhallop walked calmly down the floor to stand beside
her. He looked as calm as if he appeared before the Hierarch
every day. And if he was tired, and a bit grubby from long
travel, Makenna doubted most humans could have read
those subtle signs.

The humans were chattering like starlings, and the
guards looked from one to another to see if they should do
anything or not. The Dark One's "lesser minions" shouldn't
have been able to even appear in the palace of the Gods of
Light, and now there were two of them! But they'd look silly

threatening a man only two feet tall who wasn't even armed.

It was the Hierarch who rose to his feet and raised a hand. "Be quiet, all of you. I'll attend to this."

He stepped down from the throne and walked around Cogswhallop, studying him and Etta as if a tale in which he'd only half believed had suddenly come to life. Makenna was glad, and fiercely proud, that Cogswhallop had come to stand beside her.

If it troubled him to be stared at by so many humans, he didn't show it, returning the Hierarch's curious gaze quietly. Etta actually grinned at the man!

The Hierarch returned the girl's smile, then turned to Cogswhallop. "Why have you come here, Master Goblin? Why are you showing yourselves to humans now?"

Cogswhallop gestured to Makenna. "She's a fine gen'ral," he said. "But she's a terrible horse trader. It's time I took a hand."

The Hierarch returned to his seat, not like a man reclaiming his authority, more as if he needed to sit down. "Who speaks for your people?" he asked. "You, or her?"

Makenna's "He does" clashed with Cogswhallop's "She does."

They looked at each other, and she saw the love in his eyes—but he saw the truth in hers.

"He does," she told the Hierarch firmly. "I may lead them in battle, and sometimes be their voice in the human world, but they speak for themselves. Let Cogswhallop decide for all of us. If he wants me to lead the goblins against the barbarians, I'll obey him."

"True," said Etta clearly.

Power shifted and resettled between them, but it felt solid in its new resting place, sturdy and balanced.

Cogswhallop shrugged and turned to the ruler of the whole human Realm, Chosen of the Bright Gods themselves. Makenna suddenly realized that he hadn't bowed to the Hierarch, or acknowledged his sovereignty or holiness in any way. She hoped no one else would notice.

"The gen'ral had the right idea," Cogswhallop said. "But she was asking for the wrong thing. It's not land behind the great wall we need; it's the land we already live on and work right now. We've no more desire to move to the north woods than anyone else. And just as much reason to fight to defend our homes against the barbarians. Assuming, of course, that you'll agree they are our homes. Legal like."

Makenna suddenly realized what he was asking. The enormity of it made her dizzy.

"I don't understand," the Hierarch said. "What is it, exactly, that you want?"

Cogswhallop met his gaze squarely. "I want goblins to have the same rights humans do, under human law. I want killing or harm to any goblin to earn the same punishment, in the same courts, as harm or death to humans. And I want the property we live in and work to be deeded ours, under the law. Ours to sell, trade, or buy, with human money, just as humans do."

Jeriah, who had some idea of just how much property

the goblins would claim—property humans thought they owned—opened his mouth to protest, and Makenna pinched his elbow. Hard.

He flinched and subsided.

Makenna thought of all the court cases to come about exactly who owned what—but as long as the concept of goblins legally owning property existed, she knew her goblins would be willing to trade their labor for eventual full ownership. Goblins were always willing to bargain. She held her breath.

"And in exchange," said the Hierarch slowly, "for the right to protection under human law, for the right to own property as humans do and those lands on which you already dwell, you'll agree to help us fight the barbarians?"

"Aye," said Cogswhallop. "I'm not saying we can provide more than help, mind. We can't defeat them all on our own. But anyone who's tried to settle in the wood in the last few years will tell you that we could be . . . useful to you."

"In fact," said the Hierarch, "I've read some of those reports. And I agree to your terms, goblin. If you provide our army with material assistance against the barbarians, I'll grant you the same legal status as humans within the Realm of the Seven Bright Gods. Is that good enough for you?"

Lord Brallorscourt looked horrified, but for once, Makenna was pleased to see, the Hierarch wasn't looking at his adviser. And Brallorscourt didn't know even half of what Cogswhallop's proposal would entail. The Hierarch was too naive to understand at all. And Jeriah, who did understand, glanced at Etta and didn't say a single word.

"Agreed," said Cogswhallop. "As long as it's you yourself, Sunlord, who determine just what constitutes 'material assistance.' Not the Landholders' Council, or the priests, or some court judge. You."

"I'll accept that," said the Hierarch, "on one condition. That young Mistress Etta will assist me. Not just with this. I can think of dozens, hundreds of matters in which her . . . gift, is it? . . . might prove useful."

Now half the council looked horrified.

Etta climbed out of the pouch and dropped to the floor. She looked incredibly small as she went to stand before the Hierarch's throne, but she gazed into those sky-blue eyes fearlessly.

"I don't mind working for a human," she said. "But what for? This would be a separate bargain, between you and me. And we goblins, we don't work cheap."

"Done," the Hierarch pronounced. "The agreement between the Realm and the goblins will be drawn up, signed, and witnessed, so that none may argue later that it was not as it is. Mistress Etta and I can continue our negotiations in private."

Etta nodded.

Jeriah's hand yanked Makenna out of her farewell curtsy, and he dragged her out of the hall. He would have dragged Cogswhallop too, but the goblin, for all his calm expression, was moving to escape even faster than Jeriah was.

"Where's Tobin?" the young knight demanded the moment the great doors closed behind them. "Did you find him? Is he all right?"

Cogswhallop looked a bit nervously over the open terrace. "Is that girl really going to work here?" Already the clerks and courtiers who passed by were stopping to stare.

"Probably," said Makenna. "It's up to her. But city goblins are more accustomed to humans than we are—and frankly, I think the prospect of working with a Truth Seer who has no loyalty to any political faction is what clinched the deal. Did you find Tobin?"

"What's happened to him?" Jeriah asked. "Why hasn't he come home? Is he all right? Where—"

"I'll tell you," said Cogswhallop, "if you'll shut your yap long enough for me to get a word out."

His calm, sardonic expression had already answered the most important question, and Makenna felt a terror she'd refused to acknowledge melt away.

"Don't get too happy just yet, Gen'ral." Cogswhallop could read her face too. "He's alive, and he looks well enough from what I could see, but he's in trouble yet. The barbarians have him."

Makenna's heart stopped. "And you left him there? They sacrifice—"

"No, no," said Cogswhallop swiftly. "Sit down, hero, if you're going to faint. I shouldn't have said they had him.

Though it's hard to think how to put it another way."

Jeriah sank down on the rim of a planter, though Makenna thought it was less because he was feeling obedient than that his knees were about to give way.

"What are you talking about? *Where's Tobin?*"

So Cogswhallop explained. And explained some more. Makenna soon forgot the stares of the passersby, for the bizarre story held all her attention. If Cogswhallop had his way, they'd soon get used to seeing goblins out and about.

"You mean he's working in their camp as a servant?" she finally asked incredulously. "They think he's one of them? How could that possibly be?"

"I don't know how it came about," said Cogswhallop. "But that's certainly how it looked to me. I couldn't get near enough to ask him, either. Those barbarian warriors, some-how they always knew where I was, Gen'ral. If I got anywhere near one of 'em—as much as a hundred yards, sometimes— their heads went up like hounds scenting the wind. I had to dig into a badger burrow once, to escape 'em. I'd heard that they could sense our presence, but I'd not rightly believed it till I saw. I couldn't begin to get near him, nor sneak a writ-ten message in to where he'd find it. But if I went back with a support troop, I might. And once we make contact, well, you taught me yourself, the first step in any battle plan is infor-mation. It's going to be tricky, but I've got an idea."

# CHAPTER 11

# Tobin

TOBIN FIRST BECAME AWARE OF Cogswhallop's idea when he heard a deep voice shouting curses. He'd grown so accustomed to hearing everything through his amulet's translation that it took a while to realize that those curses were in the language of the Realm.

Tobin had been sweeping the packed earth floor of Vruud's tent, and he almost rushed out to aid whoever it was. Fortunately his brain started working, and he peered through the tent flaps instead, as a struggling knot of warriors rolled into camp.

Tobin recognized Cogswhallop's voice before he saw him; the small goblin put up an amazing fight, kicking and biting as well as shouting threats. It was incredibly courageous and completely futile—and Cogswhallop was too smart to waste so much effort to no purpose. It was also incredibly noisy.

Exasperated affection warred with fear. Was Cogswhallop creating all this commotion to attract Tobin's attention? It had certainly worked!

After some discussion, the warriors who'd captured the goblin thrust him into the cage they used to transport chickens, for the goblin could slip right through the bars of their human prison. Tobin waited till the goblin was safely stored, then went in search of Vruud.

"Friend of yours, is he?" The storyteller's single eye glinted. "Well, he found you, I'll give him that."

"Will they use a goblin in the blood trust?" Tobin persisted. "Can they? Goblins have innate magic, like the spirits, so I hoped . . ."

He stopped then, because he wasn't sure what to hope for. If Cogswhallop couldn't be used in the blood trust, the Duri might kill him immediately.

Vruud sighed. "You're going to insist on rescuing him too, aren't you? I knew it! We named you people 'soft' in truth. No, don't answer. I don't care why, or how, as long as it doesn't interfere with our escape."

"It might aid in our escape," Tobin told him. "Cogswhallop probably came to help me—"

"And got himself captured before he could even reach you. How reassuring."

"Will they use him in the blood trust?"

"No," said Vruud. "I don't know if a goblin can absorb a spirit, like a dying human can. But even if it could, it doesn't have enough flesh to pass the magic on to the warriors of an entire camp—much less two camps! So when they capture the spring spirit, they'll kill one of us. Unless, of course, another of your friends turns up."

Tobin preferred to ignore this. "Then what happens to Cogswhallop?"

"Oh, they'll eat him as soon as a shaman can set up the ceremony," Vruud said. "Probably a day or two, but it might—"

"What? You said he couldn't be used in the blood trust!"

"He can't," Vruud confirmed. "But as you pointed out, goblins have innate magic. No one is certain if consuming that magic strengthens a Duri's blood-trust magic or not. Some swear it does, some say they feel no effect. So few goblins are captured that it's hard to gather much information, but they won't waste any chance of enhancing their own magic."

"I have to get him out of there now!" Tobin rose to his feet. "Tonight!"

"Not tonight," said Vruud. "The shamans are going out to set more traps around the spring. Your friend should be safe tomorrow as well. The shamans say a ceremony is needed to make the goblin's magic compatible with ours. Some people think that's just the shamans' attempt to make themselves important, but they'll insist on it, and it takes some time. You've probably got two nights."

Tobin's racing heart slowed. "Good, that gives me time to come up with a plan."

"Well, I'd advise you not to take too long," Vruud said. "And, Softer?"

"Yes?"

"It had better not interfere with our escape."

Tobin wanted desperately to talk to Cogswhallop, but he didn't dare be seen near the cage. Even if no one was suspicious at the time, once the goblin had escaped, they might remember seeing him there.

Fortunately, Hesida had been assigned to feed this prisoner too. Unlike the bars of the human cage, nothing in the chickens' transport pen was designed to give way—and it had been built to resist not only chickens' beaks but foxes' teeth. The woven bronze wires were too strong for even Tobin to break, but they'd closed the cage with a simple iron lock.

"I can't get the key," Hesida told him. "Neither can you. The chief shaman's wearing it on a chain around his neck. I can take your friend a message—he's wearing a blood trust. But I don't—"

"He won't need a key." Tobin passed her a handful of metal scraps he'd picked up in the burned-out village. "Give him these, and ask him if they'll do. They're thin enough that he can bend them."

Hesida looked dubiously at the bits of wire and old nails. "I thought goblins couldn't touch iron. That's what Pram said when he put that lock on the cage."

"This one can," Tobin told her. "Tell him to make sure he can get that lock open fast, and be ready to run when I give him the chance."

"And how will you do that?" Hesida asked.

"I'm working on it."

In truth, he already had some ideas. The goat-pen gate faced the chicken cage, with only a small yard between them, and the goats were penned up at night. All Tobin needed was something to set them in motion, and he had an idea for that as well.

"Why do you want to come with me to the Kabasi camp?" Vruud asked suspiciously. "All I'm doing there is teaching that young idiot the whole chura song cycle, instead of the four measly verses he knows. I don't need my servant for that."

"The mules could use some exercise," Tobin told him. "Which is true, anyway. But while you're teaching song cycles, I'm going to try to convince a leopard to pee."

He couldn't get the leopard to cooperate. For one thing, it was tethered in a large pen, not stuck in a cage like Tobin had hoped. And several of the Kabasi camp chanduri told Tobin it might maul anyone foolish enough to approach it. Even if he'd been willing to take that risk, it showed no sign of needing to urinate in the entire time Tobin watched.

It was a gorgeous creature, its yellow eyes mostly shut, its tufted tail twitching as it napped in the shade. But the short fur on its legs and feet did nothing to conceal its strong arced claws. And even if Tobin had dared enter the pen, he had no idea how to obtain the result he needed.

In the end, he located the much smaller cage where the big

cat was kept at night and scraped some of the noisome earth beneath it into his jar. It might not be as intense as the pure liquid version, but it smelled pretty strong to him. It made the mules so nervous, Tobin had to seal the jar with wax and wash both the outside of the jar and his hands before he could put it back in Mouse's saddlebag.

Tobin chose the time just after sunset. The camp was quieting down and most had retired, but there were still enough people around that his presence wasn't suspicious.

He had an excuse to visit the meadow where the mules were tethered. On the way back, it took only moments to open his jar and dump small piles of the stinking dirt behind the goat pen's fence posts, where it wasn't likely to be noticed.

The goats began to bleat and mill as soon as he opened the jar. Tobin smashed the crockery and buried the pieces in the midden heap. By the time he returned, the goats had gathered at the far side of the pen, pressing against the gate, leaping, muttering uneasily.

Tobin took a quick look around. Several fires still flickered, but there wasn't much light at this end of the camp. He hadn't dared approach Cogswhallop. Hesida said the goblin was all right, and he trusted her.

Looking at the chicken cage now, Tobin saw nothing but a dark lump huddled in the center.

Had Cogswhallop opened the lock? Was he ready to run? Or was he injured, asleep, unable to pick the lock with the clumsy tools Tobin had provided?

As he hesitated, a small pale hand thrust through the wires, flashing an unmistakable signal: "Get on with it!"

Tobin strolled casually to the goat pen's gate, reached down, and tripped the latch.

He'd expected the goats to take some time to discover their freedom. He'd even thought he might have to go behind the pen and make some leopardish noise to set them in motion.

The moment the latch opened, the gate slammed wide, banging into Tobin's hip so hard, he staggered.

Goats raced out in a bounding, bleating flood, almost knocking him down as they hurtled past. Struggling to keep his feet, Tobin grabbed a fence post and looked back at Cogswhallop's cage. The door was open, the goblin gone.

Shouts erupted through the camp. Tobin didn't have time to get away from the pen, so he let out a shout of his own and reversed course, wading through the stream of goats toward the gate. There were only two goats in the pen when he reached it, so he shut them in and turned to see what he'd wrought.

Goats zigzagged through the camp, leaping wildly when anyone tried to capture them. A few forgot the leopard scent, stopping to sample a bite of the tunic someone had hung out to dry or tip the lid off a porridge pot. But most of them headed swiftly away, racing right through the camp toward the desert.

Both Duri and chanduri ran to catch them. Most of them only added to the chaos, although a couple of people were already dragging struggling, shrieking animals back to the pen.

A black ram in the center of the jostling crowd tossed its head, and Tobin caught a glimpse of Cogswhallop mounted on its shoulders, hands buried in its rough coat.

Unfortunately, Tobin wasn't the only one to see him. The ram leaped, and the young warrior who'd missed his catch froze—for a moment.

"The goblin! He's riding that goat! Stop him!"

He raced after the ram, only to trip over a spotted youngster that darted between his legs. But other warriors were running toward them—and one, more levelheaded than his brothers, stood off to the side stringing his bow.

Tobin ran toward the archer, but the Duri didn't skimp on their warriors' training. He was still a dozen yards away when the arrow launched.

It was too dark to follow the shot, but the black ram shrieked, staggered a few steps, and fell.

The goats scattered, panicked anew by the scent of blood. Three Duri closed in on Cogswhallop, who was clambering to his feet when the first of them sprang . . . and collided in midair with Vruud, who had leaped to capture a goat right in front of the goblin.

Storyteller and warrior fell in a cursing tangle, and the next Duri skidded to a stop, just as the man behind him tried to leap over them. They both went down as well, and Vruud was swearing at all three of them when Tobin bent over to extract his master from the mass of bodies.

"Let go of me, lout!" Vruud cuffed him for emphasis—hard. "Get those goats back in their pen. If they reach the desert, we'll lose half of them. You three, stop rolling on the ground and mount up! You can sense the creature's magic, so it can't get far. On horseback you can ride it down—which anyone but idiots would have realized in the first place!"

Vruud was their teacher, even if tactics for recovering prisoners weren't what he taught. The young warriors ran for the horse lines. By the time they'd saddled their beasts, Cogswhallop would be gone.

Tobin turned to the storyteller. "Thank—"

"I told you to help round up those goats!" The second cuff made Tobin's eyes water, and he began rounding up the remaining goats without another word. Vruud had a right to be angry, after the way he'd been forced to step in. Been willing to step in.

After Tobin returned his first struggling captive to the pen, he walked around the fence and kicked the leopard-scented dirt out of if its piles, hoping it would dry faster and lose its intensity.

Perhaps it worked, or perhaps the goats were becoming accustomed to the scent. Within an hour most of the flock was back in the enclosure, none the worse for their adventure.

The Duri who'd gone to hunt for Cogswhallop returned just before dawn—empty-handed.

* * *

The shamans investigated the incident the next day. They found a piece of bent wire in the bottom of the cage and deduced that the goblin had used it to pick the lock. It was twisted and tarnished, clearly from the village, and could easily have been buried in the dirt where the cage had been placed.

The goats, they decided, had been spooked by goblin magic—or perhaps others of its kind had staged the rescue. Little was known of goblin magic, after all.

The possibility of a whole band of goblins sparked a hunt that lasted three more days before the shamans pointed out, somewhat acerbically, that capturing the spirit was what mattered.

Camp chief Morovda, who led the warriors, told the head shaman that capturing the spirit was a shaman's job. He added that if the other camps' shamans beat them to it because his shamans were so busy criticizing the warriors— warriors who wouldn't have had to go goblin hunting if the shamans had been able to hold on to their prisoner—the head shaman might make a good sacrifice himself.

Tobin waited two more nights before he took off his amulet and made his way into the desert. In the direction opposite the spring, just in case.

The breeze was cool after dark, but heat rose from the rocks and earth. Tobin chose a tumble of boulders, far enough from the camp that even the most sensitive Duri wouldn't be able to detect the goblin's presence.

He didn't think he'd have to wait long, but Cogswhallop's gruff voice spoke before he even sat down.

"Not bad, soldier. The gen'ral would have planned it better, and your brother would have made it crazier, but it worked well enough."

Half a dozen goblins swarmed out of the shadows. Tobin had no idea how they'd known where to wait for him, but it hardly mattered. Several of the grinning faces were familiar, and one of them was very small.

"You brought the children here?" Tobin asked incredulously. "Your own son?"

Daroo's beaming smile turned to a scowl that almost equaled his father's, but Cogswhallop replied mildly, "I didn't bring him—he chose to come. He tumbles into less trouble than you do, these days. I've things to tell you, and there's things you need to tell me, so we'd best get to it."

The story Cogswhallop imparted left Tobin reeling. "Master Lazur was drugging the *Hierarch*? And they *hanged* him?"

But even that was nothing compared to his astonishment that his scape-grace brother seemed to have fixed everything.

"There was no other way," said Cogswhallop quietly. "That priest was convinced that if you and the gen'ral got out of the Otherworld, you'd interfere with his precious relocation, and he'd let anyone die to prevent that. But there's more . . ."

". . . So the relocation is well and truly dead," Cogswhallop finished. "And on closer acquaintance, I'd take Realm humans at their worst over these barbarians of yours."

"It was foolish to let yourself be captured, just to make contact with me," Tobin said. "I'm incredibly grateful, but—"

"That wasn't his plan." Daroo snorted. "He didn't—"

"There were many plans," said Cogswhallop hastily. "This was one of several contingencies for which I was well prepared, and don't you forget it! But since I've no desire to have yon barbarians for neighbors, we'd best turn our minds to finding a way to stop 'em. You've been living among them for weeks, lad; they have some weakness. And remember, part of our bargain with the Hierarch is that we goblins will provide 'material assistance' to the fight. So how can we bring down those bloodthirsty thugs?"

"We can't bring them down," said Tobin. "I've been living among them for almost two months, and they *have* no weakness. They can't be wounded long enough to matter, they never seem to tire, and they're cursed hard to kill. Their army outnumbers ours, and . . . they don't care. That's the worst of it. They've become so calloused, so accustomed to death, that it's become part of them. Of the Duri, at least. Maybe it's because their magic springs from death, but they're so addicted to fighting and killing that I think once they've destroyed us, they'll turn on one another and go right on killing. I don't believe we can defeat them."

The other goblins murmured in dismay, but Cogswhallop cocked his head. "You say that too calmly, for a man talking about the death of all he loves. You've got an idea."

"I do." Tobin clasped his hands around his knees. As he

was talking to his friends, in the quiet desert night, they were shaking. "But it's not about outfighting them. I gave up on that some time ago. And then it occurred to me that if we can't beat them, maybe we should give them what they want."

"What they want is to kill us all!" Daroo protested.

"They'd like that too," said Tobin. "But there's something else they want more. They want to invade the Spiritworld. They want to kill all the spirits who fled there to hide, and absorb their magic, and become as invincible and immortal as gods. I think the priests were right about one thing. I think the Duri did once worship the spirits as gods. Until they discovered they could kill them."

Cogswhallop was frowning. "This Spiritworld, that's what we call the Otherworld, aye?"

Tobin nodded. "If we open a gate, I promise you, they'll ride right in."

"But that whole world, the mistress says it's made of magic," Daroo said. "And the spirits control it. They could open a crack in the earth and bury the barbarians alive. They could send floods to drown them all. They could create nothing but sand around them forever, and they'd all die of hunger and thirst before they ever set eyes on a spirit. Once the mistress figured that out, she said they were letting us off light!"

"The barbarians don't know that," said Tobin. "All they care about is killing spirits, and they want to try. And if what you say about the Spiritworld is true, I think the spirits might be willing to give them the chance."

The goblins looked appalled; they were far less ruthless than humans. And this plan was as ruthless as they came.

"It will save the Realm," Tobin said. "It will save you goblins. It will even save the chanduri, who are still human and still care, though they've been taught all their lives not to." As Vruud had been taught—but even he cared. "The Duri are the only ones who'll die. And I'm not sure they're human anymore. Not in any sense that matters."

The goblins gathered around him were far more human than the Duri, and Tobin shivered. He wished Jeriah was here. He'd have liked to discuss this plan with his idealistic brother, to see if he was right, or if the Duris' insidious indifference had rubbed off on him. But as much as he missed her, Tobin had no desire to discuss it with Makenna. He knew she'd have approved.

Cogswhallop nodded slowly. "I think you're right. If that final battle is what they want most, it's only right to give it to 'em. And if they meet the fate they'd intended for their enemies, well, you can't say it wasn't an honest bargain. Aside from the facts that it's impossible to build a gate big enough for an army to ride through, that the spirits might well kick them right back out if we could get them in, and the small matter of getting the whole barbarian army to the spot where we can cast that gate in the first place, I think it's a fine idea."

Tobin's heart eased. Jeriah's wasn't the only opinion he valued.

"Then we'll work on it."

# CHAPTER 12

# Jeriah

JERIAH AND MAKENNA WERE IN the palace library when the letter arrived, which wasn't that surprising; they'd been spending a lot of time there. Chardane had decreed that since Jeriah was the one who'd gotten "that hellion" paroled to her custody, he was now responsible for making sure she didn't set fire to the palace. Or declare war on the Landholders' Council. Or murder the maid who was trying to keep her in proper court clothes.

"It's from Tobin!" The plump Bookerie, Master Erebus, had been working as Makenna's secretary over the last few weeks, but Jeriah had never seen the cheerful goblin so excited. "And he must not be too badly off, because it's a long letter. For a human, that is."

The humans in the library ignored them. People in the rest of the palace were still startled when goblins emerged into the open and spoke to them, but the Bookeries had taken over the library so completely that the librarians had not only grown accustomed to them, they were beginning to set them to work.

Erebus handed the letter to Makenna. Jeriah dug his nails into his palms. He could give her ten seconds, he decided, to scan the first page before he ripped it out of her hands. *One. Two.*

Makenna looked up from the letter and gave him a sardonic smile. "It's addressed to both of us."

Jeriah didn't wait for further invitation, hurrying around the table to sit beside her so they could read at the same time.

"He says he's fine!" The joyous relief of that news made everything that had happened in the last four months worthwhile.

"Erebus already told us that." Makenna was reading ahead of him. "And it sounds to me like he's taken leave of his wits."

Jeriah read onward—she was right.

He took the pages from her when she finished, and soon they began to pile up beside him. Jeriah had already learned that Makenna read more swiftly than he did, and it shouldn't have surprised him; hedgewitches passed on their craft in written notes and spells. There were gaps in her education— that was why they were in the library—but Jeriah was amazed at the speed with which Makenna absorbed information.

It took him longer than it should have to take in Tobin's bizarre story, but he finally set the last page aside and stared at her. "Could that possibly work? I mean . . . It couldn't! Could it? The whole barbarian army?"

Makenna was thinking so hard, he could feel it. After several moments dragged past, Jeriah got tired of being ignored and snapped his fingers in front of her face.

"Hey! Do you think he's crazy? Or could it work?"

"Well, if it doesn't, it won't be my failure as stops him."

"Mine either," said Jeriah, stung. "But is it even possible to build a gate a whole army can pass through?"

"I don't see why not." Her eyes were distant, calculating. "It wouldn't have to be much bigger than the gate that took us into the Otherworld in the first place. Though we'd have to hold it longer. But with enough power . . . If we had some priest mages who could replace those who tired, and if the spirits cooperate . . ."

"That's another thing! Why should they let an army of people who want to kill them into a place they created to escape from those people?"

"Leave that to me," said Makenna. "You worry about your part."

"That means you don't know how to do it," said Jeriah. "Doesn't it?"

"And do you know how you're going to convince the army to give up a large piece of the Southlands, Jeriah Rovan?"

She was the one person who had never addressed Jeriah as Rovanscourt—and his delight at finally shedding the heir's title was so great that he was willing to admit the truth.

"Well, no. But—"

"Then I suggest you set about it. Now."

Over the past few weeks, Jeriah had finally come to see her, not as the infamous sorceress who had lured his brother to destruction, but as a girl near his own age. The woman who stood before him now was Cogswhallop's general, giving him his orders. The bow Jeriah gave her before he departed was only half ironic—she was probably a better commander than the next officer he'd be dealing with.

It took him just under two weeks to reach the border, and he had to hire another horse to give Glory some relief, for he'd left Fiddle with Makenna. She'd be making this journey herself, hopefully soon. And Jeriah meant to be ready when she arrived.

The Southlanders' olive skin and curly dark hair reminded him of Koryn. She was here somewhere, presumably staying with friends. Jeriah wasn't sure if he wanted to see her or not. Part of him did—and the other part was tired of being sniped at.

He wanted to see her anyway. It took an absurd amount of self-control to ask the soldiers stationed along the road where the commander was, instead of asking them if a thin, crippled girl with big gray eyes had passed this way.

Tracking down Commander Sower took him only a few more days. But then his plan fell to pieces.

"So you failed," the commander said wearily. "I suppose it was too much to expect that he'd listen to you, any more than he's listened to everyone else we sent. But I don't know what we're going to do now. The longer it takes him to see that the relocation *must* go forward, the more lives will be lost."

The despair in his eyes made Jeriah's heart ache with pity and hope.

"Sir, there may be another way. Do you remember my brother, Tobin?"

Commander Sower frowned, then nodded. "Yes. A reliable young man."

*Unlike you.* But he hadn't said it aloud, and Jeriah pressed on. "Sir, Tobin had the misfortune to be captured by the barbarians—no, he's not dead. It's stranger than that, and there's a great deal going on in the barbarian camps that we didn't know about."

The story was so bizarre that it held the commander's attention until the sun sank and his aide came into his office to light the lamps. Tobin hadn't had time to write down half of it, but one of the goblins who'd gone with Cogswhallop was a Bookerie; he'd taken down most of the story Tobin had told Cogswhallop, and the goblin had passed that report on to Makenna as well. But there were still a number of points that didn't make much sense, even to Jeriah. He wasn't surprised that at the end of it Commander Sower sighed.

"It's clear your brother has been through a terrible ordeal, Rovanscourt. It's no discredit to him that . . . Well, if he manages to return home, time and peace can make a great difference."

"I'm not Rovans*court*," said Jeriah. "Not as long as Tobin's alive. Am I to take it, sir, that you don't think his plan will work?"

"I think living so long in that kind of danger, under so much stress . . . Small wonder he's . . . creating ways to defeat the whole barbarian army in one battle. Without even having to fight them! But assuming such a gate could be cast—which you yourself admit has never been done before. And assuming we could usher all the barbarians into this Spiritworld, why should they politely agree to go? You haven't seen much combat, Rovanscou—oh, all right, Master Rovan. But I've been fighting the barbarian army for years, and I assure you they never do what you want them to. Much less do it exactly when and where you wish!"

"The 'where' is our part, sir. You know they're constantly scouting our borders, looking for weakness. If we deliberately create one, show them a place where it looks like they might break through, why wouldn't they attack? We have nothing to lose by trying, and everything to gain! Because if Tobin's right—"

"Nothing to lose? Nothing to lose by making part of the border look so weak that it's obvious the barbarians can break through? The only way to do that is to withdraw a large number of troops, which means we *will* be weak! Suppose instead of riding obediently through this gate— which may or may not be cast in the first place!—suppose the barbarians ride right on through our lines, then launch an all-out attack on our forces? This could create the opportunity they've been waiting for to take another huge section of the Southlands."

"Tobin says they want to invade the Spiritworld more than anything else! Tobin says—"

"Tobin has been under incredible pressure," said Commander Sower gently. "It's a miracle he's still alive, and

I pray with all my heart that he escapes. I'm not inclined, however, to let him dictate my battle plans."

"Surely there's no harm in making the attempt!" Jeriah protested. "You could fortify the border just beyond the section we weaken; make it impossible for the barbarians to advance any farther."

"From what I've observed, very little is impossible for the barbarians." The commander's face was still impassive, but the despair crept into his voice. "And when you say no harm in trying, no harm to whom? Which landholder, how many farmers, do you propose to make homeless because we ceded their lands luring the barbarians in? Will you be the one to remove them from homes they'll probably never see again? Because I decline to do so."

It was clearly a lost cause, but that didn't stop Jeriah from arguing until Commander Sower lost patience and dismissed him. And then threatened to have him thrown out. The commander was shouting for his aides when Jeriah finally gave up and departed.

He never considered quitting. It was true that if the barbarians weren't stopped, the destruction of the Realm would be all his fault. And this was the final step toward saving Tobin, who clearly didn't intend to return—the stubborn idiot!—without saving everyone else first. If they couldn't bring this off, what lunacy would he come up with next? But mostly Jeriah couldn't quit because he couldn't stand the idea of

Makenna succeeding in her part while he failed in his. It should have been the least of his motivations, but imagining the ironic contempt in her eyes got him into the saddle before dawn the next morning.

It took several more days to reach Commander Malveese. He was still stationed in the same area, but the commander was out on an extended patrol with one of his troops, and it took Jeriah some time to track them down.

Seated by the campfire, Jeriah told the commander and his lieutenants most of Tobin's story and all of his plans.

The young officers looked at Jeriah as if he was crazy, but when he finished, the commander's face was thoughtful.

"You're certain, Master Rovanscourt, that the barbarians would choose this Spiritworld over ours?"

"I have no idea," said Jeriah. "But my brother's certain of it, and I trust him. And it's Rovan, sir. Not Rovanscourt."

The commander paid no attention to this. "But what if being their prisoner for so long has driven him mad, as Commander Sower thought? You can't deny—"

"If he'd gone mad, Cogswhallop would have seen it and rescued him, no matter what Tobin wanted," Jeriah told them. He was even more certain of that than he was of Tobin's judgment. "I can't say what the barbarians will or won't do. But Tobin's in a better situation to determine that than anyone else in the Realm, and this is his plan. We have to do something. You know that better than anyone, sir."

"So you'd have us put our trust in your mad brother and a

pack of goblins? That doesn't reassure me." But dry humor lurked beneath the commander's grim expression, and Jeriah held his breath.

One of the other officers stirred. "There were some goblins in our vineyards. I never saw them myself. Only a few people did, but we all knew they were there. When we did something for them, left out food, or a few feet of cloth, or a set of doll dishes my sister had outgrown—they did things for us in exchange. They never stole. They never cheated."

Several other men nodded agreement.

"What did you do when they passed the Decree?" Jeriah asked.

"Our priest was one of the strict ones." The officer sighed. "We had enough trouble getting our local hedgewitch and finder out of the village alive. We stopped setting out gifts for the goblins, and they stopped helping us, but we didn't try to burn them out like the priest wanted. I don't know if they left or not, but the yield in the vineyard where they lived went down a lot. And then the barbarians took all our land, so I hope they did get out, but . . ."

He spread his empty hands.

"I have no land now," said Commander Malveese abruptly. "If I did, I don't know if I could stand to risk it as you ask. But I have friends, and some relatives, who still do. I'll give you their names."

The other officers pitched in as well. When Jeriah rode out next morning, he had a list of names, and letters addressed to the men they knew, vouching for Jeriah and begging the landholders to listen to him.

With any luck, Koryn might be lurking on one of these estates. He hoped so—though it would be even harder to convince some Southland landholder to risk everything on Tobin's plan if Koryn was dissecting it as he spoke. He'd have to talk with her first, convince her he was right. He'd never managed to convince her of anything. Yet.

Jeriah found the first of the men on his list before midday, not riding his vineyards like the lord he was, but hoeing weeds out of a common vegetable patch. If Jeriah had paid more attention to his father's lectures, he might even have known what the small green sprouts would become.

The man removed his hat, wiped sweat from his forehead, and read the letter. When he'd finished, he looked up at Jeriah with steady dark eyes.

"Are you out of your mind? I'm not yielding one inch of my land! Not till those barbarians take it over my dead body!"

"But if the plan works, the barbarians *won't* take your land. Or anyone else's, ever."

"Then let 'anyone else' take the risk. It won't be me."

The second landholder, when Jeriah approached him late that afternoon, said much the same. The third, whom Jeriah found supervising the turning of his wine casks, not only read the letter but listened to the whole plan, why Tobin thought it would work, and why Tobin was in a position to know. It was dark when Jeriah finished.

"And there will be soldiers stationed here too, to protect the gate. And you could evacuate your family to safety first, in case anything goes wrong. And if you don't do it, sooner or later they'll take your land anyway. Living here on the border, you must know that."

"There is much in what you say," the landholder admitted. "These barbarians, they must be stopped. But the land, my winery, this is all I have. If your plan failed . . . No. You must go elsewhere."

Jeriah spent the rest of the evening arguing his point, since it was too late to travel onward anyway. But the longer he thought about it, the more fearful and stubborn the landholder grew. In the morning Jeriah rode on.

"What if the barbarians don't do as this lunatic brother of yours predicts, eh?"

"What if the sorceress can't cast such a great portal? Then my lands would be the first to fall!"

"I agree, young sir, someone must take the risk—but it must be a man with less to lose than me."

At this point Jeriah began to notice that not only was everyone turning him down, they were looking askance at him while they did it. A few refusals later, he realized why, and confronted the landholder he was talking to.

"Look, I'm not a Southlander myself, but I come from a place a lot like this. I know how you feel."

In truth, the mottled gold brick of the Southlands was nothing like Rovanscourt's somber gray stone—but loving your home was common to all people.

The Southland lord was much the same age as Jeriah's father, and he gave Jeriah the same skeptical look his father would have given a young Southland knight in similar circumstances.

"Do you? How many of your friends' estates have fallen to these invaders? How many of your neighbors have sold, at copper-for-gold prices, and run while they still had a chance to salvage something? How many of your sons are risking their lives to stop this enemy, young Norther?"

He rode away fuming, but eventually his irritation subsided. How much attention would his father have paid to a Southlander—to anyone Jeriah's age—who asked him to risk all of Rovanscourt in a wild gamble? A gamble hatched by another young outsider.

Jeriah needed an insider. Someone who could speak to these men as one of their own. Someone who believed, bone deep, that the barbarians would swallow the whole Realm unless drastic steps were taken to stop them. In short, he needed Koryn.

Now that he had an excuse—no, a valid reason—to seek her out, it took only half the next morning for Jeriah to track her down.

The friends of her dead parents, who'd taken her in, owned a small homey estate that was too close to the battle lines to suit Jeriah. She'd barely escaped one barbarian attack; was she courting another?

But he knew Koryn wouldn't court her own death, not

until the last barbarian had been wiped from the face of the earth . . . so she'd probably live to a ripe old age.

The thought cheered Jeriah as he followed the landholder's wife's directions out to the grape arbor where Koryn had taken her books and notes.

The rustling grape leaves that grew along the long poles of the shelter's roof provided a cool refuge from the pounding sun. In the fall, this was probably a crushing station, where the grapes would be run through a juice press and the results kegged for fermenting.

Now, with the grapes still green amid the leaves, only Koryn was there. The tumbled frizzy hair and moon-big eyes were the same—for a moment he'd have sworn they brightened at the sight of him, but then her expression turned cool. Here in the Southlands she wore only a light cotton blouse with a loose shift over it, and her feet were bare.

Something about those pale bony feet disarmed Jeriah, and he spoke quickly, before she could launch the first attack.

"I didn't come here to fight with you. I need your help."

With Makenna that wouldn't have worked. Koryn blinked once, then asked, "Help with what?"

"Thank you!" Jeriah sank down on the bench beside her, deeply grateful for more than just the shade.

"I haven't agreed to help you yet," she said.

"You will when you've listened." And she'd agreed to listen, thank the Bright Gods.

Jeriah told her everything Cogswhallop had told him. Tobin's report about the nature of barbarian magic had her reaching for ink and paper and making him slow down so she could take notes.

"This information is exactly what I spent the last year trying to find." Koryn had pushed her hair back several times, with ink-stained fingers, and smudges marked her temple.

"Tobin is risking his life to get it," Jeriah told her grimly. "And he's figured out how to use it, too."

He went on to tell her all about Tobin's plan. Halfway through, she stopped taking notes. By the time he finished, telling her about Makenna's promise to obtain the spirits' cooperation, Koryn was deep in scowling thought.

The silence stretched for a long time, but Jeriah wasn't impatient. He didn't think Koryn was even aware of his presence now.

Eventually the scowl faded, and her gaze found him and focused. "I know more about the barbarians by now than anyone else in the Realm. And judging by all I've learned, all I've read . . . your brother's plan might work."

"If I can persuade a Southland lord to let us use his estate to bait the trap," said Jeriah. "That's where I need your help."

She was rising, careful of her twisted leg, even as he spoke. "What are we waiting for?"

Koryn's leg wasn't strong enough to allow her to post, so they rode at a walk through the sun-drenched fields to meet with the man Koryn considered the most promising prospect. She hadn't taken time to change her clothes, only adding riding boots and a broad-brimmed straw hat that completed her peasant ensemble. But when they arrived, the Southland landholder greeted her by name and kissed her cheek when he lifted her down from the saddle.

He still didn't agree to help them, despite Koryn's impassioned plea. Nor did the next most promising prospect, nor the next.

"They're all so stubborn," Jeriah fretted.

"They're frightened," Koryn said. "In fact, they're terrified. But sooner or later we'll find someone who'll listen. Because when it comes to stubborn, Jeriah Rovan, you've got them all beaten!"

"Thank you so much," said Jeriah. "I think. Do you realize that's the nicest thing you've ever said to me?"

She didn't answer, but below her hat's floppy brim he saw her mouth twitch—surely a sign that forgiveness was on the way.

The purple Southland dusk had settled into the rolling hollows when they rode up to the fourth estate of the day. The landholder listened to Koryn and Jeriah, then read Commander Malveese's letter in silence. He was an old man, with a fringe of ragged white hair around his bald crown. His manor was small—little more than a sprawling farmhouse that had been extended and enlarged over many generations.

He said nothing for a long time after he finished reading, but finally . . .

"Yes."

"Yes?" Jeriah asked. "What do you . . . You mean *yes?*"

The old man snorted. "You hard of hearing, boy? I'm not a fool. I've seen too many estates fall to the barbarians, and my sons are fighting on the border. They tell me the same things about the barbarians that Mistress Koryn does. If no way to stop them is found, sooner or later my lands will fall. This wild plan of yours may not give us much of a chance— but it's better than no chance at all."

Jeriah hardly dared believe it. "You know you'll have to evacuate, sir? You, and all your people."

"Better now, with time to pack what we can, than fleeing for our lives with barbarian troops on our heels," said the landholder. "This way there's some slim hope we might be able to return. From what my sons say, once the barbarians overrun this land, there's no hope our army will ever take it back."

Jeriah drew in a breath. "Any chance one of your sons commands the troops that guard this section of the border?"

# CHAPTER 13

# Makenna

MAKENNA AND HER GOBLIN HELPERS had practiced the gate spell so often that drawing the runes around the cupboard door in Chardane's herbery felt almost routine, even in the goblins' absence. Makenna had no doubt of her ability to create a small gate into the Otherworld. If she wasn't able to keep her amulet, she wouldn't have enough power to get out on her own—but she'd still forbidden any of her assistants to accompany her.

One way or another, she'd escape. And if she didn't, she had no intention of allowing anyone else to be trapped with her. Not this time.

Besides, going back into the Otherworld—the Spiritworld, she should be calling it—gave her a chance to shed those absurd skirts.

"I wish you'd take me along," said Chardane. "Especially if you won't take your own casting circle with you. Between my power and your knowledge of the spell, we could probably create a gate big enough for at least one of us to get out."

"I'll be satisfied with creating a gate that lets one of us in," said Makenna.

The only way to keep her goblins from going in with her was to create this gate without their assistance. Makenna hadn't realized that sensible Chardane would give her the same problem.

"You'll have more than enough to do here," she added. "You've got to learn to cast the spell yourself, and then gather enough priests to make a gate so big a whole army can ride through it. And you'll not only have to teach those priests to work with goblins, you'll have to convince my goblins to work with priests! Dealing with a bunch of human-hating spirits sounds easy, compared to that."

In truth, it didn't. But Chardane had never dealt with the spirits, so the lie passed unchallenged.

It felt strange to create a gate with only one person feeding her power, and human magic had a different flavor than that of the goblins. Slower, stronger, dimmer, less ephemeral— lava instead of lightning.

Whatever it felt like, the whirling disk of light slowly formed in the frame of the cupboard door, and a meadow lay beyond it.

Makenna turned to the priest. "I thank you for this. For everything."

"Even court gowns?" Chardane's fascinated gaze was on the shimmering portal. "Be safe, girl. And get it done. For all our sakes."

*Don't worry. I'll manage. You can count on me.* All the easy promises flowed into Makenna's mind, but they were lies, and she and Chardane both knew it.

She shrugged and crawled through the gate into the Spiritworld.

It looked so much like the real world. The meadow stretched to the foot of some rolling hills, where the trees began to thicken. Bees hummed among the plants, birds twittered in the brush—and none of it was real, none had life of its own. Knowing what she now did, Makenna was amazed that the plants had nourished them and the water quenched their thirst. This wasn't a different world; it was a beautiful replica of the world the spirits had left behind. Been forced to leave behind? She bet they missed the real thing. In fact, she was betting her life on it. That, and one other thing.

Makenna drew in a slow breath and summoned up memories of the place she wanted to reach. If she'd had something from that area, she could have set a spell to find it. But when she'd left, she hadn't thought she'd ever return, so there'd been no reason to pick up a flower or a river-smooth stone.

She had to do it the hard way. Makenna closed her eyes, the better to see the lay of the land around the twisting curves of the streambed. The place where she'd crouched with Cogswhallop for several nights, hiding, waiting. The pattern of the stones the ice had claimed when they cast the amulets into the water.

Makenna was wearing one of those amulets now. She knew she was taking a risk—and breaking a promise too—but even angering the people she wanted to negotiate with had seemed preferable to returning to this place with no defense at all.

Holding on to the memory of the spirit's angry face, of her vivid, crystalline power, Makenna started walking. If she was right about the nature of this world, the direction didn't matter. If she was wrong, then she'd start again with a different spirit. Sooner or later, the result would be the same.

It was hard to say how long she traveled. The sun moved across the sky, but whether it moved at the same rate it did in the real world depended on the spirits' whim. Eventually the curves of the land became familiar, and Makenna found herself passing the bush where she and Cogswhallop had hidden. She walked up to the stream, seated herself on a rock, and waited.

It didn't take long. The water spirit rose out of the stream in a spinning fountain, then settled into the dripping woman shape Makenna remembered.

"You promised to go! You promised you'd go, and take that *thing* with you!" There was so much anger in the bubbling voice, Makenna half expected her to start steaming.

"Aye, and I meant it at the time. But I need to talk to you, and I have no way to summon you into the real world to meet with me. So I came to you. I'm sorry about the promise," she added politely.

"We don't care if you're sorry or not," the spirit said. "Yet another lying human has cheated us! You think the death you wear will keep you safe, but you're wrong!"

"Aren't you going to ask *why* I came back?" Makenna said patiently.

The spirit blinked, in an amazingly human expression of surprise. "I don't care about that either."

"All right," said Makenna. "But the reason I came is something you will care about. Because I can offer you a chance to get your hands on the humans who made these death amulets." She touched the one she wore, in case the stupid creature missed the point. "I can give you a chance to avenge yourselves, on humans who are still using the death of both your kind and mine to power the magic that helps them kill us. Not just some stranger who happens to be wearing the thing, like me, but the ones who do the killing. Interested?"

The spirit's arrested expression was answer enough, but the water woman shook her head—another incongruously human gesture. "I can't call a council into the presence of that *thing*. Not on the word of someone who's already broken one promise!"

"This amulet is my only way to get home. Without it, I can't create a gate." Makenna hated to say it. She hated the idea of doing it even more. "If I take this off, will you promise to give it back to me?"

"You think I'll keep my word better than you kept yours?" the spirit asked. "My promise wouldn't bind the others, anyway. So you might as well leave now. Though I wouldn't mind hearing the killing-the-death-wielders part before you go."

Makenna had always known it might come to this. She took off the amulet and held it out, dangling on its chain. The moment the medallion left her skin, she felt the Otherworld leeching her magic, taking her energy, her life joy with it. It felt like growing old, all at once, without the comfortable cushion of years.

"Don't drop it in the water!" the spirit said sharply. "Take it to that muddy place and put it down."

Makenna did so, and she watched in fascination as the damp earth softened until the medallion sank into it. Then, before her disbelieving gaze, the mud around it turned to stone. Not ice, she found as she reached out to touch it, but a solid round rock the size of a small melon.

"There!" The spirit shook herself, sending small drop-lets flying. "That's *much* better. Though I don't suppose the stone spirits will approve."

"Mind if I carry this with me?" The mud was cool and gritty under Makenna's fingers as she dug. The stone was heavy, but carrying it along was better than leaving it behind. Makenna could probably chip the amulet out of its shell, eventually—though she wouldn't begin to have time, if the earth decided to soften and swallow her up as well!

But the water spirit looked . . . thinner, somehow. Perhaps the effort of softening and hardening an unfamiliar element drained even a creature of magic. Perhaps something as large as Makenna was safe . . . as long as she had something to offer them.

"Maybe it's time to call this council of yours," Makenna added, lest the flighty spirit forget the point of this dance.

She needn't have worried.

"Certainly." A feverish light transformed the spirit's face. "For a chance to kill the death wielders, they'll all come."

Makenna had been counting on that. Known she could rely on it, that it would be a stronger motive even than the spirits' longing for the real world. She, of all people, understood the power of hate.

The spirit had told Makenna to wait while it arranged a conference. It was dark beside the stream, and those strangely patterned stars lit the sky.

If Makenna had needed confirmation that this world wasn't real, the full moon that rose many hours after the sun set provided it. The thought of a world whose people controlled the moon and sun chilled her, but at least the moon lit the rushing stream and slopes of the hills around it.

Only there seemed to be more piles of tumbled boulders than there had been before, and the woods had moved closer.

The spirits came forth, shambling, slithering, drifting on the breeze, made of tree or stone or wind-tangled grass. So many spirits pulled themselves from the stream that Makenna expected the water level to sink, but it never did.

A creature she might have taken for a pile of rock, if not for the glittering eyes, opened its jagged mouth and rumbled, "You say we can kill the death wielders? How?"

"With your permission," said Makenna, "with your help, we think we can open a portal between the worlds large enough for their whole army to ride through. If we close it up behind them . . ." She shrugged. "I know you can't directly attack anyone who wears one of these." She thumped the stone gently on the ground. They knew what was in it—every spirit who'd approached had eyed the innocent-looking rock with loathing. "And I know that their shamans can trap and kill you. But I also know that you control this world in ways their shamans can't even imagine. And death doesn't have to be direct, now does it?"

The rock spirit's quartzlike eyes were so hungry, it made Makenna shiver.

One of the tree spirits stepped forward, a white-barked sapling who moved with lithe grace. It still had too many limbs to suit Makenna.

"Why should we let them in?" The leafy whisper sounded feminine, but the body was so much more tree than human that Makenna couldn't be sure. "We live safe here. They can kill us. We might be able to slay most of them, to hide, to run as we once did. But the humans are bound to kill some of us."

A boy who looked to be made of twisting grass and flowers said, "If it gives me a chance to get my roots around their throats, I don't care." His voice was pure hate.

Makenna listened to the debate for a time. Quite a long time, for the spirits seemed willing to rehash the same ground endlessly. Some didn't want to risk losing the sanctuary they'd created, but others hated the wielders of death so much, they wouldn't mind dying if they could take their enemies with them.

Makenna understood both sides. The fiery seduction of vengeance was something she had once succumbed to herself. But in the end life had called her back to the living, and she wasn't sorry to have left hatred behind.

She'd made up her mind more quickly than these spirits, too! They really weren't very bright. So maybe she'd best help them along. Because the whole Realm could get conquered before they made a decision.

"Look here." Makenna broke into a rock spirit's plea to be left to sit in the sun and snow and rain in peace. "Some of you want to fight and some don't. Right?"

"Have you no ears?" The question came from a tree spirit who hardly had a face. Snickers bubbled and knocked and grated through the clearing.

"Then why not let both sides do what they want?" Makenna continued. "Let those who want to stay here and fight do that. For those who don't want to fight, we'll hold the gate open a bit longer and you can come back to the real world. If the bar—the death-wielding humans are all in here, you'll be safe there. Or do you like this world better?"

She wouldn't care for it herself.

"We yearn for the living world, for real streams, real earth, with every beat of our hearts." The spirit who spoke seemed to be made entirely of water, with no heart at all. "But when we went to war with the death wielders, they burned the meadows and groves to force the spirits who lived there to come out and defend their soul homes. And when we left . . . we had learned from them. The stream spirits flooded the meadow and drowned the grass. The grass spirits choked off the roots of the trees. The earth spirits poisoned the streams so that everything in or around them died. We left the killers with nothing—but they left us nothing as well. Between us we drained the land so badly that only rock spirits can live there, and they're too vulnerable to the hunters. The rest of us cannot live in a desert."

Had their war with the spirits created the drought that had driven the barbarians to cross the great desert and conquer the Realm? It sounded like it, which meant that these spirits might not make comfortable neighbors. But the Realm humans wouldn't know how to kill them, so perhaps her idea would work out. And they couldn't be worse than the barbarians. She hoped.

"The Realm's not a desert," Makenna said. "Indeed, half the Midlands are a swamp! Even the Southlands, where the gate would open, isn't a desert. And you can spread out from there."

Her heart beat fast with hope.

The contemptuous snort of a rock spirit was an awesome thing. "It's not a matter of your feeble gate. We can pass from this world to the true one at will. And we *could* live there, but we cannot. The ancient binding forbids us to dwell in the Bright Gods' Realm unless we are invited to do so."

Whose binding? The priests'? The Bright Gods' themselves? Makenna was meddling in matters far beyond the scope of a girl her age—but there wasn't much new in that, and only one question really mattered.

"Who has to issue this invitation?"

If the Bright Gods had to do it, she was foxed, but if it was just the priests . . .

"It must be issued by the humans who live there," one of the tree spirits said. "We never understood why they cast us out in the first place, for we did no harm. Well, not much harm."

"That sounds like the priests to me." And Makenna had no qualms about thwarting them. "I'm human." For the first time in years, she was glad of it. "And I live in the Realm. Can I invite you back?"

The fact that the Hierarch and landholders who ruled the Realm might not approve of her actions didn't matter to Makenna—and she didn't think it would matter to whatever magic kept the spirits out, either. The Realm's government wasn't the *Realm*, and magic would recognize that truth— even if the government didn't.

The spirits were all staring now. "Yes," a rock spirit

replied. "Any human of the Realm can permit our return. But you have to *invite* us."

And just saying "come in" wasn't enough. Makenna thought quickly. "I invite you to return to the Realm of the Seven Bright Gods. I invite you to take up your homes in meadow and stream, rock and tree, wherever a spirit might choose to dwell. I invite you to share that land with the humans and goblins and gods who dwell there, in peace and friendship, giving up your hatred of humans as long as they offer no hatred to you. Welcome home."

There. With luck, that should keep the spirits who chose to return from starting a new little war with the humans of the Realm—humans who had no reason to hate the spirits, for as far as Makenna knew, most of the Realm had no idea these creatures existed.

An excited babble sprang up among the spirits. Most were jubilant at the prospect of returning to the living world. A few grumbled about having to tolerate humans to do it. But these aren't the death wielders, others replied. These were other humans. How do we know that?

A sudden silence fell, and a tree spirit, dark barked and gnarled, pushed his way to the front of the crowd. "How do we know this isn't some death wielders' trick, to bring us back into the living world where they can slay us? Why should we trust this human, who's already broken one promise by returning here? Wearing death magic on her own body! If you want to kill humans, there *is* one human we can kill right now."

"You need me to open the gate for the death wielders," Makenna said swiftly. "And bring them to the gate. And convince them to ride through. Why settle for killing me, when you could kill thousands?" Her heart was pounding, but she had to keep calm, keep them focused on the main point—these spirits were too cursed distractible!

"She speaks the truth," said a creature made of pale, dusty stone. "You must smell it on her as clearly as I do."

Did that mean they could sense . . . smell it if she lied? Makenna was suddenly very glad she'd never tried to lie to a spirit.

"Yes," the tree spirit said. "The truth, as this Tobin human tells it. A human who, by her account, has been living among the death wielders for months! Suppose he's become one of them? Suppose he seeks to bring us back in order to obtain the death that will give him their power?"

"If you'll remember back to my original request," said Makenna, "I asked that you allow us to open a gate so we could send the barbarians into this world. You can stay and fight them, or return to the Realm and leave them here. It doesn't matter to me."

According to Tobin's letter, the barbarian shamans had no idea how to make a gate, or they'd have invaded the Spiritworld long ago. If they hated the spirits as much as the spirits hated them, they'd probably be willing to take any risk to come to grips with their enemy. She had no desire to see anyone die—but if two enemies wanted to fight to the death, that was no problem of hers. As long as they didn't destroy the world where her goblins lived in the process.

"So what it comes to," said the tree creature, "is whether we trust this Tobin human. And we have no way to know if he tells the truth or not. I don't trust any human. I think the promise breaker deserves to die."

"I can tell you that Tobin would never take power from the death of others," said Makenna. The real-world moon would reverse its direction across the sky before that happened. If they could scent the truth, they'd be smelling it now. Even those bloodthirsty trees!

"But can you swear that *he* is not deceived?" a grass woman asked. "I didn't think so. All we know is that you believe he wouldn't betray us. Can you tell us your judgment has never been at fault?"

Makenna frowned, for of course she couldn't. "Look, I know Tobin well. Betraying anyone to their death, he just wouldn't!"

"So you *believe*," the tree spirit growled, waving a number of limbs for emphasis. "Suppose you're wrong? Suppose when we go out, their spells are laid to trap us? Why should we trust this Tobin, who none of us knows?"

A silence followed. Makenna was losing them, but she had no way to prove Tobin's honesty. And her life was slipping away with their trust.

Then a new spirit welled out of the stream before her. It

looked tired and tattered, barely able to hold the shape of a human youth.

"This Tobin." The bubbling voice was ragged too. "He is now among the death wielders, in the dry lands at the desert's edge?"

"Aye," Makenna said cautiously. "As far as I know."

The left side of the spirit's face crumpled and reformed as he held out his hands, and a globe of water began to grow between them.

The other spirits were silent, and Makenna sensed pity for this exhausted stranger—if a spirit could be wounded, he surely was. But the globe between his hands became rounder and firm, and light flickered in its center.

"Is this Tobin?" the spirit asked.

The light in the water began to shift and move, and Makenna gasped when an image of Tobin appeared.

He was still too thin, and his hair was longer and a dark brown—had he dyed it, to resemble the barbarians? He looked better than when she'd seen him last, but his shoulders were tense, his face set with determination. He was moving around in the sandy bed of a stream, kicking at things she couldn't see and scuffing the dirt. It was night there too.

"Is this where he is now?" Makenna asked. It would be nice to know that the barbarians weren't on to him yet. "What's he doing?"

The spirits exchanged a look she couldn't read.

"Is this the human Tobin?" the water spirit repeated.

"It is. But what he's doing I don't know," Makenna admitted. The image was crouching now, making marks in the damp earth.

The spirit pulled his hands apart and the globe collapsed, splashing into the stream.

"We can trust him," the ragged voice said.

# CHAPTER 14

# Tobin

COGSWHALLOP CAME AT DUSK, WHEN Tobin led the mules down to drink. And it took Tobin far too long to realize that the small green scraps floating past on the current were birch leaves and not some plant that grew in the dry Southlands.

Even when he noticed, he'd had to wade out into the stream to pick one up and examine it—and then stagger back out, with his sandals and the bottom of his loose britches wet. He cursed the goblin's blithe assertion that "You'll recognize the signal when you see it." But he had recognized it . . . or had he? Maybe this was their third, or fourth, or eighth attempt to get his attention.

However, they must have seen him wade out to pick up the leaf, so they'd be waiting tonight.

Tobin fought down a surge of dread so intense, his stomach began to churn. There was no other way. Living among the barbarians had taught him that there were worse things than taking a few blows.

He could do this. He had to.

He let the mules drink their fill before starting back to camp, then curried and tethered them for the night, acting just as usual.

He thought he looked normal too, but Vruud took one look at him and said, "Tonight, eh?"

Tobin had been forced to let the storyteller in on his plans. And then he spent the better part of a night convincing the man that fleeing to the Realm wouldn't do him any good if the Duri immediately conquered it. Eventually the storyteller had to admit that Tobin was right, and Vruud had spent the last few weeks making a round of all the Duri camps. Ostensibly he went to convey the sad news that the spirit had fled, and that everyone should keep an eye out for it in their own territory. But he'd then gone on to sit beside other clans' campfires, to entertain in their men's gathering tents, spinning tale after tale of the glory and power that existed in the Spiritworld. Theirs for the taking, if only they could reach it.

For the barbarians it was more compelling than a story of some lost hoard of gold and jewels. As far as Tobin could see, their ancient myth of the ultimate conquest hardly needed Vruud to fan it. To invade the Spiritworld, to absorb all the power bound up in their enemies' lives, was the fantasy these men had been put to bed with from the time they were children. All they needed was a chance.

"It's a good plan," Vruud told him, echoing his own thoughts. "As long as your nerve holds."

Tobin's mouth was dry, his palms sweating, but the contemptuous tone still stung. No doubt it was meant to. "I'm going to try. What more do you want?"

"A bit of common sense," Vruud said. "But I suppose that's too much to expect. Take these leaves and hide them in your clothing. They'll be searching for weapons, so they shouldn't find them. Assuming you've got the brains to hide them well."

"What are these for?" The dried leaves Vruud handed him didn't look like much, but Tobin could hide them easily.

"They're a pain suppressor," said the storyteller. "Chew them up thoroughly, then spit them out—if you swallow them, they'll make you sick. Not that you won't be sicking up from nerves alone, by the look of you."

For a man raised in a culture that placed no value on kindness, this was the equivalent of a warm hug and a tearful blessing—and a lot more practical.

"Thank you," said Tobin. "For all you've done. I won't forget."

The storyteller snorted. "If you don't succeed, your memory, or lack thereof, won't matter. And if you do, I won't need your gratitude. Just make sure your army doesn't sweep in and wipe out the rest of us once the Duri are gone."

"I can promise you that," said Tobin. "At least, Cogswhallop said Jeriah would make sure of it."

Vruud grimaced. "Do Softer children play a game where one person whispers a message to another, who whispers it to the next person, all around the campfire?"

"Yes." Some games were universal, it seemed.

"Well, to my mind, adding one or two more people to your Cogswhallop-to-Jeriah chain is all that's needed to guarantee disaster. Go to bed. I don't suppose you'll sleep, but I intend to."

Tobin doubted that at the time—but if the snores the storyteller was emitting when he finally crept out of the tent were fake, they were a very good fake.

It was harder sneaking out of camp now. The Duri didn't set sentries, relying on their patrols to keep their camps safe. But there had been more night patrols lately; after they'd realized the spirit had fled, the Duri had been increasingly restless.

Several messengers had come to the camp lately, and Vruud said it looked like they were preparing for another big attack. Tobin had been terrified that attack would come before he could get his plan in place.

Now it was falling into place, and he was even more terrified.

Tobin made only one stop on his way to the meeting, to wash the dye out of his hair with an acrid solution Hesida had made for him. Vruud wasn't the only one to communicate with other Duri camps. Hesida had sent word to all her kinswomen that if "something disturbing" happened, they were to keep the chan of their camps quiet, and respect the Duris' orders. Tobin had been afraid that even so innocuous a message might warn the Duri something was up, but Hesida swore that the women would hold their tongues—and keep their camps from doing anything rash if . . . when all their warriors vanished.

Washing out the dye was time-consuming, even using Hesida's stinky solvent. The moon was waning when Tobin finally approached the tumble of rocks. Cogswhallop was waiting for him.

"It's set. And I've got the clothes here for you. They can cast the gate anytime you say. In fact, they won't be casting it till our lad's scouts see the barbarian army coming toward the trap. The gen'ral says that opening lots of gates and then closing them up might make the spirit folk nervous."

"Good." Tobin took the bundle from Cogswhallop's hands. "Then the spirits consented?"

Lightweight sturdy clothes, the kind worn by Realm knights in the Southlands—minus the church's tabard, since most spies were smart enough not to sneak around the desert clad in red and gold. The cloth was slightly worn. Tobin hoped the goblins had purchased the clothing from its previous owner, instead of just taking it and doing him some favor in return. But knowing them as he did, Tobin doubted it.

"Aye, the spirits consented," Cogswhallop told him. "More or less. Enough for our purposes, anyway."

That didn't sound reassuring, but whatever it meant, Tobin couldn't do anything about it. He'd been wearing the loose clothing of the chanduri so long, Realm clothes felt stiff and tight—particularly the boots. He was deeply curious about how the spirits had been talked into cooperating. He wanted to know what Makenna and Jeriah had been doing for the last long month and a half, and to see his family.

Soon. Or never? No, he had to believe he would survive this, or his nerve would fail. This wasn't for the Realm, not really; it was for Rovanscourt, and his chance to build a peaceful future there. For all of them.

"Do all our troops know what's going on?" Tobin buckled on the belt that held a Realm knight's dagger. "They won't go storming the camps, killing the chanduri once the Duri are gone?"

"They know," Cogswhallop confirmed. "It took an order from the Hierarch himself, but if our plan works, the Realm's army will hold its hand. Commander Sower wasn't best pleased to learn . . . Well, that's not important now, and with the Hierarch's orders in front of him, he can't go foxing it. All the commanders have agreed that if you can make the whole barbarian army vanish, they don't care what happens to women and servants. The common soldiers, who'd be doing the killing if you succeed and the dying if you fail, will be even happier to see the whole problem disappear. They won't be committing any massacres."

Tobin drew a breath. "Then we'll do it the day after tomorrow. Tell them to be ready to cast the gate from dawn onward."

Cogswhallop scowled. "Two days, soldier? Better make it tomorrow. Give 'em less time."

"They'll need some time to get organized," Tobin said. "If it's too fast, if only a handful of camps go haring through that gate, we'll barely weaken them. I want them all. I want to end it. Now. With no more lives lost."

Cogswhallop considered this. "Will they be able to set their whole army in motion on two days' notice? I hadn't thought they were that well organized."

"They manage better than you'd think," Tobin told him. "In some ways, their looser command structure makes them more flexible. If one of our commanders wanted to gather the whole army and set them to attack a specific place, he'd have to send orders to each unit telling them where to go, when to get there, and what to do after they arrive. The Duri will simply send a runner telling everyone where to gather— getting there is up to them. And they'll do it, too. I think the reason they've been so restless is that they've seen our troops moving away from the trap. They're ready to move."

He'd been praying they wouldn't strike at the weakened section of the border too soon, taking the bait before the trap was set. And pulling back the jaws and setting the lever was his job. *Tonight.* He didn't dare flinch from it.

Tobin had Cogswhallop trim his shaggy hair in the style of the Realm, and the goblin gave him information on recent troop movements and positions—the things Tobin would need to know to play his part.

He was ready to leave far too quickly, but Cogswhallop had a question of his own.

"What's to stop those barbarian shamans from figuring out how to cast their own gates once they get to the Spiritworld? You're likely right they can't do it now, but it seems to me that passing through one will give them some clues. The Spiritworld is *made* of magic. What's to keep them from figuring it out?"

"Nothing," said Tobin. "If the spirits let them survive long enough. The shamans are the ones who create the blood trusts. They trap the spirits, force them into a human body, and then wield the knife. They're going to be the spirits' first targets. And once they're gone . . ."

Cogswhallop sighed, then shrugged.

It was more mercy, more regret, than the Duri shamans granted their victims, but Tobin felt the same.

Even though he was about to become one of those victims.

He set off, moving farther into the desert. All Tobin really needed was to be captured by another camp. No one outside the Morovda camp had seen enough of the storyteller's servant to recognize Tobin in his Realm clothes and neatly cut hair. But the farther off he could get, the smaller the chance that anyone would connect a captured "Realm spy" with a runaway servant at all.

Most patrols worked closer to the Realm's lines, but they were out in force. Tobin spotted one off in the distance and managed to swing wide enough to prevent them from detecting the amulet that would keep him alive long enough to tell his tale. Hopefully long enough that he'd still be alive when, with their masters dead, the chanduri realized that they'd need to make peace with the Realm. Tobin had every intention of pointing out to them that restoring a captive knight would be a good way to start negotiations.

The desert nights were warm now, and he was sweating in his new clothes. The boots rubbed a blister on his right heel, but Tobin didn't slow down. Blisters were the least of his worries.

The moon was nearing the horizon, the night more than half over, when Tobin spotted a pocket of the dense vegetation that promised water. It was still early enough in the year that most springs reached the surface, and he'd underestimated how thirsty this long walk would make him.

Listening carefully, keeping his eyes open for patrols, Tobin made his way into the rustling bushes. He located the small seep more by its scent than by sight and bent to cup the water in his hands.

The sharp prick below his left shoulder blade told him how foolish he'd been, even before the voice spoke.

"It's always good to stake out a water hole. We hadn't expected anything larger than a deer, but the first rule of hunting is that you take what comes."

Fight or surrender? Half a dozen Duri had emerged from the brush. A hunting party, not a patrol, but still enough to take him. Having the Duri hold him in contempt was part of his plan—and Tobin figured he'd end up with plenty of bruises anyway. He held out his hands, away from his knife hilt, and felt the jerk as it was yanked from its sheath.

"Where's your sword?"

The pressure of the spear point in his back hadn't diminished.

"It was broken when my horse fell." Tobin had had plenty of time to work out the details. "Put his hoof in a rabbit burrow and shattered the bone. I had to put him down. I've been walking for almost two days now. I was beginning to think I was going to make it out."

They'd surrounded him, a fence of spears pointed at his chest.

"But I still have this." He pulled the blood trust out of his shirt, gleaming in the moonlight. "It means you can't kill me, right?"

"Another cursed spy!" one of them exclaimed. "I'd think they'd have given that up by now. We may not be able to kill you, Softer. At least, not immediately. But we don't have to let you go."

"Not much point in keeping him," another grumbled. "Not since those clumsy fools in the Heron Clan let that spirit escape."

So this was a whole different clan? Excellent. They probably wouldn't even hear about another clan's missing servant. And if they did, they wouldn't care.

"You might as well let me go," Tobin said. Despite his resolve, his heart beat hard with rising dread. "If you do, it might go easier with you when, ah . . . There's no point in holding me." And just in case they were stupid enough to miss it, he added, "I don't know anything."

His left eye had swelled shut by the time his captors dragged him into their camp, and he had a few other bruises—but it wasn't much worse than the casual abuse chanduri received every day. Tobin had refused to reveal anything about the Realm army, with enough firmness to convince them he knew something worth concealing.

It was no part of Tobin's plan to play the hero. One corner of his soul still felt he should hold out as long as he could before he "broke" and revealed all. But the rest of him was too frightened to care what the Duri thought of Softer courage. They could feel all the contempt they liked, as long as they believed his story.

The cage they thrust him into was smaller than the one in the Morovda camp, and Tobin caught a whiff of a rank, familiar scent. At some point this cage had held a leopard. He didn't bother to hunt for a weakened bar, for he had no desire to escape. At least not yet.

They weren't in a hurry to question him. It was still dark when they locked the cage door, but the camp had awakened and eaten breakfast before a handful of Duri approached. A newly captured knight couldn't have interpreted the slight distance between the warriors and an old man with lean-muscled arms. Tobin knew he must be the shaman, simply by the way the youngsters deferred to him.

One of the older warriors, who Tobin guessed was the

camp's chief, looked Tobin up and down before he spoke.

"So, Softer. My Duri tell me you know something about your army's plans."

"I know you're going to lose," said Tobin. Some of the young knights he'd known had been that arrogant, that foolish, when they arrived at the border. Their first battle usually changed that attitude. Or killed them.

"Really?" The chief sounded bored, but his gaze was alert. "You haven't won many battles so far. In fact, you haven't won *any* battles."

Tobin set his teeth and said nothing, the picture of heroic stupidity. He hoped.

The chief shrugged. "We'll know soon enough." He gestured the shaman forward. "He's all yours, Ruki."

Tobin did fight when they pulled him from the cage. It was in character to struggle mightily against the hopeless odds, and he was frightened enough that it would have been hard not to.

All it accomplished was to earn him another set of bruises. They bound Tobin spread out on the ground, with his wrists and ankles tied to the posts of one of the goat pens. Then they departed, chatting among themselves, as if tying up a prisoner for interrogation was only another chore. To the Duri, that's all it was. The accumulated knocks were beginning to add up to pain, even if he had become accustomed to casual violence.

Tobin had been flogged once, and the memory still infected his nightmares. He figured he'd take three whip cuts, maybe four or five, before he started to talk. If they brought out hot irons, he'd start talking immediately. The point was to be convincing, not brave, and the thought of being burned frightened him enough that he could be very believable.

But when the shaman finally returned, he carried . . .

"Paint?" Tobin stared at the small pot and brush. "You're going to paint me?"

"For now," said the shaman, and proceeded to do so.

Runes on his forehead, his cheekbones, down the line of his jaw. The paint was cool and black—not even blood, as far as Tobin could tell. The brushstrokes were soft, and it itched as it dried.

The shaman cut open Tobin's shirt and painted runes over his heart and down his ribs. He started to hum tunelessly as he removed the shirtsleeves to paint runes down the insides of Tobin's arms. He spread Tobin's fingers to paint the palms of his hands. Then the knife sliced up the legs of his britches, baring his thighs to the brush. Tobin's boots came off so runes could decorate his shins. The brush tickled on the soles of his feet and Tobin squirmed, but he was too nervous to laugh.

"Is this some sort of truth spell?"

If it was, his whole plan had just fallen apart. But none of Vruud's tales had contained anything like that, and the storyteller hadn't protested when Tobin explained his plan. If the Duri shamans had a truth spell, surely the keeper of their history and traditions would know it.

"No," said the shaman. "Or perhaps it is, after a fashion. I'll come back when the paint's dry."

He capped the jar and strolled off, still humming under his breath.

The morning sun shone in Tobin's eyes, and he turned his face away. He needed to piss, but he knew they wouldn't release him for that. And—the Dark One take dignity—pissing himself with fear at the right moment might help convince the Duri that he'd broken.

The goats clustered nervously at the far side of the pen. Eventually, Tobin knew, they'd become curious and come over to find out if his clothing was edible.

But they hadn't had time to do so when the shaman and the chief returned.

"Looks good," the chief said. He knelt to check the ropes that bound Tobin's wrists and ankles. They were painfully tight, and growing more painful as time passed, along with his assorted bruises. Tobin thought he could yield fairly quickly, if they'd get on with it.

The shaman snorted. "I could have botched every rune, and you wouldn't know it."

The chief glared. Some rivalry there? Something Tobin could exploit?

But then the shaman captured Tobin's attention completely by drawing his dagger.

"What are you doing?" The quiver in his voice didn't have to be faked.

"Nothing much," said the shaman. "I've already done it."

He bent down and made a small cut in the sole of Tobin's foot.

Tobin just had time to register how small the wound was before agony struck, sweeping up his leg, traveling the path of the runes and redoubling, redoubling until the only reality was blazing pain.

He couldn't think. He was vaguely aware that he was screaming, his body arching against the tug of the ropes.

He couldn't have said how long it lasted, but it faded almost as swiftly as it had come. His arms and legs jerked convulsively with its lingering echoes.

Tobin heard his own voice sobbing. His throat was raw, and his closed eyes stung with tears.

"You think that's enough?" a man's voice asked.

Tobin opened his eyes. The chief and the shaman stared down at him. The chief looked a little shaken. The shaman's gaze was interested.

He hated them, suddenly, fiercely, more than he'd ever hated anyone in his life. The plan flashed into his mind, crystal clear and edged with his determination to destroy these men.

The shaman shrugged. "He's pissed himself, anyway. Give it a try."

"Softer," the chief said, "can you hear me?"

It seemed like a ridiculous question, until Tobin realized he hadn't been able to before.

"Yes." His voice was ragged, shaking with sobs. His

rational mind, which was slowly beginning to function, told him that trying to defy these men was insane, that his best choice was to give them whatever they wanted. But the primitive part of his soul screamed defiance.

"You seem to know something you think will let the Realm beat us," the chief went on. "Care to tell me what that is?"

"No!" Tobin rasped. He'd let them threaten him a few times before he gave up.

Without another word the shaman bent down. Before Tobin could do more than gasp in protest, he sliced a small cut in the sole of Tobin's other foot.

It seemed to last longer, though he had no sense of time. He was barely aware of existing except as a body, a thing, whose only purpose was to experience pain.

Eventually it passed. Eventually he became aware of the ropes cutting into his bleeding wrists, of his own voice, sobbing hysterically now.

They gave him a few moments to recover himself, to become coherent.

That was their mistake.

"It's the spirits." Tobin spoke before they could, his voice a husky rasp. "Our priests, they managed to make contact with the spirits in some place they were in. I don't understand that part of it. But they made some sort of alliance."

He had all their attention now.

"What can the spirits do to us?" the chief demanded. "If

they stay in the Spiritworld, they can no more touch this world than we can reach them. If they emerge, we can trap and kill them."

Tobin hesitated.

The shaman drew his knife.

The scream that burst from his throat wasn't faked at all.

"No, no, don't! They're coming out! According to my commander, the spirits have figured out some way to fight you. It's something to do with magic that I don't understand, but they have to be in this world to make it work, so our priests are going to create a gate, a huge one, big enough to allow an army of spirits to come through."

The shaman sheathed his knife, and Tobin's breath shuddered back in a relieved sigh.

The chief was frowning. "How do you know about this?"

"I don't know much," said Tobin. "I was assigned to a troop in the area where they're going to create the gate, and they ordered us out. That's why they sent some of us to find out where your patrols were, to be sure it's safe to leave that section unguarded."

He sobbed again, almost believing it himself.

The shaman's eyes glittered, but the chief was still frowning.

"Why do they have to move your troops away, simply to create a gate? And why can your priests do such a thing, when our shamans can't?"

"The spirits insisted we move most of our troops away,"

said Tobin. "They didn't want any chance our soldiers might go dashing into this world of theirs. Evidently this gate can't be closed in a hurry, and even the possibility that we might invade scared them witless."

"A portal to the Spiritworld," the shaman murmured. "That must be why—"

The chief waved him to silence. "Yes, it's a dream come true. And I don't trust dreams. They're often the bait for traps, and you should know that."

"It's true!" Genuine panic filled Tobin's voice. "I'm telling the truth! Don't—"

"Then answer my other question," the chief interrupted. "Why can your priests make these gates, when our shamans have never been able to affect the Spiritworld at all?"

"How would I know?" said Tobin.

The chief drew his own dagger.

"I don't know!" Tobin screamed. "I don't know, I don't know! All I heard was that the spirits had to help create them. Something about changing the nature of something or other, but they needed the spirits' help or permission or something. That's all I know, I swear it, I swear it. Don't . . ."

They were no longer paying attention to him.

"That's why we've never been able to reach them," the shaman said. "The spirits have to change the very nature of the Spiritworld to make the portal possible."

"So how are we going to get out of the Spiritworld after we've killed all the spirits?" the chief asked. "If they have to help make this gate, then—"

The shaman glared at him. "I don't think you understand how much power the death of so many spirits would give us. If we slay even fifty of them, I could probably make a gate to the moon and back! The Spiritworld is *made* of magic. Magic they control, which is why they've been able to keep us out. Once we have their power, we'll control that world's magic too. Creating a simple portal will be *easy*."

He turned to Tobin. "When? When will the spirits open this gate?"

"Tomorrow," Tobin whispered. "Sometime tomorrow. That's all I know. Please, I swear it."

"Tomorrow? I've got to send word to the camps today!" the chief exclaimed. "If we don't know when they're going to open it, we have to be there, ready to charge, all day. You, Softer! You don't know what time of day they'll cast this thing? Will it be visible from a distance?"

*They'll open it when they see you coming. And it won't close till the last of you is gone.*

The thought held so much cold satisfaction that Tobin closed his eyes to keep them from seeing it.

"I don't know when. They only told us the date we had to be gone by. I don't know if it will be visible, either. I know nothing about magic. I'm sorry, but I really don't know."

It would have been suspicious if he had, and the chief was skeptical already.

"If we send all our messengers," the shaman said, "they

can reach all the clans before nightfall. For this, every Duri will be ready to set out before dawn. And if anyone isn't . . . Well, as long as they got the word in time, they've only themselves to blame if they find themselves chan, when the other camps bring back scores of captive spirits. We could try forcing more than one spirit into a body . . . concentration of magic . . . unimaginable . . ." His voice faded to a mumble, but his face was alight with joy and greed.

"Yes, but before we do any of that, we have to fight," the chief said. "I'll see to the messengers. You put this one back in the cage. And make sure it's solid. We don't have time for games."

"Of course." The shaman nodded. "Then I'll have to make my own preparations. Weapons that can paralyze a spirit, wire and rope to bind them, those things aren't just steel, rope, and wire."

"Don't get too elaborate," the chief said. "We'll be leaving well before dawn. And I'm putting you in charge of the Softer. Make sure he's ready to ride with us, and assign a couple of the younger Duri to guard him."

Tobin's eyes flew open, but the shaman was staring too.

"Why drag a captive along with us? We never have before. Once we've captured the spirits, it'll be easier to bring them back here."

"Several reasons." The chief was watching Tobin. "First, because I'm not as certain as you are that you can whisk us back from the Spiritworld immediately. Maybe you will have enough power to control worlds. But just getting power won't make you any smarter, so it'll take you a while to figure out how to use it. But the main reason I'm taking him along is that this all seems a bit too perfect to me. If we find he's lied about this gate, then blood trust or no, he'll die as slowly and painfully as we can manage."

Tobin fought down panic and closed his eyes again. "I wish I had lied."

He had no idea what his expression showed, but it must not have been too suspicious; the chief departed, and the shaman summoned a couple of young warriors to return him to his cage.

It only needed two of them now, and that was mostly because they had to carry him, not because he put up any kind of fight.

Even with that incredible agony gone, every muscle in his body twitched and ached. His wrists and ankles were raw with rope burns. His head pounded with pain. His heart pounded with dread.

They were taking him along. They would see the gate and know he hadn't lied. But in their rush to enter the Spiritworld, it would be simpler and safer to drag him along with them, and Tobin was too weak to stop them.

Once they got into the Spiritworld, either he'd die for their blood sacrifice as soon as they captured a spirit or he'd die from the life drain when they took his amulet to protect their gear from the spirits' meddling.

If they never captured a spirit (which was unlikely) and they left him his amulet (which they'd need to defend themselves), could Tobin convince the spirits to release him? In the midst of a raging war with the same humans he'd ridden in with? Humans, among whom the spirits didn't seem to differentiate anyway?

Saving a Realm he would never see again suddenly seemed a lot less important.

His Duri guards snickered contemptuously at the Softer knight's tears.

# CHAPTER 15

# Jeriah

HE HADN'T BEEN ABLE TO sleep. The manor had been evacuated to lay this trap. Or more precisely, in case their trap failed. But this estate had several advantages, even beyond an owner who was willing to take a chance.

The first was a stone-walled vineyard, where pulling down the wall on the far end of the field created an open cup the priests had declared was a perfect anchor for "the largest gate anyone ever considered—let alone attempted!"

Jeriah would have felt better if the master of experimental magic Chardane had talked into this had finished his sentence with "cast" instead—but honesty was probably better.

The second advantage was a small gulch, not far beyond the manor's fields, where a stream ran for most of the winter and evaporated in the summer. It was only a trickle now, the better to hold all the men Commander Sower could hide there.

The commander himself, and a band of carefully chosen

volunteers, planned to offer a token resistance when the barbarians first charged and then get out of their way. It would be suspicious to leave this important site completely undefended, and the men concealed in the ditch were the Realm's real defense.

Though if the priests failed to cast the gate, or if the barbarians chose to ignore it and invade the Southlands instead of the Spiritworld, the men Commander Sower had hidden would be lucky to slow the barbarians down—they couldn't stop them. Of course, the whole Realm army hadn't been able to stop them.

The manor's final advantage was a railed walkway on the highest part of the roof. The landholder had probably built it to keep an eye on his fields. Jeriah knew his father would have liked to look down on his land from this commanding position, particularly at harvesttime.

He wished Koryn could have stayed. She'd have appreciated the view, and she had earned the right to be here. But a crippled girl would be no use in this fight, and she'd been forced to concede—leaving Jeriah to stand alone, looking over fields that had once belonged to the landholder's neighbors and that now constituted the open disputed ground between the barbarians' camps and the Realm's border. Jeriah had volunteered to stand watch here. Since he had nothing else to do.

Commander Sower, who preferred to rely on the reports of his scouts, had agreed to Jeriah's suggestion with the deadly politeness he'd been using since the Hierarch's orders had arrived. At least the rooftop allowed him to escape the hostile atmosphere of the command post in the house below. Jeriah had been there all night, visible to anyone who cared to look, so when the trapdoor behind him creaked open, he wasn't surprised to see Makenna's short, ruffled hair. No one else was speaking to him.

She let the door bang back into place and joined him at the railing. "It's all set. The last runes have been drawn, and the priests who are to cast the arc in the air have practiced the spell so many times, they could do it in their sleep. We're ready."

It had disturbed her to rely on the priests to cast a large portion of the gate. Almost as much as Jeriah had been disturbed by Sower's refusal to let him go out with the scouts, and she concealed it better than he did. But at least she was doing something! In fact, as the person who'd cast more gate spells than anyone else in the Realm, she'd been chosen to order and anchor the whole complex spell. She hadn't been shoved aside.

"You can't blame Commander Sower for being miffed at you," she pointed out, in a reasonable tone Jeriah instantly detested. "You went over his head and behind his back to set this up. You're lucky he allowed you to stay at all."

"He can't order me to go." Jeriah didn't sound reasonable, and he didn't care. "I'm not under his command, any more than he's under mine."

At least Koryn had sympathized with his frustration.

"And yet," Makenna pointed out, "Sower's doing exactly what you want. He made the order not to attack the barbarian servants, those camps they left behind, downright ironclad. He's got his decoy troop out there, and the real troops tucked in yon ditch, out of sight. They won't interfere with us unless our plan fails completely. And then we'd be glad of them."

"So if he doesn't want me with him, I should be posted there!" Jeriah snapped. "Or out with the scouts, or running messages, or doing something somewhere! I could—"

"If you were down in that ditch," said Makenna tartly, "you'd be doing no more than you're doing here, and with a lot worse view. Which would probably make you even more twitchy!"

"At least I might be useful if anything goes wrong," Jeriah said. "Instead of sitting and watching while the greatest battle in the Realm's history gets resolved without me."

The instant he said it, shame set in. Getting rid of the barbarians was what mattered, not whether Jeriah had a hand in it. He expected Makenna to tell him so, but she only leaned on the railing, looking over the fields to the south.

"The waiting's always hard. Some say it's the hardest part. For me, the aftermath, seeing to the dead and wounded, is worse. You always wonder whether, if you'd been a little smarter, planned a little better, you could have prevented it."

Jeriah was reminded, once more, that this was Cogswhallop's general.

"If this goes according to plan," he said, "there won't be any wounded, or any dead. I know that's better than heroics."

The early-morning sun lit her skeptical glance.

"Really," said Jeriah. "I do know it."

"That's as well," she said. "Because you'll never be a hero. No more will I."

Jeriah stared. "I think we've both done pretty well so far!"

Even Koryn had conceded that he'd done a good job.

She'd ridden out with the landholder's family. Jeriah could see how much she wanted to stay, to witness her enemies' defeat. But there was nothing more she could do, and she was sensible enough to accept it.

"Not bad, Rovan." Koryn's gaze was fixed on some soldiers who were concealing themselves in the ditch. "Not bad at all. You might actually bring this off."

Even that faint praise had lifted Jeriah's heart. "If I do, will you forgive me? For Master Lazur? For . . . everything?"

The huge eyes turned to him. "Even if you don't bring it off, I have to give you credit for an all-out try."

Koryn had ridden away then, leaving him uncertain if he'd finally been forgiven or not. But if *she* thought he'd done well . . .

"We're doing a magnificent job," Jeriah told Makenna firmly.

"We've done well enough," she admitted. "But we're not heroes. You and I, we're too . . . too practical. Too aware of how things really work, of what's impossible, to ever come up with a crazy idea like this."

Jeriah frowned. "Tobin and Senna are the practical people in my family. I'm supposed to be the crazy one."

"Exactly."

"You're not making sense."

For once, Makenna's smile held nothing but friendship. "You're supposed to be the crazy one? The idealist, who doesn't let anything stop him from doing what's right?"

Heat rose in Jeriah's face. "Things stop me all the time. And what's right . . . that's gotten a bit muddled lately."

"But you didn't come up with this plan," Makenna said. "Neither did I, great general that I'm supposed to be. Tobin created it. Tobin, who'd be the first to call it madness."

"Yes, but Tobin only came up with this because he couldn't stand to leave . . ."

Suddenly Jeriah saw it, all together. The thing that made his brother a hero. That kept him or Makenna—or Master Lazur—from ever becoming one.

"He couldn't stand to leave anyone behind to be killed," Makenna finished for him. "His heart's too soft to sacrifice *anyone*, so he made up the craziest plan ever heard of, and he pushed till it might even come off. So he's the hero. You and I, we're the ones who follow behind the heroes and try to make their crazy plans work."

"Then you'd best start working on this one," said a gruff, familiar voice. "It's about to fall to bits on us."

Jeriah jumped. Cogswhallop was perched on a chimney behind them, but he'd given up complaining about the goblins sneaking up on him.

"What's wrong?" Makenna sounded calmer than Jeriah felt. "Where are the barbarians?"

"They're gathering on the other side of that hill." Cogswhallop pointed to a low rise to the southwest. "There's a gully that let 'em reach it without the human scouts seeing, but we spotted 'em some time ago. I'd guess they're waiting for the gate to go up, though as much as we can tell from a distance, they look pretty twitchy. If you wait too long, it might occur to them to ride in here, capture the priests, and force them to open up the gate when and where the barbarians choose. You wouldn't be refusing them. Not for long."

The goblin's face was grim. Jeriah decided he didn't want to know the details.

"So what's wrong?" he demanded. "They're doing exactly what Tobin said they would."

"Aye," the goblin drawled. "But they're taking Tobin along with 'em."

"With them? What do you mean?"

"He's tied hand and foot to a horse's saddle, with four hard lads guarding him," Cogswhallop replied. "So it doesn't look like they plan on leaving him behind. And if they get him into the Otherworld—"

"Right," said Makenna. "Cogswhallop, gather up all our lads who can fight. We'll—"

"You can't," Jeriah told her. His heart pounded with fear for Tobin, excitement at finally being free to do something. Utter dread, for if he failed, it would no longer matter if Koryn forgave him—he would never forgive himself.

"You've got to cast the gate," he went on. "There's no one else who can control the spell. I'll put together a troop. Humans, because if the barbarians can sense the goblins' presence, it'll give us away before we can get close."

The goblins were also too small to wage a physical fight against barbarian warriors, but Jeriah wasn't going to insult them by saying so.

"You need to stall about casting the gate till we're ready," he went on. "We'll wait till the barbarians are coming, charge out, and get Tobin away from them."

Makenna frowned, slender fingers tapping the rail. Was she going to throw a girlish fit, demand to come with him? Or—

"Put your troop in that orchard," she said crisply, pointing. "You'll be able to watch the barbarians' approach long enough to locate Tobin, then ride out while they're distracted by Sower's decoys. Take Daroo with you. He can carry a message to me when you're in position. They'll be coming in fast, so don't get fancy—ride in, get him, get out. I wish . . ."

She shrugged. Commanders didn't get wishes, and she knew it better than Jeriah did, but he still felt for her. He had no time to feel.

"Where's Dar—"

Something tugged on his britches. Jeriah reached down and swung Daroo onto his shoulder, feeling the small hands dig into his tunic. Nice, to be able to carry his friends around in the open.

He was already hurrying to the trapdoor, but he turned back as he lifted it and met Makenna's somber eyes. "I'll get him." He'd put too much effort into rescuing Tobin to lose him now. "I promise."

It was Cogswhallop who replied. "You do that, lad. But don't expect much help from him—he's in bad shape."

Jeriah wanted to ask why, but it would take time to assemble his troop, and once the human scouts located their enemy, Makenna wouldn't be able to stall for long. No matter what shape Tobin was in, Jeriah wanted him back!

He took the stairs down from the roof two at a time, with Daroo clutching his shoulder. Jeriah thought he heard a whispered "Yahoo!" but the goblin's voice was too soft for him to be sure.

The clerks and support staff stared as Jeriah ran past with a goblin perched on his shoulder. One of the commanders put out a hand to catch him. "Rovan, are they com—"

"Not yet!"

Jeriah dodged the hand and ran on. They would send someone up to the roof, who would find Makenna there, but nothing to alarm them. Unless the barbarians took Cogswhallop's advice and charged . . . No, he had to stick with the plan. Makenna would give him time. Unless the human scouts spotted the gathering horde—then Jeriah's time would be up!

He dodged through the farmyard, then sprinted down the path behind the house. A horse might have covered this ground faster, but Jeriah couldn't take it into the ditch. He was panting when he reached it, sweating in the cool morning air. He took a bit of care scrambling down the side of the shallow ravine. A sprained ankle was the last thing he needed.

Half a dozen hands reached out to steady him as he tumbled the last few feet.

"Rovan! Are they here? We haven't heard anything!"

"They're not here." Jeriah tried to catch his breath and look less panicked. "But I need some men for a . . ."

His gaze fell on a young subcommander, a friend of Tobin's from the years his brother had served in this army.

". . . a special escort," he finished. "You, Trevenscourt, meet me in the stable, mounted and ready to ride. There will be others coming to join you."

He hurried on before the troop's commanding officer could ask more questions—though he might not have had any. Squires of Jeriah's age and rank were often sent to gather men for an escort or run other errands for the assembled commanders. No one even argued as he hurried down the ditch, keeping an eye out for Tobin's friends and drafting several more before he finally reached Commander Malveese's unit.

He could have picked out the men he wanted by their expressions alone—men who'd do anything to get one last chance at their enemy. Waiting in the ditch while the barbarians escaped was harder on these men than waiting on the roof had been for Jeriah. In short, they were the worst of the hotheads. Jeriah had no fear that they'd balk at an unauthorized mission—he only hoped they'd remember that their job was to free a prisoner, instead of simply killing every barbarian they could get their hands on.

He picked out over a dozen, more than half of Malveese's unit, and met the commander's suspicious gaze steadily.

"A special escort," Jeriah said. "I was told to gather all the men I needed."

The fact that the general who'd given those orders commanded the goblins' army, not the Realm's, was a mere detail.

Commander Malveese hesitated a moment, then shrugged.

"Take all the men you like. They're not doing much here."

"Thank you, sir," said Jeriah sincerely. "For everything."

"Just bring it off." The commander's lips twitched. "Whatever it is."

Jeriah was still smiling as he led his troops out of the ditch.

Jogging back to the stables kept them too breathless for questions. When they entered the big building, Jeriah found that the men he'd sent on earlier had saddled not only their own mounts, but horses for most of the others. It took just a moment to get a bridle and saddle on Glory, who pranced uneasily as she sensed his tension.

"I have to tell you all," said Jeriah, "this isn't an escort, and it hasn't been authorized by any commander. But the barbarians have Tobin."

He kept his explanation short and succinct. They all knew it was Tobin who'd conceived this odd ambush in the first place, so the story didn't take long.

"This is against orders," Jeriah finished crisply. "In fact, coming with me might get you kicked out of the army when this is over."

"When this is over, there isn't going to be an army," one of the Southlanders said. "We might as well go out fighting, instead of hiding in a ditch!"

The rumble of approval was almost a cheer, but some of Tobin's friends looked troubled. A few of them, younger sons, had probably planned for a career in the sunsguard. But none of them said anything and Jeriah blessed them from the bottom of his heart. He needed them.

"Most of you don't know what my brother looks like—and I should tell the rest that he's been ill."

Jeriah organized them into small units, three or four Southlanders paired with each man who knew Tobin well enough to identify the man they were supposed to rescue. When he was done, almost twenty men led their horses out of the stable and across the yard. At this point, Jeriah was more concerned about being seen by one of his own officers than the barbarians. But the orchard lay just beyond the manor's gate, and the bright spring leaves soon hid them.

In a few more minutes they were staring through a screen of branches at the backs of Commander Sower's troops. Those men were supposed to look like a loose perimeter guard, assigned to protect the gate from barbarian scouting parties without getting so close as to alarm the spirits.

Jeriah had agreed that the barbarians would be suspicious if the gate was completely unguarded. He'd also agreed that it should be possible for these men to allow themselves to be swept aside when the barbarian army charged, without too many dying in the process. He still thought the men who'd volunteered for that unit were the bravest he'd ever met.

He also understood why Commander Sower had turned away so many of the Southland volunteers. The men around him looked far too eager.

Jeriah turned to Daroo, who had moved from his perch on Jeriah's shoulder to the back of Glory's saddle.

"We're set. Go tell Makenna she can start the spell."

He could feel Daroo's reluctance. The young goblin wanted to stay. He wanted to do more than carry messages. But Daroo, for all his youth, had been a soldier too.

"Aye." He slid down the stirrup before Jeriah could give him a hand and headed toward the manor.

"Daroo?" Jeriah said impulsively. The boy turned. "Tell Makenna . . . tell her I can think of worse things to do with my life than helping heroes win."

The way Daroo's face brightened was reward enough, but as Jeriah settled back in the saddle, he realized that it was true. Without people like him, people who could deal with the consequences when the plan fell apart, the heroes could end up dead. That wasn't going to happen here. Not if Jeriah could prevent it.

"Remember, we're only here to grab Tobin and get out." He kept his voice low, but all of Tobin's friends, and even some of the Southlanders, nodded.

Jeriah looked at the men who hadn't and was about to repeat himself when the light shifting through the leaves took on a silver cast. He turned toward the manor and gasped.

They'd been talking for weeks about how big this gate would be, but he hadn't expected . . . It arced from one side of the field to the other like a rainbow, but its silver-blue light was a solid, swirling curtain that descended to the earth and blotted out the sky. Then it swirled itself clear to reveal another sky, half full of drifting clouds, while the sky over the Southlands behind it still showed clear.

The sight of those clouds brought home the reality of that alien world as nothing else had, and the back of Jeriah's neck prickled at its strangeness. But he had no time for awe; a shout went up from Sower's men as the barbarian army poured over the long, low rise that had concealed them.

They'd painted themselves for battle, clay-white skin, with spikes of stiffened hair framing screaming faces. They surged across the fields like the froth of a great wave, and the thunder of thousands of pounding hooves rolled over Jeriah. He was astonished when Sower's men rushed out and formed a line in front of that charge instead of running away—he wouldn't have blamed them!

But admiration and his own terror both took second place to frantically scanning that oncoming mob for his brother. Jeriah hadn't imagined there'd be so *many* of them, and picking out an individual face in that jostling tide seemed impossible.

They completely filled the long fields as they approached Sower's line, and more barbarians were riding from behind the hill when the battle began.

Jeriah, still trying to pick Tobin out of the mass, tried to ignore the clang of metal on metal, the shouts of anger and pain. Some of the Southlanders shifted restlessly.

"Where's Tobin?" he shouted at them. "Look for my brother, curse you!"

The sounds of battle were fading, almost as swiftly as they'd begun. Jeriah saw scattered groups of Realm knights staggering off to one side of the battlefield or the other, He was relieved, in the small corner of his mind that wasn't furiously searching the sea of white-painted faces, that the warriors let them go. The barbarians headed with single-minded purpose for the great gate.

The leading edge of the barbarian force rode through. Jeriah could see them galloping onward in that other world, clearing the way for others to follow, claiming that alien place. They were probably almost as responsible as the spirits for its creation. They deserved whatever fate they—

"There!" Trevenscourt shouted. "There he is!"

One brown head in all that mob, one unpainted face. Tobin was easy to see, but Jeriah's heart sank: The entire width of the barbarian army surged between him and his brother, and Tobin's guards were leading their captive's horse at the same brisk canter as their own. They were halfway to the gate already.

There was nothing he could do except try.

"Go!" Jeriah clapped his heels to Glory's sides, and his whole troop launched themselves out of the concealing trees and into battle.

If the barbarians had cared about killing them, they'd probably all have died in the next ten seconds. Once he was inside the moving mass of men and horses, Jeriah realized that all the barbarians were focused on the shimmering curtain ahead of them.

The only time barbarians even launched a blow at him was when he got in their way. Jeriah thanked the Bright Gods for Glory's agility and guided her through the charging mob like a sheepdog through its flock.

Most of the Southlanders had fallen behind, fighting with small knots of barbarians. Jeriah hoped the fools had the sense to quit before they got themselves killed. A flash of guilt, for thrusting them into the position Commander Sower had tried to keep them out of. But most of Jeriah's attention was fixed, not on Tobin, but on reaching the place at the opposite side of the field that Tobin and his guards would have to pass in order to enter the gate.

Glory leaped aside from one determined rider's path, only to put Jeriah in front of another, who cursed and lifted his sword. Jeriah traded several blows with the man. Then one of Tobin's friends, who were still clinging doggedly to his heels, swept in and launched a blow at the barbarian's unprotected head that toppled the man from his saddle.

Jeriah didn't know or care if the barbarian died. He spun his horse, looking frantically for his brother. Tobin and his guards were almost to the place where Jeriah had hoped to intercept them. If they passed it . . .

He shouted, and Glory sprang forward once more. But there were too many rough-coated horses, too many barbarians in his path.

Jeriah saw one barbarian raise a bow, aiming at the huddle of priests gathered on each side of the gate. His warning shout died as another barbarian swung a sword that almost cut off the archer's arm. The priests who held that gate were the safest people on the battlefield, as long as that gate stayed open.

But what about Tobin? Did his guards have orders to kill him if it looked like he might escape? That was horribly possible, but Jeriah couldn't do anything about it.

One of Tobin's friends cried out as his horse stumbled and went down, rolling among the pounding hooves. Jeriah set his teeth and pressed on. He had only a hundred yards to go, but that ground was packed with a moving mass of bodies. Tobin and his guards were almost at the interception point.

He wasn't going to make it. Even as he pounded his heels against Glory's heaving sides, despair swept over him . . . and one of the barbarian horses began to buck, right in front of Tobin's guards.

A hail of stones erupted from the bushes and vines on that side of the field, and the lumpy goblins they called Stoners tumbled out of the underbrush to keep it from impeding their aim.

Jeriah shouted encouragement and urged Glory forward again, but Tobin's guards had recognized the danger.

They cut away from the goblins, away from the small, stubby arrows that were stampeding horses and even bringing down a few riders. The Stoners worked with deadly accuracy, and one of Tobin's guards dropped unconscious from the saddle. But the others dragged Tobin out of the goblins' range. It brought them closer to Jeriah, but they were also closer to the gate.

Tobin's friends had been pulled away, leaving Jeriah on his own, but the mob was beginning to thin. He was now galloping toward the gate, moving with the crowd, so the going was easier. But the barbarians who led Tobin's horse were moving faster too.

Tobin's wrists were tied to the saddle pommel and his ankles to the stirrups. He was so near the gate that its silver light illuminated the horror and despair on his bruised face.

Jeriah was too far off to stop them, but he was close enough to see a small form—hardly larger than a rabbit—that darted through the avalanche of pounding hooves and leaped to grab the saddle girth as Tobin's horse ran by.

Daroo clung to the strap for several long moments. Then Tobin's horse bucked and shrieked and its saddle slipped sideways, carrying Tobin with it as the severed girth dumped him in a tangle of leather straps.

His wrists were still bound, but that didn't stop Tobin from rolling up and flinging first the sturdy saddle and then himself over Daroo's fragile body.

They were less than twenty feet from the glowing gate. Barbarians raced past with a heedless haste that could trample a fallen man, much less a small-boned goblin boy.

One of Tobin's guards rode on through the gate, but two turned back. Jeriah's worst fears were realized when, still mounted, one of them drew his sword and prepared to bring it down on Tobin's exposed neck.

But the mob had thinned even more. Jeriah shouted as Glory charged forward and knocked the smaller horse off its feet.

Tobin cried out in protest as hooves tramped and thudded around him, but he didn't move from the crouch that sheltered his savior. Jeriah reined Glory around between Tobin and the last mounted guard.

The man who'd fallen when Glory toppled his horse looked at Jeriah, then looked at the gate and exclaimed in alarm.

The gate had begun to waver, silver flooding in spinning wisps over their view of the Spiritworld.

Clutching his ribs, the barbarian staggered to his feet and ran for the Spiritworld. His mounted companion had already made the same choice and beaten him through. The handful of barbarians who remained shouted and urged their horses to a gallop.

Peering into that strange world, Jeriah saw the leading edge of the barbarian army stagger and slow, as if their horses had stumbled into a bog. But the area around them didn't look like marshland.

The few barbarians who remained on this side of the gate didn't care about the terrain on the other side. None of them wanted to waste time fighting Jeriah, rushing instead to follow their comrades as the gate flickered and dimmed.

But it wasn't till the last of them had hurtled through that the great portal shimmered and winked out.

Jeriah thought he heard a distant echo, as if an immense clap of thunder had sounded in that other world so briefly connected to his. But then it was gone, and Jeriah tumbled off Glory's back and knelt beside his brother.

Tobin sat up too slowly, and his battered face had lines in it Jeriah hadn't seen before. But the urgency with which he struggled to lift the saddle was pure Tobin.

"Hold still," said Jeriah. He cut Tobin's wrists loose, then lifted the heavy saddle aside.

Daroo had been crouched beneath it, in much the same posture Tobin had assumed above, but he was already stirring when Jeriah raised the saddle.

"Are you all right?" Daroo asked Tobin. "Fa said you weren't in any condition to go down rough, so we tried to find another way to stop you. But toward the end I didn't see another choice. Are you all right?"

Tobin looked from Daroo to Jeriah, and his eyes filled with tears.

"I'm fine," he whispered. "I'm better than fine, now."

Tobin was also leaning against his brother so heavily, Jeriah was pretty sure he couldn't sit up on his own.

"No, you're not," Jeriah said. "Of all the idiotic, ridiculous . . ."

But someone else was approaching, and one look at the dread in Makenna's face distracted him.

"He's fine," Jeriah told her. "Or at least he's alive, so he'll be fine eventually. Thank you for making the gate waver like that. I'd have had a fight on my hands if you hadn't."

"It wasn't hard." She was pale, her short hair wet with sweat. Looking past her, Jeriah saw that most of the priests who'd cast the gate were sitting down, and those who weren't were lying down. He deduced that creating the largest gate anyone had ever considered—let alone attempted—hadn't been easy.

Tobin's friends were beginning to converge from the parts of the field where the barbarians' final rush had swept them.

There were no barbarian warriors. Anywhere.

The barbarians were gone, and his brother was leaning

against him, hurt, perhaps, but alive.

Koryn would have to forgive him now.

It occurred to Jeriah that while Tobin might be the hero, he'd had a lot of help. In real life, heroism seemed to be more of a group effort than it was in the ballads.

Jeriah opened his mouth to tell Tobin what an idiot he was for trying to do this all by himself—and nearly getting killed in the process—but Makenna's cold voice interrupted.

"I've seen more than one underplanned, reckless, half-assed stunt—but this one beats them all!"

Jeriah closed his mouth and listened with amused respect to a general's furious harangue about sacrifice tactics, and leaving your ill-informed allies to scramble after you, trying to fill in the conspicuous gaps in your plan. It was a better, fiercer scolding than a brother's. And as she reached out to touch Tobin's face with a gentleness that belied every harsh word, Jeriah realized, with a surge of stunned delight, that it sprang from the same source.

This girl loved his brother. He didn't think Tobin had realized it yet, and he was certain *she* hadn't, but Makenna was going to be his sister-in-law.

She was currently comparing Tobin's strategic ability—unfavorably—to that of a bunch of rabbits running in circles.

His father would consider her a practical person, and the girls would love anyone Tobin brought home. His mother . . . Jeriah thought of Makenna at war with his mother and cringed. Then he thought of what might happen if she *allied* with his mother, and his blood ran cold.

Maybe Jeriah could join the sunsguard. Since their mad plan had worked, Commander Sower would probably forgive him. And even if he didn't, someone was bound to mount an expedition to cross the great desert and explore the lands the barbarians had left behind. He would miss Koryn . . . but why should he have to miss her? With her insatiable thirst for knowledge, maybe she'd be willing to join him. An exploratory expedition would need clerks.

If it didn't occur to the Hierarch, Jeriah would have to suggest it. The great desert was just about the right amount of space to put between himself and the chaos that Makenna and his mother could create if they got together to . . . to enforce the goblins' entry into human society? Or find something to do with those lesser barbarians Tobin was so concerned about? Or something even wilder and worse?

Judging by Daroo's disgusted expression, the goblin boy had observed the same thing about Tobin and Makenna that Jeriah had, and Daroo was young enough to disapprove. Jeriah owed the goblins enough to stay for a while, at least. And if new in-laws, chaos, and goblin court battles weren't sufficiently interesting to keep him occupied—or if they became too horrific—a desert full of adventure would always be waiting.